Emma

Loves overpowering prison

By
ARABELLA ABEL

Table of Contents

Contents

Chapter One

June 12 1820

Miss Emma Pennington finished writing a letter to her older brother Robert, who had gone to London. Pressing her signet into the sealing wax, she extinguished the flame.

There was still a little time before her Aunt Belvedere was due to visit. So, she put her Spencer jacket onto her slender body, checked her flaxen blond hair in the mirror and then fastened on her overshoes.

Emma made her way through the door to the orangery which opened out into the garden.

Once out there, Emma thought of her dear departed Father. For it was he who taught her the names of the garden's flowers and trees, and now, how well those trees had matured.

Miss Pennington stooped to sniff the perfume of the lavender, after which she picked some, to bring into the still room to dry.

Emma was humming a tune that she was learning to play on the pianoforte when she remembered the last unkind words that her Aunt had said to her. She replayed those words over in her mind. It is time, young lady, that you were off your mothers' hands. Married to a strong husband, who will take complete control of you.

Complete control, it is those words, that frighten me. Emma shivered, as she remembered them.

Oh dear, why did my Aunt call me shameful? I only wanted to read one of Robert's new books.

As Emma carried on collecting lavender to refill her lavender sweet bags. She reflected; I wish lavender kept my Aunt Belvedere away as it keeps away the moths. She wondered, oh why is it so shocking for me to read a book about the life of an African slave? Indeed, I am curious to know about such things. Dear me, it is tiresome being under the control of my Aunt Belvedere. Emma took another sniff of the lavender flowers. I wonder why my Aunt has taken my Fathers place of authority? Can she not allow my dear mother to decide what is best for me? Emma frowned a little, I am sure my Father would have understood my desire to gain more knowledge than I dare say is usual for a daughter.

Suddenly Emma was jolted from her thoughts as she heard the rhythm of horse's hoofs. Clasping hold of the bunches of lavender, Emma rushed back into the house, taking care not to be caught panting. She put all the lavender into a flat flower basket first and then swapped her Spencer jacket for her shawl, took off her overshoes and stepped into her flat house shoes. Emma glanced in the mirror to check her hair was tidy and her hands were clean. Composing herself, she strolled into the hallway in a refined manner.

'At last. There you are. Where have you been?' Lady Belvedere snapped as she tugged at her glove. 'Why were you not here to greet me?'

'I am sorry Aunt Belvedere.' Emma Blushed pink and said, 'Sorry Mother.'

Her mother, Lady Pennington, was about to speak when her Aunt with a fearful stare said, 'You, young lady, should have been waiting for me. I have someone with me who I want to introduce to you.'

With that, her Aunt turned her large frame and beckoned a gentleman out from the Barouche.

Before Emma's eyes stood, a portly looking man, who looked to be in his thirtieth year. He had suntanned skin and was well dressed. The thing that caught Emma's eye was his very high tied neck cloth with stripes of ochre and scarlet. The gentleman bowed to her and as he was going to say a greeting, Aunt Belvedere announced his name. She rattled off, how he was an old acquaintance of her late husband.

Emma observed that her mother looked puzzled.

Their servant Smith took out a box and parasol from the Barouche. Aunt Belvedere turned and waved her fan at him while telling him to be very careful not to drop anything on the dirty path.

Lady Pennington said, 'Smith, take care.' Turning to the

Gentleman visitor, she announced. 'We are honoured to meet you, come in, welcome.'

'What a fine house you have.' said Mr Greystone the Gentleman visitor.' I hope I will also have the pleasure to cast my eye over your beautiful garden.'

'My husband has passed away; my Son Robert runs the house now. Alas, he is away on business.'

'I am sorry not to have the advantage of meeting him.' replied Mr Greystone. 'Although, I will be perfectly satisfied to make acquaintance with your pretty daughter.'

They all went into the drawing-room. Aunt Belvedere made a fuss about where to sit. She coughed loudly for Mr Greystone was walking towards the winged armchair that she preferred to sit in. He realised that it was the chair of her choice, so he took her arm and helped her into it. Lady Belvedere sat down and took out her vinaigrette from her reticule. Gave a deep sniff, and stated, 'Emma, play something soothing for us.'

Aunt Belvedere also proposed that Mr Nash Greystone should turn the pages for Emma, so, he could cast his eye over her accuracy of music reading. Lady Belvedere folded her arms and said. 'For maybe Emma has not practised enough . . .maybe she has been too engaged in reading unsuitable books.'

Lady Pennington gasped, 'unsuitable?'

Emma looked down and said nothing.

Lady Pennington's eyes widened as she looked at Lady Belvedere. But the Aunt had her lips tightly together. So, she knew there would be no further explanations. Emma's mother saw her daughter's wholesome smile, she now looked reassured.

Lady Pennington said 'I shall ring for tea.'

Mr Greystone clapped his hands together and said 'To be sure, that is a splendid idea. Miss Pennington will play the pianoforte while we wait for tea.' Addressing Emma, he said, 'I shall take advantage of observing you play by turning the page for you.' He held out his hand towards the pianoforte.

Emma blushed and checked her fichu to make sure it was in place. Mr Greystone followed behind her, as she made her way to the pianoforte and put her music book on the stand. Emma opened the page at Beethoven's piano sonata in C-sharp minor. This is not an easy piece of music she thought. This will show Aunt I have been practising. I need to concentrate, I must try and forget about him examining me.

Mr Greystone whispered, 'whenever you are ready.'

Emma could feel the man's breath on the back of her neck. She felt uneasy. For she did not even know this man.

After Emma finished playing the piece, she thanked him and

quickly got off the stool.

Her mother remarked, 'well played Emma.'

Mr Greystone kissed her hand, 'I must propose a word of praise on your music reading skill and of your music choice. 'May I say, you have a fine hand, your playing is charming.'

'I am pleased that you think so,' Emma replied while lowering her eyes to the floor.

'Charming, like this fine house. Everything in this house is most charming indeed. I must say, that your Brother keeps it very well. He raised his chin, as he commented, 'This house must take some upkeep. Although not acquainted with your brother, I feel perfectly sure that he loves his dear sister very much. To provide her, with such a valuable instrument, and the latest music. Perhaps, he is generous to a fault?'

'He truly is.' replied Emma.

'So, his allowance to you is most generous?'

'He is generous and kind,' said Emma.

'That is all very well indeed. I say we must train young ladies to have careful budgeting skills. They must learn to be very cautious if spending their annuity at all?

Emma looked around, lost for words she stroked the cover of her music book.

Mr Greystone added, 'when it comes to using allowances with good judgement females can lack wisdom. So indeed, the generous nature of a brother can be perilous for a sister.'

'Oh dear, Mr Greystone.' Emma raises her eyebrows. 'My brother and I think rather differently from you.'

'Nonsense, all women of marriageable age, must learn prudence. Once the error of his lavish ways is revealed to him. He will change, for the sake of his sister's future husband. We Gentlemen always stick together when it comes to good sense,' he spouted.

His words had vexed Emma, hugging her music book, she walked back to her chair in silence.

Aunt Belvedere chimed up, 'I do not care for Beethoven, far too contemporary for me. You should have played a piece by Haydn. By playing a piece of music, that is so dark, a young lady like you will not be improved upon.'

Just then Bess came in with the tea tray. 'thank you,' said Lady Pennington and Bess left the room. 'Will you take milk or lemon, Martha dear?' she said to Lady Belvedere.

'Milk. I do hope it is fresh.'

As Lady Pennington poured the tea, 'Charlotte, that's far too weak' articulated Lady Belvedere.

'I will pour you another,' she said. 'I will have that one Mother dear' said Emma in a consoling voice.

Mr Greystone pointed to the lemon and said, 'My dear Lady, I will have lemon and one sugar in my tea.'

Lady Pennington finished offering the tea around. Next, she offered her guests some little sandwiches, followed by apple cakes.

'I don't mind if I do,' Mr Greystone said while putting some onto his plate.

Lady Pennington enquired, 'Mr Greystone, may I ask, where are you residing?'

'I am living with-'

'-He is living with me while he is acquiring a property.' Lady Belvedere answered.

'I am Indeed. I am just about to move into Boughton House in Cheshire. Depend upon it. I saw many great houses. I thought highly of this one, for It has mature gardens and lovely grounds running down to the river. You can see right over the Cheshire plain. On a clear day, you can even see the Welsh hills.'

'It sound's praiseworthy.' Replied Lady Pennington.

Aunt Belvedere crashed her cup down onto its saucer and

exclaimed. 'Praiseworthy, my word it is. I said to Nash, upon no account miss out on acquiring that grand house for yourself.'

'Where did you live formally Mr Greystone?'

'I have been abroad for many a long year. I am delighted to be back.'

'Then the house will help you settle down.'

Aunt Belvedere added, 'What Nash needs is a polite little lady wife by his side. Yes, for I shall play matchmaker.' She said, with a glint in her eye, as she tapped the side of her nose with her finger.

Mr Greystone laughed and glanced at Emma and then at her Aunt.

Then he asked, 'Do you partake in dancing Miss Pennington? I shall hold a Ball when I move into Boughton House so I can make new acquaintances and be reacquainted with old ones. I dare say,' pointing to Emma and then her mother while announcing the news.

'You shall be my first new friends.'

'We shall be honoured,' replied Lady Pennington.

Emma gave him a half-smile but uttered no words.

Her Aunt then tapped Emma's knee with the end of her fan then said, 'Look, Emma. I have a gift for you, over there in the blue box, go and get it.'

Emma thanked her Aunt. She then opened the blue box and saw a book and a red box inside. She took hold of the narrow red box and opened it to reveal a fan. 'How beautiful, Aunt. I like it very much indeed.'

'It is a Horn painted fan.' Her Aunt informed her. She then took a sip of tea.

Emma said while opening and shutting the fan. 'The ribbon and flowers are very pretty indeed, and it is just the right size too.'

'I was told it is one of the new designs.'

'I do believe it is. There is no disputing you have very fine taste, aunt.'

Lady Belvedere lowered the cup from her lips. 'I too was a handsome young woman. I know very well, what a young lady of good breeding needs.'

Emma put the fan back into its box and placed it onto the mahogany drum table and next pulled a book from the box. The book was titled "forming the moral character of a young woman." Emma blushed a little for she knew what was inferred by this gift.

Her aunt leaned forward while waving her fan. 'Depend upon it, if you read this book, and act upon it you will be a young Lady of high moral virtue, a woman of merit. Honourable Gentlemen will desire to marry you, that is what you want.'

She then turned and addressed Lady Pennington and said, 'I do hope Charlotte, you agree with me?'

Emma's mother nodded.

Then Mr Greystone said, 'Can Miss Pennington be improved? To speak plainly, her merits, manner, and nature are clear to see.'

'Yes yes. But I want my niece to digest the books that daughters of the best families read.'

Turning to Emma, her Aunt said. 'Now Emma dear, I want you to read it with thorough regard.'

'Very well Aunt Belvedere.' Emma thanked her Aunt for the gifts.

Her cheeks blushed pink. Emma was wondering what advice; the book would hold for her.

Mr Greystone got up from his chair. He walked over to the large window draped with a silk curtain. He stood looking out at the garden.

'I would love to take a turn around your garden.' Mr Greystone caught Emma's eye and asked, 'would you do me the honour?'

'Yes do Emma,' urged Aunt Belvedere.

Emma lowered her eyes while she stroked her earlobe.

Her mother, spoke up saying, 'Indeed, we shall all have a promenade around the garden.'

Lady Belvedere replied with a heavy sigh, 'To be sure, I do not care for it.'

Stretching out her hand on Aunt Belvedere's arm. Lady Pennington said 'Martha dear, would you be good enough to come and see my newly acquired rose? It is named the "Parsons Pink China."'

'I dare say, I could be persuaded, pleasing people is my nature.' Aunt Belvedere said with an air of condescension. She then made a fuss about needing a lot of help to get out of the armchair.

So Emma and Mr Greystone supported her arms and helped her out of it.

The four of them walked through the orangery that leads out into the garden.

They all strolled down the narrow path looking at the roses.

Lady Pennington pointed to her favourite bushes and rambling roses. Then she stopped at her Parsons Pink China rose. Lady Pennington cupped its flower head in her hand while she bent over to smell it. Then asked Martha what she thought of it. Lady Belvedere glanced at the rose and said in a dismissive tone. 'To be sure, why it looks the same as my Old Blush rose.'

'I do declare,' Mr Greystone said, 'it is a lovely colour, most becoming Lady Pennington. It adds merit to your garden. I will have to acquire some roses for my new garden at Boughton House. It will make it more agreeable to the ladies.'

Emma saw some spent rose petals that had fallen onto the soil below and she without thinking started to gather them up. But then she saw, her aunt frowning at her.

She stopped and then looked at her hands. There was soil in her fingernails.

Her aunt shook her head and raised her eyebrows. Whispered under her breath, 'lacks ladylike manners?' and stated. 'Emma my dear, do leave those for the gardener.'

Lady Pennington, on seeing her daughter blush over her dirty hands quickly moved along to show off another rose. An old rose of the Lancaster variety.

Emma wiped her hands on her handkerchief. Glancing at the rose, she said. 'Mother I will pick some roses on the morrow to take to Mrs Nancy Dale.'

'Yes dear.'

'Who is this person Nancy Dale?' Questioned Her aunt.

'Mrs Dale is married to one of our workers. Sadly, her husband is ill and cannot work. With four dear children, the poor woman is struggling to feed them all.

'I dare say, a poor person would not want flowers,' her aunt said shaking her head.

'The flowers are a special gift. I propose to take food and knitted socks for them too.'

'Emma has been very industrious knitting for the family.' Her mother smiled, 'She has made a pair of socks for each one of them.'

'More accomplishments Miss Pennington?' Mr Greystone remarked.

'My knitting is not a great accomplishment, believe me, but as socks they are tolerable. Alas, they must be warm. That is why I made them. I could not bear to think that I am warm in my house, yet they are cold in theirs, that is not to be born.'

Her mother added 'My Son, Robert, allows them to stay in the cottage. As on no account, will he be the means of adding any more pain.'

Mr Greystone straightened himself, 'Speaking plain enough. We may honour such a sentiment as goodwill to all. I am only afraid that one must put time limits on doing good deeds for the poor. Or those type of people will take advantage of a good-natured Gentleman like your brother.'

'Oh dear,' Lady Pennington said, putting her hand over her mouth.

Emma then took her mothers' arm and walked in silence.

Aunt Belvedere broke the silence saying 'I propose that we see the rest of the garden another time. I feel tired. Time to take our leave, Nash. Take my arm and help me back to the Barouche.'

They walked back to the carriage in silence, broken only by the plaintive song of a blackbird.

When they reached the barouche. Lady Pennington and Emma kissed Lady Belvedere goodbye.

Smith Helped Lady Belvedere into the Barouche. But suddenly remembering, that she had left her vinaigrette in the house. Aunt Belvedere demanded that Smith go back in the house and fetch her vinaigrette.'

While Smith had gone. Lady Pennington speaking in a whisper said 'Martha dear, I want to thank you for the way you care about Emma. Your gifts are most kind and I appreciate the pains you have taken in coming here to visit us. Martha, I just want to say, dear, please, you must allow me as her mother, to decide about Emma's future. Do you not think it would be best for her?'

Meanwhile, Mr Greystone offered Emma his arm, submissively, she took it.

Staring at her with his steel-grey eyes under heavy eyebrows, he said. 'I dare say, I am right that your brother often works away from home?'

Hesitant Emma answered. 'Robert goes to London… Manchester… and Bolton.'

'Mr Greystone rubbed his chin with his hand and asked, 'Are you close?'

'I do believe we are very close. Robert is very dear to me.'

'So he watches over you.'

Mr Greystone reminded Emma. 'I will soon send you an invitation to my first ball.'

'Nash, get in.' Shouted Lady Belvedere, as Smith handed her the vinaigrette.

Mr Greystone lifted himself into the carriage. His royal blue coat matched the colour of the seat so he blended with it.

Emma thought to herself, 'he almost disappears in there, Oh, how I wish he would disappear.'

Chapter Two

The next morning, Emma had got up early and was in the library.

Her mother came in and asked. 'Emma, why are you, and all these books on the floor?'

'I am looking for a particular one but I cannot find it.'

'Is it the conduct book that your Aunt gave you?'

'No.'

'My dear, tidy up the mess. Robert will be mortified to find his precious volumes on the floor.'

Emma started to gather some books together.

'Mother,' Emma enquired. 'Do you ever feel impelled to know much more about the world? To learn about what goes on elsewhere?'

'Upon my word, Emma, what do you mean?'

'I want to understand this world and the different people in it. It saddens my heart that men do not consider it desirable for a woman to learn about history, geography, medical or science matters like Robert does. Why is it so Mother dear?'

'Old Dr Williams once told me. The brain of a female is smaller compared to a male, he also explained that women have a weaker nervous system. To be sure, we must take care.'

'Dear me, that is poor comfort. One does wonder how they know?'

'Gentlemen who go to university, do all kinds of experiments. I dare say they have the biggest brains of all men.'

'May be their heads will explode.' Emma laughed as she carried a pile of books in her arms.

'Upon my word, Emma. On no account, must you lift so many books at once, you may damage yourself.'

'I am exceedingly strong Mother dear.'

'Let me help you place them back on the shelves. If you do not lay them in the right order, Robert will be unable to find them.'

Emma stood on the library chair-cum-ladder. Her mother Passes the books to her.

I remember how much I loved it when father taught me things like the names of the flowers and trees in our garden. I would love to learn even more.

'Yes, dear. Your Father was such a good man to his children.'

Emma showed her mother a book she was reading and said, 'This is particularly interesting about Captain Cook and Joseph Banks. It explains how they collected plants from the country of New Holland, which is called Australia now. They brought samples back to England; we have a yellow Banksia in our garden.'

'Well that is interesting, dear.' Emma's mother replied.

Together, they put all the books back on the shelves.

Emma, taking hold of her mother's hand, got down from the chair-cum-ladder. 'Mother, let me show you where Australia is, on Robert's new globe.'

Lady Pennington looked first but could not find it. So, Emma pointed to it. 'Notice, it is on the other side of the world from us.'

'Such a large country.' her mother commented.

Lady Pennington sat down on the Bergere chair and patted the other seat, 'Come Emma dear, sit here for a moment.'

Emma sat down.

'I am wondering to myself, why did your aunt insist on giving you that book. Tell me, what did she mean when she made reference to an unsuitable one?'

'Oh Mother, you know what Aunt is like. How she likes to make a fuss about everything.'

'Yes, Emma. I know she does indeed. Yet, I consider there is more to it than that. Surely you can tell me, you know I care about you my dear.'

Emma looked down at her lap, but glanced up again at her mother. 'I will speak to you plain. Aunt caught me reading a book she held was shameful for a young lady to read.'

'Which book was that?'

'It was one that Robert read, called "The narrative of a slave". I want to learn about people and things of the world. The book is a true story about the life of an African who was taken from his country to become a slave on the sugar plantation. Later his life changes. I do not know anymore because I did not get the chance to read much of it.'

'Emma, your Aunt Belvedere is fixed on the correct way of doing things.'

'Women should not learn about such things. Some will view it as a disgrace for a woman to learn about a male negro. I understand your reasons were pure. But Emma dear, I dare say. It would be wise not to read the book.'

'Forgive me, mother. I would not wish to bring shame on you or myself.'

'You do not want to spoil your good reputation. Some people can be remarkably hasty in making a woman an object of curiosity by vulgar gossip.'

'Oh dear me.'

'Different rules apply. One for men and another for women.'

'I am sorry, Mother. I was foolish.'

'My dear, I am pleased with you for taking my warning to heart. There are many other things you can learn about. Only I dare say, your aunt will ask you if you have read the book, she gave you. So, I would cast your eye over it.'

'I will. Mother do you know why aunt brought Mr Greystone here with her?'

'I do not know. What did you think of him?'

'Speaking plain enough, Mother. I did not like his manner.'

Her mother reflected.' He flattered us all, he was charming, he is going to invite us to his ball-'

'But, Mr Greystone was not noticeably keen on telling us where he had come from.' Emma added, 'Abroad... where?'

'Yes.' her mother responded. 'I did not know your aunt would bring someone. I do wish she had written. As I could have picked a date when Robert would have been here to entertain him.'

Emma said. 'He seemed exceedingly interested in learning about Robert.'

'It is probably because they are both males.' Lady Pennington replied.

'I do hope, Mr Greystone does not come here often.'

'I dare say, we will have to go to his first ball, my dear.'

'Do we really have to Mother?'

'Yes, we do Emma.'

Just then the clock chimed. It was the hour of 10.

'I must pick some flowers to take to the Dale family. I have already packed the socks and food for them.' Emma kissed her mother's cheek, and they both left the library.

Emma put on her cloak and outdoor shoes. She went into the rose garden and picked some roses to select as a special gift for Nancy Dale.

Emma gathered up the roses along with her parcel. She strode down the path and through the gate, adjoining the stone wall. Then she walked down the driveway. Emma was enjoying the fresh air. The silence being broken only by the whistling of swifts overhead.

Once through the main iron gate. It was only a short walk, as the Dale family lived in one of the nearby worker's cottages.

Reaching their picket fence, Emma opened the creaking wooden gate. One of the children raced out to meet her.

'Hello Molly,' Emma said, 'come and see what I have for you.'

'Tom came out, then rushed in to shout his mother.' Mrs Dale came to the door breathless, wiped her hands on her cotton apron. She curtsied to Miss Pennington and showed her into the parlour and insisted that Emma should sit in the rocking chair.

Mrs Dale explained that her husband was in bed.

Emma whispered, 'I have brought some things for you, and gave Nancy, the flowers and the parcel.

'Mrs Dale's eyes filled up as she thanked Emma, for the beautiful and sweet-scented roses.' She then poured boiling water onto a spoonful of leaves in the teapot.

Emma reflected, 'how kind of Mrs Dale, to share some of her precious tea.'

Emma explained there is tea, bread, cheese and butter and also a jar of honey in the bundle.

The children all gathered around while their mother took out the socks from the parcel. 'They are the neatest knitted socks; I have ever seen.' Nancy exclaimed with such enthusiasm.

Emma asked how Mr Dale was? Mrs Dale rubbed her forehead. 'He is very weak I am afraid Miss Pennington. I pray   that he will get stronger so he can work again soon.' She sighed and praised Mr Robert Pennington for his forbearance towards them. Yet, acknowledged that they could not stay in the house for very much longer. They could no longer pay their rent if Mr Dale was not able to work again. Emma tried to reassure Mrs Dale that her brother would never throw them out on the street with their dear little children. The baby was trying to pull up onto Emma's knee, so she bent down and picked the little fellow up.

'John, you are becoming a big boy,' Emma laughed, as she tickled him under his chin. The children were all trying on their socks. They were a little big, but their mother said that was the best as they grow so quick.'

Emma told Nancy, her next projects would be mittens. 'John held his hands out to his mother, and she took him on to her knee. Emma then heard a noise on the stairs.

'Mr Dale, you ought not have come down.'

'I so wanted to see you, my lady. You have condescended to see us poor folk. I want to wish you God's blessings. His wife started to show him all that Emma had brought for them. Mr Dale was speechless. After a moment he said, 'I have gathered a lot of feathers over the time, I wonder if you would allow me the honour of letting me make you a picture with them? I have glue, paint, and wood. It would give me pleasure to do something for you while I remain in bed resting. Do you like birds, my lady?'

'I love birds.'

'Then I shall make a picture for you, my lady. It would be a reason for me to sit up for longer. It will give me great pleasure and a real honour to make a little picture for you.'

'As long as the feathers are not needed for pillows?'

'We have pillows enough.'

'My husband is very good at drawing likenesses.' his wife responded with a smile.

'Very well, I would love that very much indeed.'

When Emma had finished her tea, she said. 'I must go.'

The children ran to her, and Emma hugged them. They each thanked her for their socks and the food, 'I like the honey best,' said Annie.

'Please do not come to the door. Mr Dale, you need to rest.'

Mrs Dale bent over the roses and said, 'The flowers smell wonderful, like paradise. Thank you, and God bless you, Miss Pennington.'

Emma could smell the fragrance of the honeysuckle which arched over the doorway.

As she came out from the little dark thatched cottage. The sunlight made Emma screw up her indigo blue eyes until she was used to the brightness again.

Emma was just walking away from the cottage, when suddenly. A chestnut horse stopped in its tracks. She jumped. 'Oh, Mr Greystone.' Emma exclaimed 'Where did you come from?' She could not hide her annoyance in the tone of her voice.

Mr Greystone got down from his horse. 'I guessed I would see you along the road here.'

'Please, Mr Greystone, I have to think of my reputation. I must not be seen alone here with you, people will talk.'

'Be assured, fair lady, I won't let them.'

'Whatever do you mean?'

'Indeed, no one will dare gossip about you. I will see to that.'

Emma's jaw dropped, she raised her eyebrows and said, 'May I ask? Who are you Mr Greystone?'

'Me? Who am I? I am an old acquaintance of your Late Uncle Reginald. I am a gentleman and a leader of men.'

Mr Greystone bowed to Emma and got back up onto his horse. He said, 'Farewell, I will see you again sweet Lady and held one hand in the air as he rode away.

Emma was in a state of shock. She glanced all around to see if anyone had seen them. The lane was empty. Emma let out a heavy sigh. She carried on walking back home.

That man will be an arrow in my side, Emma thought. He seems to appear from nowhere.

She started to consider. If Mr Greystone was a friend of my late Uncle Reginald, then Why has Mother not met him before? Oh dear, he leaves me with more questions than answers.

Emma walked toward the elegant house that she called home. The white stone residence in its Palladian style looked bright and cheerful, and the large sash windows glistened in the sunshine. Prettiest of all were the two lilac trees both in full bloom, on either side of the doorway.

Emma realized how fortunate she was to live in such a comfortable home. She compared where she lived, with the small dark cottage that she had just been in. She wondered how they all squeezed into it. It crossed her mind that the Dale family must have to spend a lot of time in the dark, as they would not have enough money for many candles. 'Poor dears,' Emma thought. That would make one feel melancholy.

Chapter three

Emma was sitting at the breakfast table with her mother and was drinking hot chocolate and eating buttered toast with honey.

'How is Mr Dale and his family?' Her mother asked while pouring tea into her cup.

Mr Dale came down the stairs to see me. He was bright in spirits, but he looked gravely ill.

'My dear, I worry what will become of them.'

'I know Robert will not treat them unkindly. For Mr Dale and his father have worked here on this land for generations. Mother, I think I will ask Bess to collect all the leftover wax and honeycomb that we waste.'

'We waste little, my dear.'

'Even a little bit can be melted down to make new candles. It will help them, as their cottage is so dark inside. I dare say, it must make it difficult for Mrs Dale to do her sewing?'

'That gives me an idea.' Lady Pennington said, putting her cup down gently on its saucer. 'Could Mrs Dale take on some sewing alterations?'

'Yes indeed, Mother. That is a splendid idea. When Mrs Dale does anything, she does it very well indeed. All the children have clothes made by her hand.'

'leave it with me,' Lady Pennington said, 'I will see what I can organise.'

Once they had finished breakfast. Lady Pennington called Bess to take away the dishes. She then asked Bess if she could gather up all the leftover candle wax to be made into new candles.

Emma and her mother then made their way into their smaller ladies drawing room.

It was a bright room with plenty of light. Large windows dressed with gold swag curtains and pretty wallpaper with flowers and birds.

Emma and Lady Pennington sat by the marble fireplace. Emma pulled out some machine netting, from her penwork sewing table. She had planned to make a new fichu. Lady Pennington took out of her silk hanging rosewood sewing table, her fine pictorial embroidery of baby Moses.

Both women gathered their chosen threads, and started to embroider.

Lady Pennington asked, 'Are you making your fichu for your bottom drawer?'

'No, mother dear, I want to wear it as soon as it is finished. I know I have not long come out, but I do not think marriage will happen soon although, I hope I will meet the right gentleman before too long, or I will be passed my prime. It seems like us women have only a short period of time to get a husband. Unfortunately, I do not have one gentleman that I truly admire and who, in turn, admires me.'

'My dear, you mean to say that... you are not interested in Mr Nash Greystone?' Her mother hid a faint smile.

Emma looked up and saw her mother was being playful.

'Especially, Mr Nash Greystone.'

'He is wealthy, I think? Although Emma, to be sure, he troubles me a little.'

'Speaking plain enough, he troubles me too, mother. May I ask, have you ever met him before at Aunt Belvedere's house?'

'Never, I can not even remember your Uncle or dear Father speaking of him.'

'How odd.'

'Look, Emma, I have just finished baby Moses. How sweet he looks.'

'How perfectly rendered. Which part will you embroider next?'

'The basket.'

'How dreadful for a baby to be taken from his mother and all his family. To become the son of a female who is unlike his mother, who speaks a different language and has a different culture.'

'Yes, imagine Emma. Sailing across a river in a basket, to an unknown future. All because of a powerful man who is seeking his revenge.'

They both carried on stitching for a little while in silence, with just the gentle ticking from the clock.

Lady Pennington noticed that her daughter was sighing from time to time.

'Emma, I know something is vexing you. What is it?'

'How can you tell?'

'Your sighing gives you away. Emma, my dear, look how tightly you are pulling your thread.'

'Oh dear. The net is puckering up a little. I dare say, I will have to undo the last few stitches.'

'So you see, that is how I know.'

'You are right, Mother.'

'I am listening dearest, tell me.'

'Do I have to?'

'Yes, dear.'

'When I was coming back from the Dale family's cottage, I met Mr Greystone. He got off his horse and spoke to me. He had no regard Mother, no regard, to how that would have looked to anyone, who may have seen him talking to me. I was completely alone. I dislike him.'

'This is a disgrace. I will have to have a word with Aunt Belvedere. She can have a word with him, as it was her, who introduced him, to us.'

'Mother please, no. Please do not allow Aunt Belvedere to be involved.'

'I am astonished by Mr Greystone's behaviour. His forward conduct would seem ungentlemanly. I propose then that we talk to Robert and ask his advice.'

'Robert?'

'As a man. He will know the best way to deal with this situation.'

'It may never happen again, Mother dear?'

'I want to make sure it does not.'

'If it happens again, then we can tell. I would be perfectly satisfied with that.'

'I will give it some thought.'

Emma said looking up from her work. 'I can hear horses and a carriage.'

'Look out the window Emma and see who it is?'

Emma went over and looked out.

'It is Robert, and he has a Gentleman with him.'

Lady Pennington clapped her hands together. 'Dearest Robert has come home early. What utter astonishment that we were just talking about him.'

Emma could now see the other gentleman. 'He is a young man, tall, very smart. I am certain that he is not wearing a ridiculous brightly coloured high neck cloth.'

Emma and her mother laughed.

'Emma, you go down to greet them.'

Emma ran downstairs. She stopped for a second on the last stair to get her breath back. Her cheeks flushed with sudden excitement.

'She walked into the hall just as the Gentlemen came through the doorway followed by Smith carrying in a portmanteau.

'Look at you, Em.' Robert said, as he spun her around.

'Her brother introduced the young man to her. This is my business partner and a good friend. Edwin Sinclaire.'

'I am honoured to meet you.' Emma said with a curtsy.

'The honour is all mine,' Mr Sinclaire replied and bowed. 'Your Brother Robert has told me good things about you, Miss Emma.'

'Emma smiled,' then her mother appeared and greeted their new visitor.

'Robert dear, we are so glad to have you back safe.'

'Bless you, Mother. You do worry about the roads. Mother dear, meet Mr Edwin Sinclaire. He will stay here overnight before getting back.'

'You are very welcome, Mr Sinclaire. I will get Sarah to make a bed up for you in the blue room.'

'Come and have some tea in the drawing room first, while Sarah makes your room up. We can have a chat and hear all about London.'

The Gentlemen removed their coats, and Bess took their coats from them.

'Bess, bring a tray of tea.' Lady Pennington continued. 'Then after, will you help Sarah prepare the Gentleman's rooms?'

'Yes Lady Pennington,' Bess said and left the room.

Robert asked. 'Did you get my letter a few days ago?'

'Oh yes, Emma moved to the edge of the chair. We loved all the descriptions of the fine buildings and shops that you wrote about.'

'Robert, I never realised that the river Thames was so long and busy,' commented his mother.

'Although I much prefer to see you in person, brother dear.' Emma faked a frown. 'I have just sent a letter to you.'

'Oh, how wretched for you Em. They will keep it for me. I will read it next time I stay in London. Did you make any requests?'

'Only to let me know what the fine ladies in London are wearing?'

'Ah.' Robert rubbed his hands together. 'My dear little sister, it happens that my new business venture is in selling machines that will print designs onto cotton fabric. Which I sell to mills. So, Em, that is a subject that interests me.'

'My dear boy, how do you manage all this. On top of running the house and the estate?' His mother asked while holding her palm in the air.

'That is why I have my right-hand man, he pointed to Edwin.'

'Tell me, Robert, what are the fine ladies in London wearing? I am at pains to hear.'

'Women are wearing darker coloured cotton fabric. Also, long sleeves are replacing short ones. Waistlines are dropping a little lower. Aren't you impressed, Em?'

'Upon my word, I am Robert, I am.'

Robert tapped Edwin's shoulder.

'Edwin's Father was a master weaver. Edwin has learnt about fabric from the cradle.'

'Yes, I did indeed. In fact, my Father taught me how to weave when I was very young. He always used the finest threads that you could get at the time. He made wares for the highest of society.'

'How perfectly interesting.' Emma said, clasping her hands together.

'It was the weaving loom. Then it was the weaving machine which I loved the most.'

Bess knocks on the door and comes in with a tray of tea and little plum cakes. She then leaves the room.

'Mr Sinclaire, do you take lemon or milk?' Asked Lady Pennington.

'Milk, thank you,' he replied.

'sugar?'

'No thank you, Lady Pennington.'

'Em, I have a gift for you,' said her brother, getting up from the tub chair. He handed Emma a large silver and white box.'

'What do you think, Em?'

Emma undid the white ribbon and opened the box. There was a beautiful long sleeved green dress with a printed floral pattern on it. Around the hemline, it had pleats and applied silk leaves.

'Oh Robert, it is very attractive. I do thank you.'

Emma kissed her brother on the cheek.

'I did not forget you, my patient mother. I am sure you can guess what is in this bandbox.'

'It looks hat-shaped,' said Lady Pennington, while smiling and undoing the gold ribbon. She took off the lid, and there was a lovely straw bonnet, with red ribbons. She placed it on her head and looked at herself in the walnut carved mirror.

'It suits you, Mother,' said Emma, and everyone agreed.

'The ladies are happy now,' Robert said to Edwin.

'Now you are in good spirits. I have something I wish to speak to you both about.'

Emma and her mother sat down. They both looked at Robert with curious interest.

'While I was in London,' Robert began, 'I have been in the company of a people called Pamela and George who have a delightful daughter called Belinda.'

'Robert dear, who are they?'

'George is a consulting physician.'

'How did you meet them?'

'When I tell you Mother, please do not upset yourself.'

'You worry me.'

'I took ill while in London.'

Lady Pennington put her hand over her mouth as she listened to his tale.

'Mother, the Doctor was called because Edwin insisted. However, it turned out to be food poisoning, nothing more. I recovered very quickly. I wrote a letter to you, as soon as possible after, so as not to worry you both.

'My poor boy, yes, we got your cheerful letter, we did not suspect a thing.'

'Speaking plainly, Mother. The next day, I fainted while taking a walk around Vauxhall Gardens. A kind lady saw me and got a man to fetch her husband, who was a doctor. The Lady and her daughter stayed with me. When her husband, the doctor came and saw who I was. He recognised me as the same gentleman he had called on only the day before. He rendered help to me, for the second time. The next day, I went to see him for I was concerned that I had not paid him. I also wanted to thank the ladies personly, for taking pity on me.

'I see.'

'That was the moment I saw Miss Belinda for the delightful creature that she is.'

'Do you have an understanding with Miss Belinda?'

'No Mother. I have not known her for very long. The reason I am telling you this is I am going to London again in a few days so I can get to know her better.'

Emma questioned, 'What is her family name?'

'I need not say for now, for I do not completely know my own mind as yet. I can assure you both, that Belinda seems a sweet, honourable and caring young lady.' I believe she has feelings for me.'

Emma looked rather distressed.

'How could she possibly have feelings for you? Upon my word Robert, she is not acquainted with you or your family?' Emma snapped. Then, seeing that Mr Edwin Sinclaire was watching her. Emma's lips fell into a smile, she continued. 'Well, I am sure she is very sweet. You would not admire her so if she were not.'

'Mr Sinclaire, have you met her?' Lady Pennington enquired.

'Yes, I have met her a few times. She is indeed, a lady of merit. I dare say, if you saw her and your son together you would see that their natures are well suited, Lady Pennington.'

'Robert dear, I have been hoping you would meet a suitable lady.'

'I wanted to tell you both, as I may ask Belinda's Father's permission to court her. Mother, if I do, I do not want it to be a shock to you and Em.'

'Son, I am more than happy for you. I have been hoping so much that you would soon find a desirable lady who will have to fill the role of your wife, and mistress of this wonderful house.'

'I too have an admirer.' Emma informed her brother while pointing to herself.

'Take no notice of her Robert.' Lady Pennington added quickly.

'I do indeed. He is called Mr Nash Greystone.'

Emma's mother held up her hands. 'Upon my word, Emma, you dislike the man.'

Robert said, 'Em, you are telling me there truly is someone?' His eyes held a puzzled look. 'Tell me my all grown-up little sister, you have my ear.'

'Aunt Belvedere brought a gentleman here. He has been living abroad but is now living back in England. This gentleman showed a great deal of interest in me and praised me.' Emma said while she inwardly winced.

'Do you like him, Em?'

Emma rubbed her lips with her finger.

'Em?'

'It is not important.'

'Why pray?'

'It does not matter whether I do or do not like him. We women can never ask the gentleman we would choose. We only get to refuse a man's offer.'

'Ah, I have the picture.'

Emma stood up. 'Please excuse me.' Emma went out of the room.

Robert said. 'I think Edwin and I will get freshened up. Please excuse us too Mother.' The two of them also left the room.

Emma sat down on a rattan chair in the Orangery. Her cheeks were flushed pink. As she leaned back, in the chair Emma felt something firm behind her that was not a cushion. It was a book. It was the very book Aunt Belvedere had caught her reading.

'How did it get there?' she wondered to herself.

Just then, Emma heard footsteps behind her. She turned around and saw her mother.

'I wonder where I have left that book?' Lady Pennington said.

Emma held up the book for her mother to see. 'You Mother?'

'I confess, I too was curious, dear. Yet Emma, it mortified me to read about slaves, men, women and children who have endured terrible treatment. But I am glad to tell you that gentlemen of the government have passed a law that makes it unlawful now to transport slaves to this country. They are putting an end to slavery. I just wonder, what will they do with all the slaves?

'Oh dear Mother. If they have been treated cruelly. Then I could not love or marry a man who worked with those poor slaves. You can depend on that.'

'A lot of gentlemen have slaves, Emma. I have even known some women who do.'

'I am surprised indeed... women?'

'The sooner there is an end to it. The sooner they can call themselves Christian again.'

'True.'

'My dear, you seemed upset by Roberts news?'

Emma's chin quivered 'I will no longer matter to Robert anymore,' she looked down.

'Upon my word, No, that will not be true. Robert will always love his little sister.' Her mother stroked Emma's hand.

'I will never get used to another lady being in this house with us in your place.'

'It is true, dear. His wife will be Mistress of this house, but Emma, that will not change his love for you. I am sure that Belinda is as good-natured as Robert and Edwin say she is. In time she will become your friend and sister.'

Emma looked at her mother. 'Indeed, I do not mean to be selfish. I am foolish, talking nonsense. Sorry, I just get so upset about things. Oh Mother, I dare say you are right.

'You will soon marry my sweet child. I am sure with your pretty face. You will not lack admirers. You will be loved by a desirable gentleman and he with you in return. I am sure of it.'

'Oh Mother dear, I want to be happy. If only I could meet the right gentleman. I would love to be his wife.

'You shall be a good wife. To be sure, you will see.'

'Before you are 9 and 10 years you will meet someone and get married. Depend upon it.'

Her mother squeezed Emma's hand.

Lady Pennington then left the room taking the book with her.

A little time later, Emma heard strident manly footsteps behind her. She turned around, this time, it was Mr Sinclaire.

He nodded to her and said, 'May I sit here with you while I wait for Robert to come down?'

'Yes , of course, Mr Sinclair.' Emma said.

She had flushed pink cheeks, and her indigo blue eyes had misted.

Edwin Sinclaire spoke to her in a low, quiet voice.

'I see you are distressed, Miss Emma. If I had an older sister who had just told me that she wanted to marry. I think I would feel melancholy too. For it is not the person getting married, It is the fact, things will never be the same again. Do you not think?

'You understand.'

' I think I do. Robert often talks about you. He loves you very much. I think he believed that he was holding you up from marrying because he was not yet married. Your brother said to me, that he was quite sure, that you must have had offers.'

'Upon my word, I never knew that. Please, may I confide in you, Mr Sinclaire?'

'Call me Edwin. Yes, you do me the honour.'

'I dislike Mr Nash Greystone. Believe me, I am not flattered by him at all. The truth is, he makes me feel uneasy.' Emma rubbed her left arm with her right hand as she spoke. Edwin, I was just vexed that Belinda may take my dearest brother away from me. Dear me, it was out of my mouth before I could stop myself. I am a silly creature at times. She looked straight at Edwin and said, 'I am not always that childish. I hope you believe me?'

'You miss your Father Miss Emma?'

'Yes, I do so very much.'

'So, Robert is like a Father and a brother to you.'

'Indeed, I see you perfectly understand.'

'Yes, I can see that.'

'My dear Father never objected to me reading books or learning. My aunt, who is dictatorial, says, women should not worry their delicate heads about learning matters which do not belong to the female mind.

'Ah.'

'I would love to learn the things that men like to learn. Geography, science, nature study. Those sorts of things. I think it would be very exciting to go on a ship and sail to different countries, collecting shells, plants, or gemstones. Do you not think so Edwin?'

Putting his hand on his stomach, he said.'Ships are not for me. I get very sea sick I am afraid to say.'

'You could never be a sailor then?'

'No, not at all, Miss Emma. I will stick to fabric, and printing machines. On land is where I like my feet to be.'

Emma smiled at him.

Mr Sinclaire said, 'There, you are smiling again.'

I am delighted with my new green dress,'

'The dress makes you look very elegant, forgive me if I be so bold, as to say so.'

Smiling again, Emma said. 'You may indeed.'

'Robert has told me, you play the pianoforte very well Miss Emma. I would be rewarded with great pleasure, if you would play for me.'

'Then it will be my pleasure to play for you, Edwin.'

Emma got up, my new piano is in the drawing room. Come with me, while we are waiting for Robert and I will play for you.'

Once in the drawing room. Emma sat on the piano stool and found a piece of music.

'Do you like Ludwig van Beethoven?'

'I do indeed. He is a new breed of living composers.'

'I have a little Bagatelle here, in A minor.'

'I have not heard that piece. Would you like me to sit down over there and listen or stand here?' Mr Sinclaire asked.

'If you would be so kind and sit on the winged chair over there.'

Emma smooths her dress with her hand and then closes her eyes for a moment. Then lifting her hands, she plays the short piece by Beethoven.

When Emma had finished playing. She looked over to Edwin for his thoughts on her playing and the composition.

'What a pretty tune and so well played, by a lady who does justice to the instrument. Thank you. Do you play anything else by Beethoven?'

'indeed, I like to play the Beethoven piano sonata number 14 in C-sharp minor.'

'Ah, now that is one of Beethoven's finest.'

'If you like it, I will play it for you, as I am very fond of it, too.'

Emma found the music behind the piece she had just played. She places it in front of her.

Emma started to play. She was halfway through when Robert entered the room. He too sat down and listened to his sister play the piece.

When Emma had finished. The two listeners clapped.

Robert spoke first. 'For sure Em. You have improved since I last heard you play.'

'I do like to practise every day.'

'I am glad that you get pleasure from the instrument. I do think the pianoforte is an improvement on the old harpsichord.'

'Ah. Because the hammers hit the strings, rather than the strings being plucked.' Edwin said.

'For sure, there speaks a fellow who likes to know how machines work.' Robert winked at Emma.

'Yes, I do indeed. Your sister understands the merits of the pedals on the pianoforte.' She used them with great merit during the Beethoven Sonata.' His eyes lit up as he spoke. It was a pleasure to listen to you play, Miss Emma.'

Robert said. 'Em, I need your help. I would like to buy a gift for Belinda. I would be delighted if you would advise me .'

'I will, how could I say no? I am only afraid that I do not know her or her desires, having not had the privilege of meeting her yet?'

'I thought all ladies liked the same things?'

'We ladies, may like similar things, but Robert. We are all quite different, you know.'

'Let us all go to Chester and see what you recommend?'

Just then. The door bell rang.

Bess came in.

'It is Lady Belvedere with a gentleman, Sir.'

'Ask them to come in,' Robert answered.

Emma's eyes widened. She quickly sat down and took out her white work embroidery. Head bent she worked with her needle.

Lady Belvedere could be heard from the hallway, 'I well know Nash they will understand, these things happen to one, I will do the explaining.'

Mr Sinclaire noticed Emma's anxious face. So he sat down on the chair next to her.

Emma kept her eyes down on her needlework.

Aunt Belvedere and Mr Greystone entered the room.

Robert kissed his aunt on the cheek, but she just stood like a statue.

Robert then bowed to Mr Greystone.

Mr Greystone held out his hand to Robert and shook his hand heartily. He said 'I am honoured, and I dare say-'

'Yes yes, Nash,' said Aunt Belvedere. She then turned and glared at Emma. 'Young lady, are you not pleased to see us?'

Emma got up from her chair and quickly kissed her Aunt on the cheek. Silently nodded to Mr Greystone. She then sat down quickly and again picked up her needlework.

'Let me help you to the wing chair, Auntie.' Robert said while taking hold of her arm. He then said to Mr Greystone, 'Take a seat.'

Robert asked Bess to tell his mother about the arrival of Lady Belvedere and Mr Greystone.

Lady Belvedere fained a cough and asked. 'Who is this person?' Pointing to Mr Edwin Sinclaire.

Robert scowled. 'I was about to introduce you. Auntie, this is Mr Edwin Sinclaire, my business partner and a good friend.'

'Business fellow! I am all astonished. So your workers have rights to our private family life now, do they?'

Lady Belvedere's face held a formidable look as she shook her head.

At that moment, Lady Pennington entered the room.

Robert had exasperation in his voice as he said under his breath, 'such humiliation.'

Emma lowered her eyes.

Aunt Belvedere ignored Robert's vexation and carried on.

'Now listen to me, Robert.' She cleared her throat and waved her finger. 'Nash and I have come here with an invitation to a Ball.' She flicked her fan open and waved it furiously.

Mr Greystone was just going to explain when Lady Belvedere cut in. 'Let me explain to you. Here are the invitation cards. Pass them around Nash.'

Mr Greystone rose from his chair and offered an invitation to each one. He lastly offered one to Edwin Sinclair.

Lady Belvedere with a sour tone of voice said.'I mean, we do not desire my nephew's trade business personnel at our ball.

Robert scowled, he was just about to retort when his aunt continued.

'I dare say, you will notice that the address for the ball is at my house. The reason is, Nash was about to move to Boughton House. Which I must say is a magnificent house. I am sorry to have to report that someone, someone I must say with no scruples. Has excepted a higher offer on Boughton house from another personage.'

Robert looked at Mr Greystone who looked unmoved by this.

'This is why I came to the rescue. As you all know, pleasing people is my nature. So now Nash's first ball will be held at my address.' She tapped her knee with the end of her fan. 'I shall expect you all to be there.'

She then looked over to Mr Sinclaire and drew her eyebrows together. 'most of you.' She then looked away.

Robert drew an audible inward breath.

Then Mr Greystone said, 'A word of praise for your dear aunt. She is the queen of kindness.' He got up from his chair and kissed Lady Belvedere's hand. She hid her face by opening her fan.

Emma glanced at Robert and caught him rolling his eyes.

Lady Pennington quickly broke the silence by announcing that Robert had brought her a splendid bonnet from London.

She got out of her seat to get her new bonnet to show Lady Belvedere. But Lady Belvedere followed her out of the room.

Robert said, 'Mr Greystone would you like to come into the library? You must see my new globe.'

They too left the room.

Emma put her embroidery down and said to Mr Sinclaire, 'I feel quite mortified that our aunt was so insensitive to you. Please forgive us? We should have stood up for you.'

'Dear Miss Emma. It is no matter.'

'She can be so unfeeling and discourteous.'

'Please, do not upset yourself. After all, your Aunt Belvedere is of a higher social standing than I.'

Lowering her voice, Emma said. 'The other day I went to see a man who was ill. Who is a worker on Roberts estate? He had more respect in his work-worn, grimy finger than my aunt has for people?'

'It is kind of you to be concerned about my feelings.'

Emma watched Edwin's hand as he slowly ran it through his chestnut brown hair.

Her eyes became fixed as he lowered his hand down and rested it on the first gold button of his brown waistcoat.

He spoke again. Emma felt herself drift gently back to what he was saying.

'I do not come from the land-owning gentry. I am a self-made man through the skill of designing machines.' He paused then continued. 'I am most grateful to your brother, for his confidence in me and my skills.'

Emma's eyes lingered on the movements of his lips.

As her conscious mind drifted back, she became aware of her long pause and quickly said, 'Robert is sensible, not like Aunt Belvedere.'

'My grandfather and father explained to me that a Master Weaver once had a high status. His weaving knowledge was kept a secret. Only passing on the skill to the male members of the family. The men were highly skilled members of society. The paradox is that machines eroded the status of the weaver's position. That is the reason I had to change the direction of my career.'

Rubbing his chin, he said. 'So, now, I make and design machines.'

'Oh, please do tell me how does the printing machine work?'

'His eyes opened wide in surprise. You, a Lady, want to know how a machine works?'

'I am interested. Indeed I am.'

'Upon my honour. I have never met a lady, not any female who wanted to know how a machine works.'

Edwin's brown eyes glittered as he smiled at her.

He leant closer to her and said in a quiet voice. 'I will draw you a diagram to help me explain it to you.'

'A perfect idea.'

Just then Robert appeared in front of them. 'What are you two scheming?'

Emma blushed, while getting out of the chair and asking Robert to sit in her vacated seat, so he could converse with Edwin. Emma sat on another chair.

She noticed Mr Greystone standing at the other end of the room. He was examining a group of portraits of the Pennington Family on the wall.

She then looked back to Robert. Emma could see that he was fidgeting.

Then she overheard Robert say to Edwin. 'My dear fellow, forgive my Aunty's impoliteness.

Emma heard Mr Sinclaire answer. 'It is forgotten.'

'You are a good man, Sinclaire.' Replied her Brother.

'My Auntie is a formidable female.' Emma heard Robert say. 'Even so, I am alarmed by this unfamiliar Nash Greystone character. He leaves me with so much to be guessed at. I invited him to my library to have a chat with him, but for sure Edwin, he is a slippery fellow.'

'Who does your Lady Belvedere say he is?'

'She claims, he was an acquaintance of her late husband who was my Uncle Reginald, he was a ship's captain.'

Emma then saw the door open.

Lady Pennington came back into the room with Lady Belvedere, followed by Bess and Sarah, who were carrying trays with glasses of whipped syllabubs and drinks of ginger beer and soda-water.

Lady Pennington handed out the drinks. While Bess and Sarah gave out the syllabubs.

'Why is this drink bubbling?' Lady Belvedere asked with alarm.

'It has gas in it, answered Lady Pennington. It is a new drink, called Ginger Beer.'

'No, no, I do not care for it,' said Lady Belvedere as she thumped it down onto the tray. The cold liquid ran down the side of the glass. She put her hand to her throat, then said 'You do not know what it does to your delicate insides.'

Then Aunt Belvedere went over to Mr Greystone, who was examining the pictures.

Emma could see they had their heads together whispering.

She had just finished her dessert when Emma saw her Aunt beckoning with her finger, to come over to them.

Emma went over.

'Tell me,' demanded Aunt Belvedere, 'have you read the book I gave to you?'

Emma felt like a child in front of a judge, putting her hands behind her back She said. 'I have only cast my eye over it, as yet. I have not had time to read it thoroughly.'

'Good gracious, I entreat you not to be idle in this matter.'

'No Aunt, I will read it if you wish me to.'

'After Miss Pennington has read it. She will be all charming delightfulness' gushed Mr Greystone.'

Emma looked down and said nothing.

'I see your likeness framed upon the wall there. Was it perhaps a couple of years ago?'

'Yes.'

'Miss Emma, I feel you are ready to be painted by Thomas Lawrence himself.'

'Thomas Lawrence?'

'The president of the Royal Academy.'

'Good gracious, Nash,' Lady Belvedere gasped.

'May I have a moment alone with Miss Pennington?'

'Very well, Nash.'

Lady Belvedere went to the other side of the room to talk to Emma's mother.

Emma felt uneasy, as Mr Greystone's cheeks were bright red, matching his red neck cloth. He seemed excited when he said, 'Just step into the hallway for a moment, Miss Pennington.'

Emma walked subdued into the Hallway.

Mr Greystone then bowed and said, 'I have a gift for you fair, Lady.'

That flurried her. He put into her hand a little red velvet box.

Emma gazed at it and said, 'I am all astonished, Mr-'

'-Open it.'

Blushing, Emma pulled on the end of the ribbon while her heart began to race.

'I can see you feel excited my dear, the thrill of it.' He said.

A cold shiver ran through Emma's body as she took out a gold heart-shaped pendant on a chain.

'Let me...' Mr Greystone took the necklace from Emma's hand.

'Whatever do you mean?' Emma blurted she continued to say, 'You do me the honour Sir, but I-'

'-I mean, He answered, that a pretty slender neck like yours should be gifted with gold.'

Emma suppressed the urge to recoil because she could feel his clammy hands touching the back of her neck as he fastened the necklace. He seemed to take such a long time. Emma wished that someone would come to disturb him.

'At last, she felt him remove his hand, and Emma turned around swiftly and said 'Mr Greystone, I am honoured and sensible of your kindness... But-

'-There there, I do not need your thanks or praise. I can see that it overcomes you with delight. All I ask is that you wear it at my Ball.'

Emma started to look towards the doorway, praying that someone would come.

Just at that moment. Mr Edwin Sinclaire came into the hallway. He glanced at Mr Greystone, and Mr Greystone glanced back at him.

Emma, keeping her voice steady, asked. 'Mr Sinclaire may I be of help?'

Edwin studied them both with his dark, curious eyes. 'I was just going upstairs to gather my things together to get off in the next hour Miss Emma.'

She felt her stomach churn.

'Dear me, Mr Sinclaire is that the time? I entreat you, do not leave until I have had the chance to say a proper goodbye.'

' Ah.' Mr Sinclaire looked at Emma quizzically. Frowning, he went up the stairs.

'Speaking plainly, my dear miss Pennington.' Mr Greystone declared. 'You do not have to concern yourself with a person who is decidedly low in origin, a fellow in trade.'

Emma asked herself. Has Edwin noticed the gold heart? I must get rid of this necklace. But, how do I get rid of this odious Mr Greystone?

Her cheeks flamed. Emma said, 'Mr Greystone it is time we joined the others in the drawing-room.'

'Do not forget sweet Emma, that you promised to come to my ball. I would be perfectly delighted to see you wearing my love token.'

Emma's body stiffened. The words, a love token, kept running around her head.

She stormed into the drawing room and sat down.

Her Aunt said loudly 'Oh there you are Nash, it is time you helped me out of this chair. We have stayed here long enough.'

Nash Greystone held his arm out to help her. Lady Belvedere took it.

Emma kept her hand covering the heart necklace, while her brother and Mother said goodbye to their visitors. She saw the opportunity to unfasten the necklace, and she quickly hid it inside a cushion cover.

They all went outside to wave goodbye. Emma stood behind Robert and her mother, so Mr Greystone would not see that she had removed the gold heart pendant from her neck.

Emma was extremely relieved to see the barouche and its occupant's leave.

Then Robert asked Emma to go into town with him to help him choose a gift for Belinda.

Emma remarked, 'Belinda will love any gift that you choose for her because it is from you Robert. A gift is more about the person who gives it than the item itself.'

'You never cease to be dear to me Em, with your sensible advice. Do be sure, if I marry. I will always look after you and Mother. You will stay under my roof until you yourself wish to get married. Indeed, I plan, as Father did, to give you a generous dowry. Whether or not I marry Belinda. I shall organise the making of a will when I come back, I do hope Em, this has put your mind to rest on this subject?'

'You are the brother every girl should have. Does Mother know?'

'I have spoken to her about it. But you know Mother gets distressed if you talk about wills, because of our Father.'

' She does so. When is Mr Edwin Sinclaire leaving?'

'Soon, for he has an appointment in Bolton. He is a fine fellow do you not agree Em?'

'fine indeed.'

'For sure, I need to have a strong word with our Auntie.'

'Oh.'

'I'll leave it until the right moment.' Robert cringed as he said, 'You would think we live in the Tudor times. The way she spoke about Edwin.'

'I am only afraid our Aunt is indifferent to how her conduct seems to others,' Emma pointed out.

'Speaking plain enough. That ghastly fellow Greystone she has paired herself off with. Is not even half the Gentleman that my friend Edwin is.'

'Robert, did you find out where Mr Greystone comes from, when you spoke to him while you were both in your library?'

'He muttered, something about being in Africa. I asked him to show me where on my globe. But he quickly moved onto another subject. So, I never found it out.'

With that, Edwin and Lady Pennington came into the hallway.

'Mr Sinclaire is taking his leave now dears.' Lady Pennington wished him a safe journey and told him she was very pleased to make an acquaintance with him.

Just then the carriage arrived and Smith strapped Mr Sinclaire's luggage to the carriage.

Mr Sinclaire bowed to Emma. She felt him gaze at her with reproving eyes.

Emma surveyed inquiringly into his large brown eyes.

He saw the necklace. Emma thought to herself. Mr Sinclaire thinks I am a vulgar double-dealing creature. Her eyes misted.

Smith open the door of the carriage. Mr Edwin Sinclaire got in.

Lady Pennington said, 'Come again soon. You are always welcome.'

Emma bit her lip, waved her hand and then called out. 'Please, do not forget the diagram of the machine you promised me.'

The carriage swept Mr Edwin Sinclaire out of sight.

Lady Pennington said, 'I will have a little walk around the garden for some fresh air before luncheon.'

Emma and Robert walked back inside the house.

Robert looked at the clock. He then said, with the shake of his head. 'I will not have enough time to go into Chester with you, Em.'

'Oh dear.'

'I have just remembered an appointment with a landscape artist and our head gardener in a little while about some improvements I have in mind. I want the garden to look more natural like the surrounding countryside?'

'How perfect.'

'Yes, I will have some trees moved and replanted. To give a view from the house down to the grounds beyond. I want them to create a lake and build a folly. We will also need more gravel paths.'

'Will you have more plants planted in the wilderness garden too?'

'Yes.'

'You are very good Robert. We are blessed to live in such a delightful house. Emma requested, may I speak to you concerning the Dale family please?'

'What is it you want to say?'

'Mr Dale is still very ill. He has not worked on the land for a month now. I know you have shown Christian charity to him and his family. What makes me feel uneasy is that Mr Dale may not be able to pay his rent. I know these things should not concern me. Forgive me Robert, but I wanted to draw the problem to your attention.'

'You need not concern yourself, I will deal with it.'

'I entreat you, my dearest brother. I put myself in their situation and wonder, how would I cope?' Emma's chin quivered. 'They have such sweet little children.'

'Men can handle these problems. It is much too difficult for a woman to do so. Leave it Emma. I will visit them when I get back home from London.'

'Will you be leaving soon?'

'Yes, Em. However, I am disappointed; We can not go to town together to purchase the gift.'

'I dare say, I may have the answer to your problem.'

'What do you mean Em?'

'I have a gold heart pendant, a friend gave to me as a gift. I have never worn it. The heart is too large for my taste. Please do take it as a gift for Belinda. I shall get it.'

'I could not take it.'

'Robert, please do, It would mean a great deal to me.'

Emma left the room. She went back into the drawing room where she found the hidden heart necklace inside the cushion cover.

Emma went back to her brother and passed him the velvet box.

He opened the box and took out the necklace. He gulped and said. 'This is worth a great deal of money Em. You must have a very good friend.'

'Do you like it? Does it have a merit?'

'Yes, it has a lot of weight to it. It must be gold.'

'Indeed, but, will you take it?' She shuffled her feet, while waiting for his answer.

He replied. 'I can not take such a beautiful necklace from you.'

'I have so many jewels, Robert, I will not miss it. I own that it will give me much pleasure to help you out.'

'Then, I will give you a contribution towards it. Then you can get yourself something that you like better. Let us settle on that.'

'So be it.' Emma thought, 'I am relieved to be rid of it.'

Just then, Sarah knocked on the door and announced that the landscape artist had arrived.

Chapter Four

Emma was ready to go to Chester with her friends. With her reticule around her wrist and her parasol in her hand, she climbed into the Berlin Carriage with Dudley's help.

Her friends were already in the carriage, so Emma got in and squashed herself up against them.

The sun was shining, although, there were some grey clouds. Emma hoped it would not rain and ruin their picnic.

'Shall we go to the drapers first?' asked Phoebe. They all agreed to go and buy lace and fabric first.

Emma told her friends what Robert had revealed to her concerning the long sleeve dresses that were in fashion in London and Paris. She told them she wished to make some changes to some of her existing dresses, that still had a lot of wear left in them. She needed some ribbon and lace to enhance one of her bonnets too.

The young ladies got very excited, when they walked into the shop and saw all the different fabric and lace they could choose from.

Dudley stayed outside with the horse while the young ladies bought their wares of lace, wool, silk, and fabric.

Next, they called at the shoe shop, which was an old black and white timber-framed building. Julia got a pair of new shoes in yellow silk. Emma purchased a pair of silver buckles for her favourite shoes. Dudley bought himself a new shoe horn. Isabella bought nothing; She was happiest in the confectioner's shop; She loved cakes and sweets. Dudley was also willing to spend money on sweets too.

'I say, I am hungry,' said Dudley. 'Let us go down to the river and have our picnic.'

They got back into the carriage, and Dudley drove them past the Roman red sandstone walls. He started to tell the girls about how Chester was a Roman fort known as Deva in AD 79. Emma wanted to know what else Dudley had learnt from his schooling about the Romans. But the other girl's face's wrinkled in disgust and they complained that, on no account, where they interested in Roman history. Emma was disappointed not to hear more, but she kept quiet for they outnumbered her. The carriage went down towards the river. They saw Chester bridge over the water and they could see the meadow on the other side. So, they went over the bridge and they got out of the carriage and looked for a place to set out a picnic.

Dudley gave the horse some water. Then he took his net with him to see if he could catch some butterflies, while the girls got the picnic organised. As all the friends had servants at home, it was fun for them to get the food and dishes out from the baskets to lay them in an attractive manner. It was freedom that they never really felt when in a house behaving with politeness and restraint.

Dudley came back with no butterflies. There were grey clouds gathering overhead, although the sun shone. Wasps buzzed around the food, which Dudley swiped away with his net. The girls deliberated about the lovely fabrics they had bought and what they planned to do with them. Emma asked

Dudley to tell her more about Italy where the Romans came from. Emma's friends complained. Phoebe said, 'Most assuredly Em, you should have been a boy.' 'Whatever do you mean, sister? asked her brother. 'I mean, Em seems to be more interested in boys' subjects.'

'Dear me, Phoebe. I like girl's things very much indeed. I desire to get married and have children, like you. I just desire to learn about the world like boys do at school.' replied Emma.

'Upon my soul, I would not want to study like boys do,' said Julia, 'What lady would want to know about women being carried off by armies or arrows flying from a castle to kill your husband or your children being taken from you?' Julia started to laugh and say with her eyes twinkling. 'Maybe, just maybe, Emma wants to know about the Romans so she can spend more time with Dudley.'

'Julia, I have known Dudley since I was little. We have been friends for such a long time. We have always talked freely together.'

'Dudley replied. Yes, Julia we have. Dear Em, I am very fond of you. What is more, you are more like a sister to me. I say, marriage would be just a foolish fancy. To be truthful, I dream that my fine lady will have black hair and deep brown eyes. I am sorry Em, not flaxen blond hair and blue eyes.'

Emma with her arms crossed over her chest, said mockingly. 'Whatever can you mean, you horrible scoundrel...' With her hand she swept a curl back from her brow and laughed.

Then they all laughed, except for Isabella, who asked, 'I have seen a distinguished-looking gentleman riding a fine horse. Is he new to the area, do you know who I mean?'

Emma felt her cheeks burn.

Julia said, 'Yes, I have seen a man who looks smart, yet is rather plump and plain looking.'

Dudley added. 'I think he must be an unmarried gentleman, as I have never seen him with a lady.'

 Phoebe then thought and said, 'I think I have seen him once, he came to our village. He looks rather like the dull sort to me. Although, the colours he wears are not dull, indeed they are very bright on the eyes.'

Julia agreed, 'not a desirable type of man, I think.'

Isabella said, 'I like the look of him. Why should he not be a fine husband, especially if he is wealthy with a fine large house.' She continued, 'It is all very well when you are pretty like Emma, Phoebe or you Julia. Men will fall in love with you and ask for your hands in marriage. But confound it, when you are too wide and plain like me, you certainly do not get the choice of handsome men!'

'No dear me, Isabella You are not too wide or plain,' Julia responded. 'You have a very pretty face you certainly have great merit, and you look very fine to be sure.'

 'I dare say, you are just being kind to me.'

'No,' the three girls said in unison.

'I say, I will go and give the horse an apple.' Dudley remarked then made a quick exit while the girls discussed the topic of Gentlemen.

Isabella said with conviction. 'I imagined that he might not be so interested in thinner girls, being strong and large and wide himself. He does look dignified and although I have never spoken to him. He looks like a fine Gentleman to me.'

'I wonder what his name is?' asked Phoebe.

'Do you know, Em?'

'Oh, it maybe Mr Gravestone or... Greystone Emma answered,' as she pulled a daisy out from the grass.

'Do you know for sure?' Isabella asked while examining Emma's face.

'I dare say... I heard him being called by one of those names... I think... I may have done.'

'Do you like him?' enquired Isabella.

'well, I-

'I don't believe it,' said Phoebe, 'we have received a ball invitation from a Mr Greystone and we wondered who he was.'

'Have you Em?' asked Julia.

'Oh, I... I do remember now, we did. Robert is away in London so he will not go. I did not want to go. Alas, my mother said, we must. Depend upon it, I am so happy, that you will all be there.' Emma said, while stroking the grass with her hand.

'Upon my soul,' Said Isabella. 'Is that the puzzling invitation my mother received? She said we could not go. As we have not been introduced to the gentleman. She would never connect herself to a stranger. Whatever am I to do? I must go to his ball?'

Julia frowned. 'What I want to know is why would a stranger invite people to his ball? ones, who he does not know?'

'I wonder why?' whispered Emma under her breath.

'Dear Isabella, you can come with us,' said Phoebe. Your mother will let you come with us as she will think we must know the gentleman.'

'I will, that is a splendid idea.' Isabella said with delight. 'I need to look for a husband before my mother and grandmother chooses some terrible one for me.'

'Then that is what we shall plan. Dudley can take us, so the three of us can go together.'

'Will your Mother and Father go Phoebe?'

'Father hates balls. It is unlikely he would go to a ball of a gentleman he has no acquaintance with. I could not say for sure, if Mother will? If she does, there will be room for us all. Isabella, we can get the master of ceremonies to introduce you to Mr Greystone or whatever his name is.'

'I do hope he is not engaged to some wealthy, pretty girl,' Isabella said, 'her eyes looking upwards with thoughtfulness.'

Emma broke into the conversation and said. 'Isabella, do not let your imagination run away with you. As he may be a blockhead or not have moral scruples. Perhaps he may not even be the sort of person who he claims to be.'

The three girls stared at Emma.

Julia broke the silence, 'time is getting on. Black clouds are coming over. Let us tidy up and go to the circulating library.'

'Yes, lets.' The girls cleared the picnic things away. Then Phoebe waved to her brother to come back.

Dudley helped the girls put the baskets away into the carriage.

'Are you going to make a daisy chain with all those daisies you have pulled up?' asked Isabella.

'Daisies?' Emma then realised she had not been aware that while she was talking, she had pulled out a bunch of daisies. So, gathering them up she said. 'Yes, I will.'

All the friends got into the carriage.

Dudley stopped the carriage for a few minutes to watch the flowing river. Dudley spotted a kingfisher. Which thrilled them all.

Dudley drove the horse and carriage back toward the newly built Georgian building, which contained the Library.

He told the girls that he would sit and have a nap rather than go into the circulating Library. As he had enough books waiting to be read next to his bed and in his study.

Julia and Phoebe had subscriptions. So, Emma and Isabella paid their pound for their year subscription.

Emma felt very excited. Now she could read books and learn about the wonders of the world. Whether Aunt, Mother, Brother or friend approved the books or not.

Emma paid the gentleman and asked him. 'Sir, where are the books about geography?' The gentleman showed Emma to the shelf displaying the geography books.

Emma thought to herself. I will find a book about the Romans in Chester.

She saw that her friends were looking at novels. Emma liked to learn about real life.

Emma tilted her head to one side to read the writing on the spines. Seeing the one she wanted she felt the shiver of excitement. It was so nice to make one's own decision about something. Emma picked out the book, opened it, flicked through the pages. She saw some maps and one or two engravings. The writing looked very sharp and clear. She took the book.

Emma saw a little area with gloves for sale which Emma enjoyed looking at, even though she was not in need. 'I must start my next knitting project, mittens for the Dale family,' she thought.

Emma saw the girls; They had found some novels they wanted to borrow. They all went to the desk to have their books noted, they were given a card with the return date.

'Shall we look and see what the reading room is like?' asked Isabella.

They agreed and followed her through the heavy wooden door. As she pushed herself hard against it to open it. They all gasped with surprise, because sitting at the table with lots of books spread out over it was Mr Greystone.

Emma got hold of Julia's arm and pulled her back. Too late. Isabella had walked up to Mr Greystone with a wide beam. He looked up.

'What is it?' He said, with a grunt.

'You do not know me Sir but-'

'-Go away then.'

'Sir, please allow me to explain. I have received an invitation to your ball.' Isabella said. Mr Greystone raised his head and saw the four young ladies. He caught sight of Emma discreetly leaving the room. As she was quietly shutting the door behind her, she felt a strong tug against the door, it opened and there stood Mr Nash Greystone right in front of her.

Emma's spine tensed as he said, 'Miss Emma Pennington. How desirous of you to do me the extraordinary honour of finding me.' There was a wide grin on his face. He kissed Emma's hand and continued, 'To bring your friends with you, to have it out in the open. To me, this is not a small matter, this means a great deal to me.'

He then pulled a chair out for her and said, 'Please, you and your friends must join me.'

Emma's friends were standing opened mouthed. Emma was so shocked she could not speak.

Julia said. 'We are pleased to make your acquaintance Mr Gravestone.'

'Greystone,' he corrected her.

Turning his attention to Emma, he said. 'I have invited all the people of your acquaintance. Your Aunt Belvedere has been a great help to me. She gave me a list of your circle. I dare say, I presume these ladies are your close friends?'

'Yes indeed we are,' said Phoebe.

'Splendid, then you will all come to my first ball.'

Isabella said, 'Only, my mother would not let me go to a ball of someone to whom I had not been introduced.' Isabella sighed, 'forgive me Sir, for you cannot know how much I would wish to go to your ball.'

Julia said to Isabella, 'No dear, your mother will not stop you. For now, Emma has introduced you to Mr Greystone.'

'Glad to hear it,' Mr Greystone said with cheer in his voice. 'I want all Miss Emma's friends to enjoy a jolly evening.'

Phoebe surveyed the books on the table. Books about English law. Opened maps of England and Scotland, books about Australia and ships of the high seas. Great houses of England and a newspaper.

'What a lot of books your reading, Mr Greystone.'

'To be sure, I have a thirst for learning,' he answered. Miss Emma Pennington, I know is also fond of reading books as he tapped Emma's hand with his.

She withdrew it quickly. Emma felt her head spinning she could hardly think straight.

A Lady and Gentleman came into the reading room.

Emma could feel her heart beating so fast it made her feel faint and breathless. It gave her an idea. She would pretend to swoon so she could leave the room.

Emma, let her body sag against the chair, 'I feel faint' she said, pressing her fingers to her forehead.

'Em are you ill?' Isabella asked.

'I need air.'

Phoebe and Julia took hold of Emma and helped her out of the chair.

The lady came over to help the girls get Emma outside. 'She needs more air,' the lady said.

'More air.' Emma said in a soft voice.

'Em dear,' Julia said, 'Keep walking, we shall soon have you back in the carriage.'

Phoebe thanked the lady for her help.

Julia asked, 'Do you want to see Mr Greystone, Em dear?'

'No, NO.' Emma answered firmly.

Isabella enquired, 'Are you in love with Mr Greystone?'

Emma replied, her voice showing signs of agitation. 'Keep him away from me.'

Dudley saw the girls holding on to Emma, opened the door, and helped the girls into the carriage.

Mr Greystone then appeared and asked. 'Is miss Emma Pennington very ill?'

'No Sir. We shall get her home,' Phoebe answered. 'I dare say it is nothing that a good night's sleep will not mend.'

'Take good care of her, for I feel sick to my heart. She must be well for my ball...'

Soon, the carriage then sped down the road at great speed.

Dudley asked, 'What is wrong?'

His sister answered, 'We just do not know. Upon my life Dudley, I do not know.'

The girls sat in silence. Emma sat motionless with her eyes closed. She was breathing calmer now.

Julia stroked her face. 'Em, Emma dear.'

Emma opened her eyes. There were three faces looking at her.

'Thank you, my dearest kind friends. Depend upon it, I had no part in encouraging that man. It is his contrivance, not mine. My Aunt has encouraged him with some foolish fancy that I could be his. Speaking plainly, my Aunt is taken in by him. I do not believe he is the person who she thinks he is?'

'I do not understand you Em.' Julia said. 'He spoke like a perfect gentleman.'

Phoebe added, 'He likes you very much indeed. I can see that with my own eyes? I will say, it may be true he is not so very handsome. Yet, he is most kind. He has gone to a lot of trouble by inviting all your friends to his ball. I wish I could find a man who thought of me that way.'

'Oh dear me, you have been taken in, also have you?' Emma said with her eyes opening wider.

The girls did not know how to answer. Isabella broke the silence.

'If you do not intend to have him. Please, acquaint him with words of merit about me.'

The other two girls shouted, 'Isabella. You have no conscience!'

'I entreat you, Isabella.' Emma said with earnest. 'He is not the Gentleman you think he is.'

'I think you are wrong.' Replied Isabella, folding her arms and blushing up.

'Attach yourself to him at your peril. There is a falsehood, believe me.'

Julia said, stroking Emma's hand. 'He seems like a charming gentleman who has just fallen for you, a younger lady. You must throw him over quickly. It will grieve him at first. Yet afterwards, he will soon see it as a fleeting small matter. Then, Em dear, you too, will see it was just a foolish fancy of his. That is all.'

Emma realised that she had not convinced them.

They sat in silence the rest of the way back.

When Dudley stopped the carriage outside the gate. Emma said, 'Please dear friends do not speak of my foolish outburst to my mother. I do not want to distress her.'

They all agreed to keep it quiet.

'Will we see you at the ball?' asked Dudley.

'You have all been very kind. Only, please do not ask me.'

Emma thanked Dudley and the girls for their care. Then she walked up the drive alone.

Chapter five

After breakfast, Emma was sitting at her little satinwood desk, writing.

'Emma.' Lady Pennington called.

'I am in the study mother.'

Her mother came in.

'Emma dear, we have a letter from Robert.' Lady Pennington passed the letter to her daughter.

Emma took it and read the letter, then said, 'He seems to be having a lovely time in London with Belinda and her family. Oh, he is asking us to take some foodstuff to the Dale family.'

'Yes, we shall go together.' said Lady Pennington.

'Indeed, we shall go.'

Lady Pennington noticed that Emma had her hand over her letter.

'Are you writing to Robert dear?'

'I will.'

'You are writing to someone else?'

'I...'

'Emma, what are you hiding?'

'Why Mother? It is no matter.'

'Emma, what is it that you are so keen to hide from me?'

'Just... Aunt Belvedere.'

'Emma?'

'Mother dear, I cannot, on no account, can I go to the ball.'

'So you are writing to your Aunt, Emma, it will not do. You will bring her reproach upon me if you do not go. Depend upon it, young lady. You will be going to the ball with me.'

'Dear me, Mother, I am old enough to decide for myself.'

'Emma, do not refuse the invitation. Believe me. I shall not be put off by any inducement in the world, from making you go to the ball.'

'Oh, mother. Why do you always do what Aunt Belvedere desires you to do?'

'I have a thorough regard for your Aunt Belvedere's kindness.'

'Kindness?'

'Yes, young lady, her kindness.'

'I do not understand...'

'Emma, if you must know. Your father came close to losing most of his fortune. Aunt Belvedere and uncle Reginald saved us by lending your father a substantial amount of money. They also helped your brother Robert, paying his school fees for the first three years. Your father had to take some risk, but he paid back all his debts. He paid back the money that your kind Aunt and uncle lent him. I am so grateful and will never forget their kindness.'

Emma put her hand to her mouth. Fear hit her and despair washed over her. Feeling trapped and yet she felt pains of guilt.

Her toes curled. Emma looked at her mother and said, 'Now everything makes sense.'

'So I say, Emma, you can rip up the letter. Then check you have your things ready.'

'You never told me?'

'Could you have the goodness to think in a more generous way towards your aunt in future Emma?'

'Yes, mother.' She said as a weight settled on her heart. For Emma knew that escape from Mr Nash Greystone would be impossible now.

Chapter Six

The evening of the ball had arrived.

The Pennington's carriage drew into the crowded, noisy driveway of Lady Belvedere's grand house.

It surprised Lady Pennington and Emma that so many carriages were queuing to park.

'It must be a very large ball.' Emma's stomach was knotting.

'Indeed, Mr Greystone must know a lot more people than we thought,' Lady Pennington said.

Once the groom had helped them out of their carriage. They walked up the steps into Mollington house. Their cloaks were taken from them by a female servant and a footman directed them into another room. Emma and her mother weaved in and out through groups of people and found two vacant seats to sit on while they changed into their dance shoes.

As they left that room, they were directed to a table in the hallway where Mr Greystone had set out a guest book. For he had made a request that all his visitors sign it as they arrived for his ball. So, Emma and her mother signed their names.

They could hear the musicians tuning up and there was sounds of chatter from every room they passed.

As Lady Pennington and Emma arrived into the ballroom itself, it seemed as bright as if midday, for it was alive with so many wax candles.

Lady Belvedere reserved this room only for special functions and Balls. It was a wonderful large room with a very high Rococo stuccowork ceiling. Which was painted in gold, aqua and white. Everywhere one looked on the ceiling and walls was stucco of Shells, flowers, palm trees and birds. The room was full of chandeliers glowing with candles which were spitting rainbow stars from the crystal glass.

Emma had not been in this room before; It had been wrapped over in dust sheets. The door had been locked since her Uncles' death. Her Mother had explained to Emma, that her Aunt, never saw the need for holding balls, since she had no husband nor children.

Emma looked around and saw large windows draped with gold swaged curtains. There were large full-length mirrors between the windows, which made the room look even bigger. She could observe lots of oil paintings with pastoral scenes hung here and there. Beautiful large displays of fresh flowers along with guilt cages with stuffed birds and wax flowers. There were also a few pieces of fancy fine wood furniture with marquetry, prettied with swirls and curves in gold. With the fine Rococo fireplace standing prominently at the far end of the room.

Lady Pennington and Emma had their names announced, which were at once dampened in the sound of many voices. Emma's mother fanned herself. 'With all these people it will get very warm in here.'

'A real squeeze. 'Emma nodded.

'Emma dear, can you see your Aunt?'

Just as Lady Pennington said that. Emma caught sight of a very large ostrich feather weaving its way towards them, when it arrived, Emma smiled, as she saw it adorned her Aunts fancy headband.

'Splendid, You are both here.'

'Indeed, Martha dear, we would not have missed your ball.'

'Nash longed to hold a ball in his new house as I told you. I was desirous of coming to his rescue. As you are very well aware, that pleasing people is my nature.'

Emma now understood why her aunt always said that, a little more, than she did before.

'Yes, you do Martha dear.' Lady Pennington then kissed her cheek.

'Emma, do you have anyone down for the first two dances?'

'Not yet, Aunt.'

'Upon my word, that is no good. No, no. The music will start soon. You must spend the evening dancing.'

'I know someone who wanted the first dance with you. Can you guess who?'

Emma looked down and fingered her earlobe. Her heart started to thump loudly. She asked, 'who is it?'

'A friend of yours called Dudley Gilpin. He told me he wanted the first dance with you, so I will take you to him, as he did not spot you first.'

Lady Belvedere held out her arm to Emma. She took it and went with her aunt to where Dudley was sitting.

'Dudley boy, here she is, stand up, the music is going to start.'

The master of ceremony announced the start of the ball. Mr Greystone was standing next to him with his face beaming. He spotted Emma and gave her a wide grin.

Everyone got in a line including Dudley and Emma. The musicians began to play, then everyone moved in unison. The dancing had started.

'Are you feeling well?' Dudley enquired.

'Yes, perfectly well now. I am delighted that you have asked me to dance with you.'

They parted to dance with a different partner then came back together again.

'I did not think you would come Em after the scene with Mr Greystone in the library.'

'My mother would not let me decline.'

'If I may inquire, what will you do Em? He is most likely to ask you to dance with him.'

'Oh, Dudley. That is going around and around my mind. I feel sick with uneasiness.'

'I was thinking Em. I know they set rules to dance only two dances with the same female. However, I am agreeable to cut in and save you from having to dance with Mr Greystone. As it is not a matter of much consequence to me to dance more often with you. As I do not have a sweetheart.'

They parted to dance with a different partner then came back together again.

'You are a fine fellow, Dudley. I do thank you with all my heart.'

'We are very close friends you and me Em, we go back a long time.'

'Yes, indeed. Have you seen the girls?'

'Yes, Phoebe and Julia are dancing with our neighbour friends.'

'I have not seen Isabella since we got here.'

They parted again to dance with a different partner then came back together again.

'I must say Emma, Mr Greystone has a very fine house.'

'Upon my word, this is not his house.'

'No?'

'To tell the truth, this is my Aunt Belvedere's house.'

Dudley raised his brows. 'Well, confound it. This plot gets thicker.'

'Yes, even my aunt has been taken in by Mr Greystone.'

The music ends. All the dancers take their seats around the edge of the room.

Emma was hot, so she got out her fan that her aunt had bought her. She vigorously fanned herself.

Emma looked over to the other side of the crowded room and sighed, seeing Isabella talking to Mr Greystone. Poor Isabella, thought Emma, she is completely taken in; She does not understand.

Emma also saw Julia was talking to Doctor Solomon Sherborne who was Emma's family doctor and a near neighbour.

Dudley said to Emma, while pointing to the next room. 'Let us go and have some ices.'

'Indeed, it will cool us down.'

Dudley led Emma into the next room where the ices were being served. They both tucked into their lovely cool ices. Julia came in with her neighbours and another girl they had brought, and introduced them to Emma and Dudley.

The girl caught Dudley's eye, and he asked her for a dance. She was a pretty girl with ebony black hair and lovely chocolate brown eyes, a petite person called miss Susan Roscoe. She said yes to Dudley's request.

Julia and Emma and two of the other girls ate their ices and talked about their dresses and jewels.

Emma forgot all about her anguish until she heard the music stop. Then the master of ceremonies clapped his hands and asked all the ladies to come into the ballroom.

Julia and the neighbours obediently put their ice glass down onto a silver tray and went into the ballroom. Emma turned around and slowly walked in the opposite direction, hoping not to be noticed, but a gentleman said 'you are going the wrong way miss.' Pointing, he said, 'The Ballroom is this way.' Everyone was walking towards the ballroom so Emma was compelled to go in the same direction as the flow of people.

Mr Nash Greystone was standing next to the master of ceremonies who clapped his hands and called for everyone to be quiet. He directed all the ladies to stand in a circle on the dance floor.

'Mr Greystone,' The Master of ceremonies continued, 'will choose the prettiest Lady in the prettiest dress. There shall be a prize for the winner.'

There was a whisper and the ladies all stood in a circle. They ushered Emma into joining the circle.

Looking over to the other side of the room, Emma could see her mother sitting next to Aunt Belvedere. What is going on? Emma thought as she looked left and right. Just then she heard Dudley whisper from behind her. 'Em, I am here at the back of you.' Miss Roscoe came and stood beside Emma in the circle. She said, 'This is like a cattle parade at our village market.' Emma wished she could disappear.'

Mr Greystone was walking around the circle and looking at each lady, then too soon, he stood face to face with Emma. She tried to look past him but Mr Greystone lips fell into a grin, as he moved on to look at the next lady.

Mr Greystone then whispered the winning name to the Master of Ceremonies. Who called for everyone's attention and said in a loud voice, 'And the winner is – Miss Emma Pennington.'

Everyone in the room clapped and the Master of Ceremonies presented the prize to Emma.

The music started up again. Couples got in line to dance.

Emma became surrounded by Dudley, Julia, and Susan. Lady Pennington and her aunt came over. They all wanted to see the prize that Emma had won. She looked inside the box, with hands lightly shaking. Emma took out a gold and turquoise stone bracelet. Everyone agreed that it was such an amiable prize, very generous. Lady Pennington kissed her daughter and said, 'Emma, you do look splendid indeed.'

Emma placed the bracelet back into its box and stood frozen to the spot. Everyone dispersed to get a drink, for it was airless and hot.

'Can I get you a drink, Em?' asked Dudley.

Emma was lost in thought and was immobilised to the spot, so she did not hear Dudley ask. 'Em, Emma, I entreat you, are you well?'

Emma did not seem to hear, so Susan and Dudley helped Emma sit down. Susan fanned her. 'Dear sweet girl, are you ill?'

Dudley looked at Susan and said, 'Don't forget you have promised a dance with Mr Fox.' 'Oh, Sweet Heaven, you are right. Will you be able to watch over Emma?'

Yes. You go and dance. I will help Em into the library. There should be fewer people in there. It will be quiet for her she can take a rest.'

'Shall I get her mother?'

'No, not yet, let her have a little rest first.'

'You are a good friend to her.'

'I say, Susan. Would you care for another dance with me, later on?'

'I would be delighted.'

'Mark me down for the dance after the next one.'

Miss Roscoe hid her smile with her fan and walked away.

'Come into the library, Em,' Dudley whispered. 'It will be cooler in there.' He helped Emma walk to the library.

Dudley opened the door. They saw two middle-aged ladies playing cards.

He helped Emma sit on a couch where she would not be disturbed. She quickly fell sleep.

Dudley left the room so he could have another dance with Miss Susan Roscoe.

One of the ladies who was playing cards said to her partner, 'It is time to eat dear, I say, we better go and see.' So, they left the library room.

Just then Lady Pennington put her head around the door. 'Emma, my dear there you are, it is time for supper. What is wrong, have you come down with a headache?

'Yes, Mother.'

'Do you need to go home, or would you like supper?'

'My headache is dreadful. I need to go home.' Emma said, pressing her fingers to her forehead.

'Of course dear, I shall go and ask for our carriage to be called for.'

A few moments later, Emma saw the door opening and in walked Mr Greystone.

He came over to Emma. Cupping her face with both hands, Emma groaned. 'Please leave me alone.'

Mr Greystone knelt down by her side and said softly, 'I love you. Do not sent me away for I am in love with you Emma Pennington.'

'Please.' Emma jerked out her hand. 'Mr Greystone do not say another word.'

'He grabbed hold of her fingers and kissed the back of her hand.'

Emma pulled her hand away and stood up.

'Mr Greystone this has gone far enough.' She raised her hand again in protest.

'I dearly love you,' he professed.

He took hold of her right hand and said, 'Miss Emma Pennington will you marry me?'

Emma quickly replied, 'I am sensible of your offer. But Mr Greystone, upon no account can I marry you. We would make an imprudent match you and I. We are not alike. We think differently, so I must decline your offer.'

She shook her head in disbelief. Wild pink flushed her cheeks.

'Why? Why do you refuse me?' His eyes filled up.

It cannot be, for you do not know my desires. I own that I certainly do not know your desires or even your true nature, Sir.' Emma said in a firm tone.

'Is my ardent love not enough for you?'

'It is not enough for me.'

But... you came, you came to find me, in the reading room, at the library in Chester.

'I am sorry but I did not. Please, Mr Greystone. I do not wish to marry you. I am sorry. I see I must put it plainly to you.'

'So, so... you will not marry me? You will not marry me why?'

'Mr Greystone, you are a mystery to me. I do not even know where you come from?'

'I was in Africa; how can that be important?'

'What did you do in Africa?' Emma asked, with a tremble in her voice.

'A slave overseer on a sugar plantation.'

'I could never marry a man like you.' Her heart was sinking as Emma realised, she had spoken her mind at last. 'I do not endorse slavery. I rejoice that they can no longer bring Africans across the seas. Depend upon it, I know there will be an end to slavery. I sincerely hope it will be soon.'

'He was not listening to her, every inch of him craved her love.'

Emma hurried to the door and said, 'Please leave me alone.'

With a dejected tone, he said, 'You are not wearing my love token heart necklace or your prize, Emma?'

Ignoring the question. Emma quickly left the room.

Chapter Seven

L ady Pennington called out, 'Emma dear, we have a letter.' She looked at the initials in the wax seal. 'Where are you Emma?'

'Coming.' Emma entered into the women's drawing room. 'Is it from Robert?'

'It is from E.S.' Her mother broke the seal. 'Upon my word it is from Mr Edwin Sinclair.'

'Oh?'

'He says, that Robert has asked him to call in on us when he is next in the area. To check that we are well and not in need of anything.' Mr Sinclair says, 'He shall call on us later today.' I shall be very glad to see that nice young man, again.'

A feeling of energy filled Emma. 'Yes Mother. We shall both be delighted to see him again.'

'There is something else in here.' Her mother pulled out a folded piece of paper with a drawing of a machine on it. With arrows pointing to different parts of the machine which led to drawn boxes with tiny neat writing in them.

Emma smiled. 'It is a diagram of the printing machine. Edwin remembered.'

'What a funny thing to send a young lady.'

'I asked Mr Sinclair to draw me a diagram of how his printing machine works.'

'I dare say, he must think you are a strange female.'

Emma thought to herself. I am only afraid he must think; I am a double-dealing sort of creature. She then said aloud. 'I shall have a walk around the garden. Mother dear, do you wish to come with me?'

'I would have, except, I have some things I must do this morning.'

Emma put on her overshoes and spencer jacket and went out to have a stroll around the garden.

Emma was standing near to the iron gate when she saw Isabella on the other side of it.

Who said. 'Em, I was just coming to see you.'

Emma opened the gate and let her friend into the garden. 'Come and sit on the bench with me under the oak tree.'

Isabella sighed and said. 'Em, I want to ask you if Mr Greystone has any intentions towards you. Be truthful with me. Do you have an understanding with him?'

'Why do you ask?'

'I ask for one reason only. I am rather interested in Mr Greystone. Marrying a fine gentleman like him would make all my dreams come true. I feel though, from my observations. That there may be an understanding between you and Mr Greystone. As you are my friend Em, I need to know for sure.'

'Why do you think that?'

'Because every time he danced with me all he did was ask questions about you or your brother.'

'What did Mr Greystone want to know?'

'He asked, did I know if you and Dudley were engaged, or have an understanding? I told him that you were not. Mr Greystone also wanted to know when your brother Robert was due back home. What puzzled me the most was that Mr Greystone seemed to think as you were not engaged to Dudley Gilpin you must have been talking all the time, to me, all about him.'

'Him?'

'Mr Greystone?'

'Dear me, what did you say in answer?'

'I drank a little at the ball, so I was feeling a little more relaxed than usual. I told him what I knew. Mr. Greystone seemed upset that you had said little to me about him. In fact, I am vexed with you Emma Pennington. Why did you not warn me at the picnic that you knew Mr Greystone well? You let me embarrass myself, in front of our friends. How could you do that to me? I feel mortified just thinking of it. It is well for you being pretty, for you can play with Gentlemen's hearts and still have the pick of the best gentlemen.'

Emma frowned and said. 'Upon my word, I do not play with men's hearts. I am telling you plainly. I do not have an understanding or engagement with Mr Greystone, nor with Dudley Gilpin.'

'You do not?'

'No, absolutely not. Believe me Isabella, I have no intention ever to have an understanding with Mr Greystone.'

'You do not like him?'

'I dislike him. Mr Greystone was a slave overseer. I have found out that they treated their slaves cruelly.'

'How would you know that?'

'My mother read about such goings on, in a book.'

'So, maybe one particular overseer was harsh. It does not mean that Mr Greystone was. Goodness me, Mr Greystone looks a kind, dignified gentleman. He is a friend of your own aunt, and she thinks highly of him. I do not understand you

Emma Pennington. He chooses you from all the ladies at the ball. He praises you. Are you sure you are not mistaken in your thinking towards him?'

'You think I am wrong or that I am being malicious about him? Yet Isabella. I have a rather strong negative feeling about him. So why would I feel that way?'

'All I can say is. I would be so thrilled to have a gentleman like him thinking well of me. I wish it was me that Mr Greystone thought of.'

'You would not wish it.'

'I do.'

'Are you sure, after knowing this?'

'Yes, Em.'

'I will invite you to meet him the next time I learn of his coming with my aunt.'

'Sadly for me Em, he will not notice me because he will only have eyes for you.'

'No Isabella, for I know Mr Greystone must look for someone new.'

'Whatever do you mean?'

'Isabella, I will confide in you. I turned him down.'

'Down.'

'Yes.'

'Please no, it gets worse. Mr Greystone has asked you to marry him?'

A flash of temper lighted Isabella's eyes. 'That is that then,' Isabella pronounced. 'There is nothing further you can say.' she stammered. 'I must, I must go.'

Isabella put her hand over her mouth, tears fell from her eyes. She hurried and left the garden crashing the iron gate closed without turning around. Isabella hurried away.

Emma called her name, but Isabella was gone. Emma stood for a moment and let out a sigh. She knew she had to calm down.

Sitting down again and looking up at the fluttering leaves of the oak tree, Emma's mind went over and over the conversation, until she was distracted. She spotted a siskin shifting from branch to branch, his yellow feathers brightening the Green hue.

The sound of the breeze rustling the leaves soothed Emma until the bird flew off and she next heard a robin singing from another tree which helped her to shut her eyes and relax.

What seemed like the next moment? She heard someone speak her name. Emma opened her eyes. There before her were a pair of deep brown eyes, gazing straight at her.

'Miss Pennington?'

'Mr Sinclair.'

'Yes, I have come to call on you and Lady Pennington. Although I am sure you do not need me here. I have come out of respect for your brother Robert. He asked me to come and see you both to make sure you are well.'

'You are very kind. I am delighted to see you again. I know Mother will be too.'

'I wonder...'

'Oh, most assuredly.'

Emma extended her hand towards him. 'Come into the house.' She said again with conviction. 'Mother will be pleased to see you again, as am I.'

They walked together along the drive towards the house.

She said, 'Mr Sinclair, the last time you saw me, I was in the hallway with Mr Greystone-'

'-I entreat you Miss Emma, do not concern yourself with me or what I think.'

'Please, I have been desirous of speaking with you since we last met.'

'Very well.'

'You saw me speaking with Mr Greystone. Perhaps you took it, that I was intimate with him?'

'Please, it is none of my concern. It just took me by surprise. I was confused, I mistakenly believed you did not like the gentleman...'

'I assure you. Mr Greystone tricked me. I did not know he was going to give me a gift. I saw that you discerned the heart necklace around my neck when you passed me in the hallway.'

Emma put her hand against her throat. 'Please, believe me, I felt mortified when he fastened it around my neck. You need to know that I did not speak falsehood when I told you; I dislike Mr Greystone.'

'Miss Emma Pennington, may I appeal to you?'

'Of course. Please do.'

'I do not understand? May I inquire? Why is it so desirous for a fine lady like you, to tell someone like me, your feelings?'

'I would hate you to go on thinking of me as a deceitful person.'

'Dear Miss Emma, that would be a great reproach indeed.'

'My peace would be shipwrecked. If I thought you thought so badly of me.'

'Most assuredly not.'

'Indeed, Mr Sinclair. It would be very distressing to me.'

'I am perfectly persuaded. I shall not be the means of giving you any pain.' Edwin smiled. 'If you must know, I think most well of you Miss Emma.'

'You are very kind. I thank you. Edwin, I turned him down. He asked for my hand, and I turned him down flat.' She sighed. 'Now, I am afraid of Mr Greystone.'

'You are afraid of him, and now you have been distressed by me. Ahh, I am sorry for you. So, you refused to marry him then?'

'I will never marry Mr Greystone.'

'Miss Emma, I hope I too, have not upset you, when I sent my drawing of the machine with the letter. Forgive me for my presumption.'

'Oh dear me. No, it was me who asked you. It was charming, most charming. I understood the diagram and can see how the machine would work.'

'Miss Emma, you are most amiable. Although I believe you need someone to take care of you. Edwin held his hand out and asked, with a twinkle in his eye. Shall I call him out and fight a duel with Mr Greystone?'

'No, indeed no.' Emma smiled back at him.

Edwin was near the front door when he stopped and turned.

'Emma?'

'Yes.'

'Did you really understand my drawing, of how the printing machine works?'

'It took me some thought, yet, once I imagined it working in my mind's eye, I understood it.'

'You have intellect, which most women that I meet, scarcely know that they possess. You are different.'

'Is it wrong in your eyes?'

'No, it is wonderfully right.'

'Emma blushed a little.'

'I encourage you wholeheartedly. To be sure, I admire you.' Edwin's face turned serious. 'I promise no harm will come to you.'

'Oh, how I wish I had never met Mr Greystone.'

'Mr Greystone may have been drawn to your pretty face, your feminine form. But I do not think he would have loved or understood your wonderful bright, enquiring mind… but forgive me for speaking my conviction when I say, I do.'

Emma's eyes gleamed.

They both stood silent for a moment. Edwin put his hand on the handle. But slowly, he removed his hand and turned again. He gazed at Emma. His lips moved, he almost said something.

Emma wondered what he was going to say. She smiled and raised her eyes to look up at him.

Edwin grasped her hand and drew her towards him. Enfolding Emma into his arms. He confessed to her. 'I have fallen in love with you.'

She closed her eyes for a moment.

'Dearest Emma, I hope I have not frightened you. I told myself repeatedly that I should hold back. Ahh, but now that you are near me. Forgive me, for I cannot hold back from telling you how I feel.'

They both held a lingering gaze.

'I have released my burning heart. Emma, I can no longer

hold back how I feel.'

'Dearest Edwin.'

'Am I right or wrong? Tell me Emma?'

'I feel the same.'

'Are you sure? You do not wish me to go?'

'No, please stay.'

'Dear, dearest Emma, I love you even more than that wretched Mr Greystone does.'

With tenderness, Edwin cupped Emma's face in his hands. 'It is not a cold chain with a gold heart that should drape your pretty neck; it ought to be swathed with warm affection with lips from a loving heart.'

He caressed her right hand, pressed his lips to it, and whispered. 'All I hoped for was, that you could open your heart a single hair's width to my love?'

'Edwin, you have breached my heart. You have opened it wide.'

He let go of her hand and stood a small distance away so he could look at her.

Emma said, 'Yet, Edwin, we have only been in each other's

company for a few hours?'

'What are a few hours when love feels so irresistible between us?'

Emma's own sensations reacted to his words. She stroked his cheek with her finger. 'I have thought about you over and over again, yet I believed that all chance had gone. I dared not even reveal my true feelings to myself.'

His eyes smiled at her. 'Upon no account could I believe that a fine precious Lady like you would have any feelings for a working artisan like me. Yet, I could not think of any good reason why you would care so badly about what I thought of you.'

'I believe a title is not what makes someone a Lady or gentleman. My feeling is, they must act in a Gentlemanly or ladylike way.'

'You are a fine lady, from a good high family. Alas, Emma. I do not have a rank or title.'

'You have one special thing, which all the other gentlemen do not have.'

'Upon my honour, what is that?'

'My beloved brother, Robert, thinks highly of you.'

'Dearest Emma, that seals it.'

'What do we do now, Edwin?'

'I will have to write to your brother, for permission to court you.'

'What shall we do about Mother when we go into the house?'

'I could speak to your mother if you wish, or I could wait until I write Robert?'

'I do not think my dear mother will oppose us. I know she likes you, she told me so.'

'Are you sure? Do you think I should ask your mother first? Upon no account, do I want to shock her. I don't want to put her into a faint or anything worse.'

'Dearest Edwin, Mother will love you, because I love you. The good thing is, she knows Robert thinks highly of you. She seems to trust Robert's judgment.'

'I do not have a title. I am a weaver's son, although not poor, I earned my own wealth. I can support a wife but... I do not come from the gentry class, I do not have a title as one from the top mode.'

'If this is how real love feels, matchmakers of our class know nothing,' Whispered Emma.

'I am the happiest man alive. I could not feel happier even

working at my father's loom, or on a throne in a palace.'

'Edwin, I am extremely happy too, but dear it is time to go in and see. I am sure Mother will love you as much as I do.'

'Dearest Emma. You know your mother best. I shall take your direction on the subject. I will tell her, if you wish it. Shall I be valiant and tell her?'

'Oh, that is the spirit. No fear anymore.' Emma's eyes were glistening with pleasure.

Edwin kissed each of Emma's hands. 'I adore you.'

Emma threw her head back with delight and laughed. After, calming, she smoothed away some creases from her dress.

Edwin put his hand onto the handle and opened the door.

They walked into the hallway, 'There you are Miss Emma,' Sarah said. 'Lady Pennington has just asked me to find you.'

Emma and Edwin glanced at each other. 'What room is Mother in, Sarah?'

'The drawing room, Miss.'

'Carry on Sarah. I will take Mr Sinclair into the drawing room.'

They both took a deep breath. Edwin winked at Emma as she opened the door and walked into the room.

'Mother,' Emma said, 'here is Mr Sinclair already.'
Lady Pennington smiled. Mr Sinclair bowed. She asked him to sit down.

'It is nice to see you again. Mr Sinclair, would you like tea?'

'Why yes, thank you.'

Lady Pennington pulled the cord for Bess. She asked for tea and seed cake. After which Bess closed the door behind her.

'Mr Sinclair, it is very good of you to call on us like this. Robert worries about us so when he is away. Please reassure him we are perfectly well.'

'Is there anything you wish me to get for you, Lady Pennington?'

'No, thank you. Other than a little news about Robert and Belinda.'

'Yes, Lady Pennington. Robert is greatly occupied in London. I know he has seen much of the young lady.'

'Mr Sinclair would you reassure me, if you can, that she is not the pretentious or the ostentatious sort?'

'Quite the opposite. Belinda is a well-bred young lady, with an elegance of manner and is refined in taste. She plays the harp and speaks with a well-modulated voice. She is interested in medical science and helps her father, who is a consultant physician. I have found her to be a woman of merit.'

'I can see that you are in love with her too.'

'Oh no, no. Upon my honour, I-'

'I am playing with you, Mr Sinclair.'

Edwin coloured up.

'Do you have an attachment Mr Sinclair?'

Emma bit her bottom lip and looked at Edwin.

Edwin looked over to Emma. Emma communicated by the movements of her brow and eyes to Edwin that she wanted him to answer her mother truthfully.

'Ahh.' Edwin pulled himself up erect. Glanced again at Emma. Then said. 'I must speak plainly to you Lady Pennington. Your amazing daughter, Emma, has been in my thoughts since we first met. I was astonished to find that she too has been thinking about me.'

'Oh.'

'On meeting again today, we have formed a strong attachment. Lady Pennington. I love your daughter very much indeed.'

'I am never more astonished.'

'Your daughter is everything I desire in a woman. She has a lively mind which I wish to nurture, rather than control.'

'Oh.'

'I understand, that I may not be the ideal eligible sort that you would have wished for. But, Lady Pennington, I can assure you that I shall always behave in a gentlemanly way. I wish to ask you if you would allow me, Lady Pennington, your permission to court your dearest daughter Miss Emma Pennington? With the view that it will lead to an engagement then marriage?'

Edwin audibly breathed out again.

Emma felt her cheeks burning as her mother's questioning eyes swept over her. 'I am confused.' Her mother confessed.

Lady Pennington picked up her fan and started fanning herself, 'Is it hot in here?'

There was silence.

Lady Pennington frowned and asked her daughter. 'Is this true, Emma?' Her eyes narrowed as she searched her daughters face.

Emma answered, 'Yes, perfectly true Mother.'

'This is an immense surprise to me.' Lady Pennington said. Even a shock to me, as Mr Sinclair, you have only just arrived here.'

'Yes.'

'I do not understand. You have only seen one another for a short time, in fact, for hardly a days' worth of hours before now?'

'True.'

'Mr Sinclair, 'can one discern love so quickly?'

'I know I love Emma.'

Emma declared, 'Edwin is wonderful.'

Lady Pennington frowned, 'Mr Sinclair you are a little older, I think. You should know better?'

Edwin shifted around in his seat.

'It will not do, upon no account Emma... It cannot be.'

'Oh dear me. What is wrong?'

'I have only just opened this letter.' Emma's mother held it up. 'It came early this morning, from Aunt Belvedere. She says she is coming over to congratulate you on your engagement to Mr Greystone?'

'Aunt is wrong Mother. She is mistaken. I am not engaged to Mr Greystone.'

'Your Aunt says, 'Nash Greystone proposed to you at the ball.'

'Mr Greystone did propose. But I turned him down. I said I would not marry him. I told him no in a clear way. I left him in no doubt at all.'

'May I speak up for Miss Emma?' asked Edwin. 'Lady Pennington, Emma told me the same. Mr Greystone asked her for her hand, but Emma refused.'

'That is all very well, Mr Sinclair. Except you were not there.'

Lady Pennington picked up the letter and read it aloud. 'Mr Greystone has left me and gone abroad for a short time, to add to his fortune. So, upon marriage to Emma, dear Nash will be able to keep her well provided for, with the best of everything.'

'Upon my word, Mother, Edwin. Please believe me. I have never said I would marry Mr Greystone. To put it plainly, I deeply dislike him.'

Emma held out her hand to Edwin. He took hold of it.

Her mother looked displeased at seeing their hands touching. Edwin slowly withdrew his hand away.

118

Lady Pennington stood up shaking her head. 'What am I to do?'

Emma put her hand in her mother's. 'Please, Mother dear, please, you know me more than anyone else. You know I always speak the truth to you. Believe me. Mr Greystone is obsessed with me. But it is Edwin I admire and love, not Mr Greystone.'

'Yes, Emma, but what will your Aunt think of us, she has been so good to us in the past. Remember, your kind aunt is your father's sister. She may choose a husband for you and not you yourself, you have been undoubtedly foolish.'
'Please mother dear, do not call me foolish.'
'You are foolish-
'Mother I cannot bear you to be vex with me.'
'Vex...no I am not vexed, I am angry with you Emma, yes angry with both of you.'

Edwin lamented. 'I have done wrong I am to blame.'

Lady Pennington shook her head in disbelief. 'My daughter is a dreamer, wanting to make her own decisions. Learning about things she ought not. Mr Sinclair, as good-natured as you are, you would not understand these things. I have brought Emma up, to be a Lady, she has learnt life's rules from the cradle.'

Emma said with a sob, 'Life's rules. Rules. All I want is a happy life with Edwin.'

Lady Pennington's voice croaked a little, betraying her angry feelings.

'It cannot be. Upon no account, have you known each other for long enough? You are from different situations in life.'

Edwin replied, his voice growing increasingly shaky. 'Dearest Emma. It will break my heart to say this, but your mother is right. We have only just met. It is true, I have fallen in love with you. Please, Emma, believe me when I say. It is because I love you that I must leave. I will not cause pain or come between you and your mother. I would not be acting as a true gentleman. Edwin looked at Emma with a meaningful look in his eyes. 'You must believe me, it is with such an agonising heart, that I must now leave...'

'No, oh no, please no... Edwin, please I beg of you please stay.'

'Sometimes in life, sweet Emma. A man has to do what we deem to be correct.'

'No, please-'

'I am so sorry, dear sweet Emma.' He took her hand, kissed it tenderly, then uttered the words, 'Forgive me. It is the right thing to do.' He slowly released her trembling hand.

Tears ran down Emma's cheeks. 'Oh, please... I cannot concede our separation...' Emma's body felt limp. Her heart felt like it had been shot with an arrow.

Edwin raised himself and bowed. His eyes filled up as he wished both of them all good health and future happiness. Edwin turned and paced out of the drawing room.

Chapter Eight

'Where is she?' Lady Belvedere summoned on entering the hallway. That girl should be here waiting for me.

'Emma is in bed, Martha dear,' Answered Lady Pennington.

'In bed, in bed this time of the day?'

'Yes...'

'I require my niece here, get her up. What is wrong with her, anyway?'

'Martha dear. Let me explain-'

'-Did you get my letter?'

'Yes, I did dear, that is what I wish to talk to you about before you converse with Emma.'

Lady Belvedere sat down on the bench and folded her arms across her chest. 'Tell me.' She said in a controlled, tempered voice.

'My Emma says, she is not engaged to Mr Greystone. She told me she even turned down his offer of marriage.'

'Good gracious me. Such an impertinence of the girl. Is Emma so unfeeling that she would treat Nash and me in this dreadful way?'

'Martha, she does not wish to marry him.'

'Wish? What are wishes? Are young girls going to decide for themselves who they should marry? She must have set her cap for someone else. Foolish fancy. Emma does not know what is best. We are wiser, she must defer to us.'

'Why do you believe Emma should marry Mr Greystone?'

'Nash is my dear friend and a fine gentleman. To be sure, he worships the very shadows of her footsteps.'

'Yet, Emma dislikes him and his profession.'

'Someone has to watch over the slaves.'

'But-'

'That is not a subject for a young lady to have any personal opinions about.'

'I dare say. Martha.'

'-Charlotte, you need to put your foot down firmly, about the books she reads. They put silly ideas into her head. Ideas that are not proper for a young lady. Your Emma will end up on the shelf. Robert will bear the cost of keeping her. You need to be firm, firm, I say.'

'I do not know what to do?'

'Make her marry Nash.'

'Are you sure Mr Greystone is all that he purports to be? Is he trustworthy? Does he have enough wealth to keep her secure?'

'Yes, Nash is looking for another house as fine as Boughton House.'

'Does he pay his way, while he is staying with you Martha?'

'He has not yet had the opportunity to pay me back for his ball. I well know he will. Depend upon it, he will pay me when he gets back.'

'You mean, from Africa?'

'He told me he has a different, new profession now.'

'So what is it?'

'I never asked him, Charlotte. I am not interested in men's occupations. Only in their yearly income and their social standing.'

'Martha, may I ask you. Had you met him when your Reginald was alive?'

'I am old dear. Upon no account can I remember all the people, I have had contact with over the years. This is getting tiresome. It is Emma we are sorting out, not me.'

'Martha, listen to me. Emma has another admirer.'

'No, she cannot.'

'Yes, Martha, I have heard the declaration from the man's own lips. He confessed as he spoke to me in this very house.'

Lady Belvedere snapped her fan shut. 'Who is this person?'

'Mr Edwin Sinclair.'

'No, no, Charlotte. It is not to be born. He is low, from trade. He was not born to become a fine gentleman.'

'He is tremendously gentleman like. Mr Edwin Sinclair is not without wealth. Robert thinks highly of him. Emma loves him. Yes, Martha, even though I sent him away, I am still persuaded to like him.'

'Where is she? I am going up to her room to have a word. I do not care if she is asleep. This girl needs a strong husband to take control of her and Nash is the one to do it.'

Lady Belvedere thrust herself up the staircase, with Lady Pennington following behind her.

The Aunt flung open the bedroom door and charged around the bed. In the loudest voice she commands, 'Emma, awaken now.'

Emma shot up into a sitting position before she had time to think. 'Aunt Belvedere, what are you doing in my room?'

'Your hair looks a mess girl; it never normally looks a mess. What is the matter with you? Are you mad or something?'

Lady Pennington stood at the foot of Emma's bed and said, 'Tell your Aunt what you told me, Emma.'

'I beg of you, leave me alone, please.'

'No, no.' Lady Belvedere pulled the bedcovers off her.

'You have been a foolish girl. Whatever are these imprudent fancies about Emma? This trade person? This Sinclair creature?'

'I love Edwin, Aunt Belvedere, and I do not love Mr Greystone.'

'Love, Love, what makes you think marriage is all about romantic love? Books are the problem. You read silly books and believe them. This is real life, not a play. Do you want to damage your reputation? Become a servant? Make debt your only friend? Starve to death?'

'Why should I have to suffer those things upon marriage to Mr Edwin Sinclair? He has wealth, regular yearly income and a house. He has a loving heart. He has knowledge and understanding of the world. He loves me. He is the man I want-'

'You have spoken hastily. Mr Nash Greystone has all those qualities and more. I will ask you to hold your tongue young lady.'

'Mr Greystone does not have a house.'

'Not yet.'

'Mr Greystone does not have a loving heart.'

'Nash's high regard is lost on you. Hold your tongue, I demand .'

'Emma, Martha, please...' Lady Pennington pleaded with them to keep their voices down, so the servants would not hear them.

Emma got out of the bed and sat on the side of it and said in a quieter voice. 'Aunt, please do not become angry over this.

You have only known Mr Greystone for a short while, just as I have only known Mr Sinclair for a short time, too.'

'Now you listen to me. I have known Nash Greystone for longer than you have known Edwin Sinclair.'

'True, but Robert has known Edwin for more than a whole year. If Edwin Sinclair were not trustworthy, my brother would never have asked him to come and check on our welfare?'

'I do not care for him, he is not one of our class.' Lady Belvedere's face wrinkled with the look of contempt.

'Aunt, tell me, why do I have doubts about Mr Greystones character? Why do I feel that way?'

'Thoughtless girl, it is because you are young and do not know what is best for you.'

Emma's mother raises her hand, 'We should leave this until another time when we are all calm.'

Lady Belvedere continued with exasperation in her voice. 'Emma Pennington, I want you to give up Mr Sinclair.'

'Edwin Sinclair has gone. Please do not ask me to engage myself to Mr Greystone.'

Lady Pennington waved her hand to attract attention. 'We can talk about this tomorrow after a night's sleep.'

Aunt Belvedere took another deep breath. 'I am telling you, Emma Pennington. Nash has gone abroad not because he needs to, but to build up his fortune, for you. That poor dear man has taken on a new profession. Determined to acquire a large fine house for you, and supply everything and more that you need as fineries. Why? Because, he worships you, and yet, you do not deserve it.'

'With respect, Aunt. I think he had to find a new profession because slavery is ending soon, which I am very pleased about, indeed Aunt, I really am.'

Lady Pennington said. 'Emma, I request that you give your Aunt a kiss and we shall all leave the subject alone for today.'

Emma stood up and kissed her aunt on the cheek. Aunt Belvedere stood stiffly clenching her hands at her side, after which she stormed out of the bedroom, with Lady Pennington following her. Aunt Belvedere strutted down the staircase into the hallway she then turned and said to Lady Pennington. 'That was a disgraceful scene. Your daughter is quarrelsome and uncivil to me. Why do you allow it? I am her elder. I demand respect. Poor Nash, I was so desirous of them getting engaged. I am deeply vexed that girl is a foolish creature.'

'I am sorry, Martha.'

'I am going now. No need to kiss me, Charlotte. I am too cast down.'

Due to all the distress of yesterday, Emma could not face her breakfast. She got up and was dressed. Her hair was styled with Sarah's help.

Emma sat on a stool by the window. Watching the men dig up the ground for the garden landscape improvements.

Emma reminisced to herself about how happy she has been living in her childhood home with her brother and her mother. She even started to think. A very rare thought. Emma was asking herself. Would it be so bad if she never married? If she remained unwed and lived with Robert and Belinda if they married? Emma loved Edwin, and he had left her. How miserable she felt thinking she would never speak or see him again. Emma wondered. What would she do if she happened upon Edwin Sinclair unknowingly in another town or in the countryside? Would she fall into his arms? Would she hate the sight of him? These questions looped around and around her mind. However, Emma could not give an answer.

Chapter Nine

There was a knock-on Emma's door.

'Come in.'

Bess came in. 'Miss Gilpin is asking for you, Miss Emma.'

'Upon my word, it is not visiting time yet? Did Phoebe say what she wanted?'

'Your friend seems determined to speak with you privately, Miss.'

Emma went down the staircase and saw Phoebe in the hallway. Hugging her she said. 'Come into the study, Phoebe. Sit down and tell me, is there anything wrong?'

'Em, I felt I must be the one to come and tell you what has happened to Dudley.'

'I fear you bear no good tidings.'

A tremor shook her friend's lips. 'Dudley has been hurt.'

Emma cried out, 'Hurt...'

'Yes. He was attacked on his way home from a concert.'

Emma covered her mouth with her hand. 'Oh, dear Dudley. Who did it?'

'Someone hit my brother from behind. Fortunately, he managed to get home. I sent for Doctor Sherborne, who reassured me that although they bruised him, Dudley will recover with a good rest.'

'Thank heavens.'

'You asked who? Dudley told me, although he was attacked from behind. He managed to turn around and caught sight of someone running away.'

'Who was running away?'

'The man who ran away was a tall thin man, a stranger to him. 'Phoebe clenched her hand. 'Em, it is not the man who ran away that I need to tell you about. It is the man who that man ran to; was no other than, Mr Greystone.'

'No. Nash? You say that Mr Greystone has paid someone to attack Dudley?' Emma felt a shiver run down her spine.

'I am mortified to say, Em, I believe it is true.'

'But why?'

Phoebe lowered her voice and said. 'Are you sure you can bear it, Em?'

'I know I will hate it and it will frighten me. But why dear Dudley? I must know.'

'The thin man accused my brother of being in love with you. He believed Dudley was stopping you from marrying Mr Greystone. My Brother was told to leave you alone, at once, with verbal threats.'

'I am mortified.'

'I think the offensive thin man had been told or paid to attacked Dudley because he was seen spending time with you at Mr Greystone's ball. So, Mr Greystone believes that you are in love with Dudley, and he with you.'

'Oh, ... I see.' Emma cast her eyes down. 'It is all my fault that your dear brother is caught up with this. I must see him.'

'Is that wise, think of it Em. It could be dangerous. What if the thin man catches you?'

'I dare say, you are right. Oh, dear Phoebe, what if your father finds out?'

'Rest easy, dear. Dudley told our father that the man was a drunkard. My brother told me he could smell whisky on the thin man's breath.'

'Oh dear me.'

One thing that has come from this is. Susan Roscoe has paid a visit. She came along with three other fine young ladies who were sisters. All the young ladies were pretty, but I think Dudley is growing in fondness towards Susan.'

'Susan seems a sweet girl and there is no one better than your kind brother.'

There was a look of bemusement on Phoebe's face. 'I think my brother is enjoying Susan's attention.'

'Good.' Emma's eyes had a distant look.

'Dear Em. Depend upon it, it will all blow over. Mr Greystone will soon get over you and come to his senses. Maybe he will even find another Lady to bother over.'

'Oh... dear me.'

'What is it?'

Emma pressed her fingers to her forehead. 'Isabella likes him.'

'I would not wish Mr Greystone on her.'

'I must warn Isabella about him.'

'Quite so.'

'You and Dudley have always been such good friends to me. Indeed, I love you both.'

They both hugged each other.

'I must go. Take care of yourself Em. I will call again soon.'

'Give your dear brother all my best wishes,' begged Emma.

Chapter Ten

A little later a letter arrived, Emma paid for it. The communication told of Roberts homecoming.

Emma rushed to find her mother. 'Mother, Robert is due home tomorrow. He says he has some happy news for us.'

'We need some Emma dear. For now, it is time for our visit to the Dale family.'

'I do hope, they will not notice my heart-breaking sorrow.'

'I know you are upset about Edwin Sinclair. But it will help you, to think of others.'

Emma and Lady Pennington got ready. Gathering up the gifts, they left the house.

Emma and her mother were walking towards the Dale family's cottage. Lady Pennington wrinkled her brow and asked. 'Why do you look all around Emma?'

'Oh, ... just looking at the lovely bushes Mother.'

'You give the impression as if you are looking for someone to appear out of them?'

Emma caught her bottom lip between her teeth and looked straight ahead.

Her mother chuckled. 'Your aunt Belvedere perhaps?'

'Dear me. What an image I have in my mind. My Aunt jumping out from behind the bushes.'

Lady Pennington's looked serious again. 'You remember Emma. We still have to face your aunt later today.'

'Mother? I do wish she would not interfere with my life. I know she cares for me. But even so. I have lost my true love.'

They walked in silence to the little cottage, as Emma opened the gate, young Tom ran out and asked if he could carry their loads in for them.

Annie took Emma's arm and pulled her into the dark little room, where her mother and her Father were sitting.

Mrs Dale sprang up and told Annie to let go of Miss Emma's arm.

Nancy Dale pointed to a chair and asked Emma to sit down. Mrs Dale quickly wiped the seat of her own chair then begged Lady Pennington to sit down too.

Lady Pennington smiled. 'We are delighted to see that you are looking a little better now Mr Dale.'

'Thank you, my Lady.'

'I am so glad. I was in great concern for you, Mr Dale, when I last set eyes upon you.'

'God has been kind to me.'

Mrs Dale added, 'Doctor Sherbourne says he'll be back to work on Monday week.'

'We are most pleased to hear of it.'

'Yes, we shall report the good news to my brother,' added Emma.

'I have your picture, Miss Pennington.'

'I look forward to seeing it.'

'You are both very kind to us. We are so grateful to you, for the sewing work you arranged for Nancy, which has saved us my Lady.'

Mr Dale handed Emma the picture, of two real looking birds. She could see he had painted the two birds first and after added the real feathers. He had put it in a little wooden frame.

A smile lit up Emma's face. 'I am delighted Mr Dale, thank you.'

'Mrs Dale asked her children to stand in line and said to the children, Say thank you to Lady Pennington and Miss Emma Pennington.' All the little voices said in harmony, 'We thank you from the bottom of our hearts for your kindness to our family.'

'Very well-done children,' Lady Pennington said, as she clapped her hands.

Emma felt a strong attachment to the children. She thanked them and said. 'You must have been practising hard to say such a wonderful thank you in unity.'

The children grinned while they sat on the rag rug by their mother.

'Would you care for tea, Lady Pennington?' asked Mrs Dale.

'No, thank you. We cannot stay.' Lady Pennington rose from her seat.

Emma continued. 'We have to get back as we have a visitor.'

Mr Dale thanked them very much for the kind gifts.

Mrs Dale went with them to the cottage door.

After the door was shut, Lady Pennington said to her daughter. 'You need not tell them we have a visitor, Emma. It is none of their business why we have to leave.'

'I am sorry Mother.'

'Now they will look out of their window to observe who is coming to see us.'

They walked home in silence. Emma could tell her Mother was flurried about their dreaded visitor, Aunt Belvedere.

Her heart sank with the thought of it.

Once back home they went to their separate rooms.

Chapter Eleven

E mma came into the women's drawing room. She brought in a jug of glue and placed it on an old cotton cloth, covering the games table. Emma was covering a tea caddy with paper filigree quilling, and was trying to keep her mind off from her distressing sadness and fight away the exasperation she so sharply felt in her mind.

Emma felt great pain while contemplating the fact she would never be married to Edwin Sinclair. She now realised that she had in a deep way fallen in love with him; Emma now knew what real love was.

It also crossed her mind. Mr Nash Greystone would be feeling this way too. But Emma kept wondering why he had hurt her by attacking Dudley Gilpin? Nothing made sense.

Emma asked herself over and over, if Edwin loved her, why did he so easily leave her?

She curled a thin strip of paper around the stiletto quilling tool then carefully removed the circle, pinching one end of it to make a tear shape. As she glued the loose end of the strip to secure it, Emma contemplated how many real tears she could shed, a frown clouded her face.

She next reflected on Robert and his happy news. Did it mean that Belinda had agreed to marry him? Emma knew she would have to cope knowing her brother had found the woman of his dreams. Yet, she also knew when Robert tells her his news, she must look happy.

Emma contemplated. Shall I ever be happy again? She considered, all I desire is to be happily married with children and be allowed to educate myself from books.

She realised that the paper art was not helping. So, Emma abandoned it for now and made her mind up to go into Robert's library, as she thought, maybe reading will help a little more.

As Emma opened the library door, the smell of the leather book covers hit her nose. Emma noticed an open book on the desk; It was a book about garden follies and fountains with ideas for settings. As Emma flicked through its pages, she saw it had a detailed diagram of how a fountain worked. Upon my word, that is how the water comes out of the top, she comprehended after spending some time looking through the book. She went over to the window and saw the workmen busy putting markers in the ground for the new gravel paths. Others in the distance were clearing away soil, to make a deep hole for the foundations of the new folly, which was the one thing that Robert had always wanted. Emma watched the men for a while, until one man looked up at the window and saw her, she moved away immediately.

Emma thought, I hope the garden will be finished when Belinda sees it. I wish Belinda was coming today rather than Aunt Belvedere. Yet, I would have expected my aunt to have stormed in here by now. Emma sighed, how relieved I am that she has not.

She looked at the clock. Robert will be home soon and he will be on my side. My beloved brother will stand up for me. Oh, how I long to see him. His coach must have left London two and twenty hours ago. I must tell Mother that he will be due home soon. I do hope he gets here before Aunt Belvedere arrives.

Lady Pennington was in the drawing room arranging some roses in a majolica pitcher.

'They look pretty Mother dear.' Emma said as she came into the large drawing room.

Just then, Bess rushed into the room without knocking. 'Please my Lady, Doctor Sherbourne, Lord and Lady Gilpin and a Mr Morrison are here. They say they must see you, as it is dreadfully important.'

'Show them in Bess.' Replied Lady Pennington.

Emma and her mother were standing by the table, as the four people blew into the room in all of a flurry.

'We have some, we have news. I am afraid it is not good news. we are so very sorry.' Said Lord Gilpin taking off his hat. 'My dear Ladies, you better sit down.'

'My goodness.' Lady Pennington dropped the rose in her hand onto the table.

Emma Cried out. 'What is it?'

Lady Gilpin helped Lady Pennington to a chair. She sat down and raised her eyes slowly to Lord Gilpin's lips as he said, 'I am sorry to have to inform you that your Son Robert is... He... I am so sorry... Robert is dead.'

Emma Shrilled, 'Dead. Robert!' She collapsed.

Dr Sherbourne picked her up into his arms and laid her on the couch. He put his fingers on her wrist and took his watch out and listened carefully.

Smelling salts were used to bring Emma around.

The doctor said, 'These Ladies have had a most terrible shock. I am concerned about how this will affect their tender nerves. It is most unwanted news for a strong man, but for two delicate Ladies, it is not to be born.'

Lady Pennington sat rigidly, staring and asked in a weak voice. 'How? Oh, how?'

Lady Gilpin stroked Lady Pennington's hand, and Lord Gilpin said. 'Mr Morrison was the Gentleman who sadly found Robert on the road when he had been thrown from the coach.'

'Did my… did my poor boy feel any pain?'

'No Lady Pennington, he seems to have hit his head against a stone wall,' said the Doctor. 'I can assure you it would have been instant as he never moved at all.'

'Was, was anyone else with him?'

'There was one other gentleman in the coach going to Chester. All the other passengers had already departed.'

Lady Pennington, with a blank gaze muttered, 'a glad day for them, but not for my darling boy.'

Lady Gilpin stood and stroked Lady Pennington's hand.

'Emma is asking for someone called Edwin?' doctor Sherbourne relayed.

Lady Pennington murmured, 'I am afraid, he has gone too.'

'I am not sure who they mean,' said Lord Gilpin.

'I think the servants need to help the Ladies to their beds,' Doctor Sherbourne said. 'I will give them something to help them sleep and keep calm.'

'I will stay the night with them,' suggested Lady Gilpin.

'Yes, my dear, quite right,' replied her husband.

Mr Morrison looked shocked. He was rubbing the brim of his hat with his hands. 'I offer my condolences to you, Ladies. I must report the accident now. I shall take my leave.'

Lord Gilpin went to see the Gentleman out.

Meanwhile, Lady Gilpin, Bess and Sarah helped Lady Pennington to her room.

Emma was still calling for Edwin to come. So, the doctor gave her some liquid medication to help calm her.

Lord Gilpin came back into the room and whispered to the doctor. 'Morrison says, the driver died too. He reckons the carriage was going far too fast around a bend. The luggage started slipping off the roof, and that threw the coach off balance. Morrison was travelling in the opposite direction on horseback when he saw it all happen before him.'

'Poor fellow.'

'His account must have some weight, I say.'

'It would indeed, Doctor Sherbourne said, 'Lord Gilpin. Miss Emma Pennington looks a little sleepier now.'

Just then someone was at the door. One of the servants came down the stairs to answer it. They heard her burst into tears as a female voice demanded. 'Let me pass, out of the way, where are my dears?'

Lady Belvedere opened the door and stood at the mouth of the drawing room. 'Who are these people?'

The doctor rose to his feet. 'I am Doctor Sherbourne, and you are?'

'Sister-in-law and Aunt. Lady Belvedere. Where is Charlotte Pennington?'

'I have met you before,' said Lord Gilpin, as he took a bow.

'That silly female servant talks nonsense. My nephew cannot be dead.'

Sit down, dear Lady, requested Lord Gilpin. 'I am sorry to have to tell you that your nephew Robert has died in a terrible coach accident almost an hour ago. He was on his way home from London.'

Lady Belvedere got out her handkerchief from her reticule. 'Get me a cup of sweet tea,' she ordered, waving her hand.

Lord Gilpin called Sarah. She came into the room sniffing.

'Sarah, I request that you bring in tea.'

Lady belvedere walked over to the couch where Emma lay asleep.

'Poor young creature. Such a strong will, brought low by this terrible thing.' She felt Emma's forehead with her hand.

'Stone cold. She is such a handsome creature, golden hair and very feminine. No wonder poor dear Nash loves her so.'

'She is a rather pretty looking young lady,' Doctor Sherbourne echoed.

'Yes, indeed.' agreed Lord Gilpin. 'My Son Dudley thinks the world of her too. Yet, she does not seem to know what effect she has on young men, for she has a sweet innocent nature.'

Lady Belvedere asked. 'Doctor, will she recover from the shock?'

'I am sure she will. Most people do recover.'

'My dear Lady Belvedere, Lady Pennington is upstairs in her room if you wish to see her? My wife is with her.' Explained Lord Gilpin.

The doctor added, 'I must advise you not to talk to her so that she can rest. It would be for the best Lady Belvedere.'

Sarah came in with the tea, then burst into tears and ran out again.

Aunt Belvedere wiped a tear from her eye with her handkerchief and drew a deep audible breath. 'They will need to get in touch with their solicitor.'

'Please, allow me the honour.' Requested Doctor Sherbourne. 'To arrange the conveying of Robert's body.'

'Yes,' Lady Belvedere answered. I will help his Mother; Charlotte make arrangements for his funeral. There are few living gentlemen left in the family. However, there is a cousin, Charles Pennington, who is Robert's late father's nephew. So, we need to inform Charles.

'I can be at your disposal. This is not a time for ladies.' Said Lord Gilpin. 'Roberts Father was a good fellow and a friend of mine. I dare say, it would be my honour to help.'

Aunt Belvedere said, her voice husky with tears. 'I shall make sure mourning rings are designed and made. Also, Charlotte and I shall have to decide on what favours we are to give out at the funeral.'

Doctor Sherborne added, 'I shall check on what the coach company reports. Also, what the magistrate has to say on the matter.'

'Sad, sad time.' Groaned Lady Belvedere.

'Shall I write a letter to cousin Charles?' Lord Gilpin asked.

'Yes do. I think a night funeral would be the type of funeral I would like for the darling boy.'

'I do not wish to distress your sensibility, forgive me if I do. I only want you to understand that a night-time funeral will cost twice as much than an afternoon one.'

'Doctor, I would not have any less for my darling nephew, he was of first-rate importance to me. He shall have a funeral fit for a prince.'

'I will write to Charles right away.'

Emma let out a soft groan, but went back to sleep.

The doctor said, Miss Emma needs to be taken upstairs and settled into a comfortable bed.

So, with a great deal of sadness in their hearts, they sat in silence as they one and all stared into their teacups.

Chapter Twelve

Emma and her mother were dressed in black garments waiting in the drawing room for the gentlemen to come back from the funeral.

It was darkening fast, and the rain was tapping against the windows. The two women sat in silence. The candles had been lit which created flickering shadows on the walls.

Lady Pennington was reading her Bible. Emma was writing a poem as a tribute to Robert.

Emma's mother put the Bible down on her lap and said, 'My dear, I have to tell you something, I have been wondering how to put this to you all day.'

'Just tell me, Mother. I will bear it. I can endure anything now.'

'I have received a letter informing me, ... Robert had not made a will. Dear Emma, we do not have the right by law to stay in this house. I am afraid that your cousin Charles Pennington is next in line to inherit our lovely home.'

Emma slumped in the chair. 'Dear Robert was too late.'

'My darling boy never thought he would die, he was in the prime of life.'

'I think it is wrong, so wrong, that we as women cannot

inherit. Father would never have desired us to suffer distress about our housing.'

'I do not know what sort of man your cousin is. I worry that he may not wish us to stay with him,' Lamented Lady Pennington.

'He is family; indeed, I am sure he will help us, he is my cousin.'

'You will not remember him. I remember a very spoiled child.'

'He may have changed, Mother dear. Emma rolled up the paper in her hand, pray he has changed.'

'I feel it is us who should brace ourselves for an immense change. I only wish Mr Sinclair had been a personage with a title, who could have been worthier to marry you. I feel rather dashed to pieces my dear.'

Emma put the paper down on the little pedestal table.

'Mother, I still love Mr Edwin Sinclair. Please soften your heart towards him. I would run to him right now if you did.'

'He was not the right sort of man for you and I have to remind you that he left you Emma. Mr Sinclair did not have the strength of character to stand up against me and fight for you.'

'I forgive him. Oh, indeed I would forgive him if only we could have our chance again.'

'He may leave again, dear.'

Emma's eyes burned with conviction. 'Mother dear, I shall believe, Edwin would talk you around next time.'

'My dear one, we may not have very much to live on now. I will not have land or property. How is a good dowry ever to be had?'

'It is no matter if we love each other.'

'You must remember Emma; he is a man of business. Edwin is a man who wants to better himself, make his wealth by hard work, and move up the social hierarchy. So, he may need your dowry.'

Emma's eyes lowered. 'Mother dear, do you think our lives are lost to happiness now?'

'I lost my happiness the day your darling Father died.' Lady Pennington lowered her head. 'Now, Robert... It is too much.'

Emma knelt down by her mother's side and stroked her hand.

'My Dearest mother... I do not know what to say. It breaks my heart.'

'It will all depend on cousin Charles Pennington now.'

Lady Pennington's friends were helping Lady Gilpin and Lady Napier and their daughters, to arrange the food and the flowers in the dining room ready for the gentlemen's return from the funeral.

Aunt Belvedere with another Lady was sorting out the funeral rings by putting a name tag on each of the ring boxes.

Just then the ladies heard the gentlemen coming back. So, all the ladies joined Emma and Lady Pennington.

The gentleman came into the drawing room, bowed and kissed the hand of Emma and her mother one by one. They offered condolences and told them that it was a well-conducted funeral which had gone ahead with no upset. They reassured the ladies that there were many gentlemen in attendance and all who worked for Robert were also there.

Lord Gilpin said. 'A Mr Sinclair was there. He wanted us to pass on his most sincere condolences. He said he would not come to your house, but he stressed that if you were in any sort of need, you must write him without hesitation. Here is his card, he insisted that I gave it to you. Mr Sinclair is very sad that the business with your late lamented son will not be realised. He asked me several times to stress on his behalf that if you need him, please send word he will be honoured to help.'

Lady Pennington thanked Lord Gilpin for passing on the

message. She put her handkerchief to her eyes. Lady Gilpin took her arm to support her.

'Shall I call Mr Sinclair for you?' asked Lord Gilpin.

'I shall decide what I need to do first. You are very kind.' replied Lady Pennington.

Just then, Sarah showed Charles Pennington into the room. He was looking around as he entered. Standing before Lady Pennington he said, 'I am exceedingly sorry for your loss. I have not seen you, dear aunt, since I was a boy. I live in York now. Believe me when I say, that I miss charming old Chester. I do not care for the Yorkshire lot.'

'Oh.' replied Lady Pennington.

'Shall we eat, Aunt?' said Charles.

He took Emma's arm and Lord Gilpin took Lady Pennington's arm and they walked into the dining room.

'Cousin Emma, would you give me a tour around the house after we have eaten?'

'Do you like the look of the house?' Emma asked Charles.

'It is a very fine house.'

'It is somewhat large. Do you not think?'

'Believe me, cousin, it is just fine.'

'As it is a family house. I think one person would feel cold and lonely in a house of this size.'

'Well, I do not think-'

'It has been my happy family home for most of my life.'

'Ah, Believe me, cousin Emma. I know what you are doing.'

'What I am doing is, grieving over my dearest brother Robert. His family and I loved him very much indeed. All those who knew him loved him too.'

'Believe me, Cousin Emma. It is of first-rate importance to me. As I have come a long way, all the way from Yorkshire.'

'You only knew Robert as a child, is that true?'

'I seem to remember we went fishing together a few times.'

'Indeed.'

'Cousin Emma, Did your brother have a will?'

'Dear me, what a question, you must know, gentlemen of law do not divulge to Ladies about such things.'

'Quite right.'

Aunt Belvedere was helping Lady Pennington to give out the funeral rings.

She went over to Emma, kissed Emma on the cheek, and gave her a little white box. Emma, in return, kissed her aunt. Lady Belvedere said, 'Do not fear, Nash, and I will look after you both.'

Emma's chin trembled.

She opened the box and saw a gold ring. It had the symbol of a wheat-sheaf fashioned from Robert's hair and covered by a fine layer of crystal.

Emma kissed it and put it on her finger and it fit perfectly.

She whispered, 'I loved you so much, my dearest brother.'

Her mother came and sat down next to where she was standing. 'Emma, is the ring to your liking?'

'Yes, indeed thank you.'

'Emma dear I cannot help but feel sad, that we do not know who Belinda is or where she lives. I asked Lord Napier if he could find out where she lives. Alas, he tried in vain, as he could not find her.'

'Upon my word Mother, Belinda will think Robert has abandoned her, and does not care for her anymore.'

'She will never know what has happened to him. It is all too sad.'

They then went over to talk to others in the room. However, cousin Charles kept standing behind them all the time. After a while, Emma turned around and asked in an irritated voice. 'Cousin, what is it you want to say to us?'

'Cousin Emma, it is nothing. Believe me, it is fine.'

The room went quiet. Emma retorted. 'You wish to have a tour of the house?'

Everyone looked at the three of them and cousin Charles coughed and said, 'I would very much like to see the house.'

'No, no, you blockhead,' Aunt Belvedere bellowed. 'This is not the time or place.'

Lord Gilpin said, 'Can I be of service?'

'Who are you, sir?' Charles frowned.

'Lord Gilpin, one of their oldest friends. Please do not upset the Ladies.'

'Well Lord Gilpin, I believe there was no will made. So, I am in line to inherit this house.'

'Whether that is false or true. What sort of gentleman are you that you bring such a subject up at a time like this? Do you have no regard for the lady's feelings? What sort of fellow are you?'

'As Robert's relative, I wish to offer my condolences. Furthermore, I need to explain to the Ladies that I intend to exercise my right by making a claim for the estate. Now, I shall bid you all good night.'

Charles Pennington kissed the hand of Lady Pennington and said to her, 'You will receive word from my lawyer soon.'

He rushed out of the room so fast he knocked a fan out of Lady Gilpin's hand. Phoebe saw it fall, so she picked it up for her mother.

Everyone stood speechless in the room. Then one by one murmured against the behaviour of the young man, towards the widow Lady Pennington and her sweet daughter Emma.

When things had settled down again. Everyone ate and talked about the times they had with Robert. For they all agreed, that he was an honourable gentleman and that he would be sadly missed, by them all.

Chapter thirteen

The next morning, Emma and her mother both dressed in black were sitting in the breakfast room.

Sarah knocked on the door and then came in with a letter.

'Thank you, Sarah.' Lady Pennington took hold of the letter and looked at the seal as she broke it. 'This is the letter we have dreaded Emma.'

'From cousin Charles's lawyer?'

'Yes.'

Emma's mother studied the letter and passed it to her daughter. 'read it dear.'

'He has not given us very much time to find another home...' Emma gave the letter back. 'Oh dear, I could box his ears.'

'It is his right.'

'Law made by men. Oh, depend upon it, I shall miss this house very much.'

'We will both miss this delightful house.'

'Poor you my dear Mother. You have all your memories of father and your two children as babies, in this house.'

'I do.'

'Mother, shall we write a begging letter to Cousin Charles? To see if he will allow us to still live here with him in the smaller rooms.'

'beg him?'

'We could offer to pay a small rent?'

Lady Pennington got up from her chair and walked over to the wall where a drawing in a frame of her husband with Robert as a small child hung. She stood and looked at it and said, 'Robert was such a good little boy. He always wanted to be like his Father. Yes indeed, he was growing more and more like him too.'

Emma went over to the picture to take a closer look. 'They would hate to see us thrown out of our fine house.'

Her mother sighed. 'Robert should have made a will sooner. He told me he was thinking of making one, shortly before he went to London. Speaking plain enough, I wish I had paid more attention to him. I should have encouraged him sooner. Now it is too late and we shall suffer for it.'

'Mother, Robert also told me he was about to make his will. I think he was waiting to see if he would marry Belinda. Afterwards, he had in mind making a will to benefit us all.'

'I have been a foolish parent. She bit her lip. I should not have said to him that he was too young to need such a thing.'

'He knew you did not enjoy talking about wills or death. He understood it was because of Father. His delay was not caused by your feelings towards the writing of wills. He had planned to make one, whether Belinda had agreed to marry him or not. Depend upon it, I do know that for sure, so Mother, do not blame yourself.'

Lady Pennington wiped a tear away from her eye. She turned to Emma and looked steadily at her and said, 'we must prepare to retrench dear.'

Emma sighed and took her mother's hand and said. 'Mother, we must be strong and stick together.'

'How will we find a property that suits our new situation, do you have any ideas?'

'I do have one idea.'

'Well, my dear. What is it?'

'Would you write Mr Edwin Sinclair? He travels to different areas for his work, so he may have knowledge of a cottage or a small house for rent.'

'That may be a good idea, Emma. Although I feel uneasy, as the last time we met, I was rather ungracious to him and would it not be hard for you?'

'We are in a dreadful predicament. We need help Mother dear. He sent the message to us via Lord Gilpin, offering his help if we needed it.'

'Yes, he must be a forgiving man. Could you bear seeing him again, Emma?'

'I shall not pretend to say that it will be easy. But I do have a deep regard for Edwin Sinclair.'

'So be it then. I shall sit and write a letter asking for Mr Sinclair's help. I also need to write to our lawyer and the family accountant.'

There was a Knock on the door.

Sarah enters the room. 'The Landscape gardener would like a word with you Lady Pennington.'

'Thank you, Sarah. I shall be there in a moment.'

'Emma, I will have to cancel the work contract. It had slipped my mind. I dare say, they will want paying for the work that has already been carried out.'

'For sure, Cousin Charles will not pay for it.'

'What will he say about the holes in the ground? Or a half-built folly?'

Just at that moment, they heard Lady Belvedere's voice

booming. 'What are you waiting for my little man?' They could hear the landscape gardener giving the aunt an explanation. Lady Belvedere replied. 'Go away, get your workmen off from here and leave these poor people alone to grieve. Now listen, send your bill to me. Here this is my card, my auditor will deal with it. We will hear no more about it.'

'Good old Martha,' Lady Pennington said, with a relieved look on her face. 'Martha has saved me.'

Lady Belvedere walked into the room. Emma and her Mother kissed her on the cheek. Then they listened to the Aunt tell them about the deed she had accomplished on their behalf.

So they made a lot of fuss of Aunt Belvedere, and they saw that she loved every moment.

'Listen to me.' Lady Belvedere exclaimed. 'You cannot possibly stay here. That impertinent young cousin of yours will throw you out of this house and without bread or a penny. So, your old beloved aunt will take care of you both. You are to come and live with me. I shall not take no for an answer. I have a large house, we will all do just fine.'

'What can I say, Martha dear?' Lady Pennington forced her mouth into a smile.

'You can say, yes. For I am getting old and I need help.'

Emma glanced up enquiringly. 'Aunt, does not Mr Greystone live with you still?'

'Poor dear Nash. He has gone abroad, and he kept saying to me, I must buy a grand house for my sweet Emma and I.'
'But, Miss Emma Pennington... does not know what is best for her?' Her aunt shook her head. 'In any case, I do not know when he is coming back. He comes and goes. Yet, I miss him so. To be sure, I have rooms for us all.'

'But, oh, Aunt. It will be so uncomfortable for me if Mr Greystone comes back. If he comes while I am residing at your house.'

'Nonsense, you will be ready for him.'

'Aunt, I never intend to marry Mr Greystone. I need you to understand.' Emma raised her eyes in protest.

'I know you have foolish ideas. Like ridiculous romantic love between personage who are part of the top classes with those of the low. My girl, that is all very well in books. I say in the real world. You need to be very careful or you will end up starving to death.'

'No, Aunt.'

'You will be thrown out of your house for you have very little money of your own. Your mother has very little to live on. You need to understand Emma that marrying well is very important to your future. Do you wish to see your sweet Mother, walk around in rags, begging for food on the street?'

'Martha, do not paint such a black picture.'

'You would believe it, if you have seen what I have seen in the past... People have slipped down the ladder of life into debt, poverty, even death. I have witnessed it. I lost my childhood friend that way.'

Lady Belvedere got her handkerchief and wiped her eyes.

'Martha dear, we did not know.'

'Charlotte, I have seen these things happen. So, I am making sure they do not happen to you and Emma.'

Lady Pennington said. 'Thank you for your kindness, Martha dear. I shall think about your kind offer. I shall give you our answer tomorrow, if you would indulge us, in giving us a day to make our decision.'

'A whole day? I thought it would be settled now. I cannot waste my time here, pleading with you two. Good gracious I hope you know what is good for you.' Lady Belvedere sniffed. 'I shall call back tomorrow then.'

'Thank you, Martha. We both want to thank you for your extremely kind offer and warm regard.'

Aunt Belvedere withdrew from the room.

'Emma, I found that most ghastly. Your aunt gives us a most generous offer. Which would help us enormously. Then you hint, you do not want to take it up. Why? Because of whatever foolishness lies between you and Mr Greystone. I feel sick of heart over it. I entreat you, Emma. Just marry the Gentleman. He is always agreeable to me and charming to you. I think it is time for me to put my foot down hard. Emma, Marry Mr Greystone. If he will still have you, he is a gentleman who cares for you wholeheartedly, what more could you want? Women have married for far less; you no longer have a choice. We are poor. We need a roof over our heads and food in our stomachs. I have decided… Yes, we shall live with your Aunt and you will marry that gentleman.'

Emma grabbed her mother's hand and kissed it and said, 'Mother dear, may I please say one last thing to you, please?'

'One, then there shall be an end to this madness.'

'If you would agree please, to write one, just one letter to Mr Edwin Sinclair. If he does not help us or no longer wants to know me. I will live with Aunt Belvedere, even in the company of Mr Nash Greystone, when he returns.'

'Emma, you are pushing my patience.'

'Mother dear, I beg you, please. Just one letter.'

Her mother looked up and sighed heavily. She then went over to the desk, sat down and taking her quill pen she dipped it into the ink and wrote to Mr Sinclair.

Emma looked over her mother's shoulder as she wrote. She

163

wrote quickly and blotted the ink and turned around to Emma.

'I feel very disturbed about this letter, Emma. Your aunt gives us the answer to our problem. What do we do? We write to a person who is not even our relative for help. Every time you go against your aunt's wishes. I end up smoothing things over.'

'I only want what is best for us', Emma said, trying her best to appease her mother.'

'I dare say, but is this the best for us? Aunt Belvedere will soon lose patience with us and then what will we do?'

Sarah knocked on the door and hands over a letter to Emma. After closing the door, Emma opened the letter.

'It is another letter from Charles. He says he is coming to look over the house and the accounts. He then adds that he shall allow us to pick some things out to take with us. Very obliging of him. He also says he will need to lay off some workers. Oh, dear... he will bring his agent and secretary along with his lawyer. Emma looked at her mother.' What will happen to the likes of Mr Dale and his family? Mother, this will be a loathsome business.'

Emma passes the letter to her mother.

'Reading, she exclaimed.' It will not do. It will bring shame on our good name. Those families have been here for

generations. Even before we were here.' She scanned more.'
Charles says he is getting new machines. He explains that the
new farming machines can do the jobs of many men. OH, we
can never lift our heads up around here again.'

'Please, Mother, do send the letter to Mr Sinclair. For if we
stay with Aunt Belvedere, we shall live too close to here. How
could we bear to be talked about by our neighbours? We
would become their sport. It would be too distressing for you
to bear. The answer for us is to move far away from here,
where we are not known.'

'There is some merit in what you say Emma.'

'I do believe we would manage in a small cottage with just
Sarah and Bess.'

'I dare say we could... although, depend upon it, it will be
difficult... with just two servants.'

'Yes indeed, but think of it, we would be happy together and
we would have peace.'

'How I need peace.' Lady Pennington shut her eyes for a
moment.

'I will look after you Mother dear. I promise I will always look
after you. Please send the letter to Mr Sinclair. I am sure he
would have seen a cottage for rent.'

'What about your Aunt Martha? She will be mortified. After

all, dear, she has been so good to us in the past.'

'Aunt can come and stay as often as she wishes, we will always be thankful to her. I know our future will be hard for us. But we will live in peace and make our own decisions. You do not want trouble or reproach from Charles or the neighbours. You need a quiet life, my dear mother. I promise I shall make sure you have everything you need.

'So, you think we should retrench to a small cottage in the country?'

'Yes, Mother dear. We shall take our most treasured things with us to create a comfortable home, and we shall make some new friends. How many books we will read? We will find pleasure in growing flowers and fruit... and depend upon it. I promise to knit you shawls to keep you warm.'

Lady Pennington listened to her daughter's words and picked up the letter, lit a candle and melted the wax to seal it. 'Well, my dear. Let us see what Mr Sinclair can do for us then.'

Chapter Fourteen

E mma and her mother had just arrived back from a shopping trip. They were greeted by Sarah who told them that there was a gentleman waiting for them in the drawing room. Sarah said she had taken the liberty of letting the gentleman wait for them, seeing he had some very important news.

'A Gentleman?'

'Yes Lady Pennington, I hope I have done the right thing? Only, I have met the Gentleman before.'

'Was his name Mr Greystone?'

'No, the gentleman named-

'Edwin!' Emma said with the biggest smile on her face not seen since before her brother had died.

She was just going to march into the drawing room when her mother stopped her and said, 'Emma, calm yourself.' She stopped and looked at Sarah. 'Was it Mr Edwin Sinclair?' Emma asked as she glanced back.

'It is, Mr Sinclair.'

'Thank you Sarah.' said Lady Pennington. 'Please bring tea and cakes.'

'Right away, Lady Pennington.' Sarah left.

'Now, Emma dear,' her mother said, 'remember that Mr Sinclair is only here because we wrote to him, asking him, for a large favour. He is showing kindness to us, on account of his regard for dear Robert. Please hold yourself together with manners and decorum.'

Emma blushed. 'Yes, Mother.'

Emma's face was burning, and she felt her breathing becoming rapid. How can I hide how I feel, she thought?

She noticed her mother was uncomfortable too.

They took off their spencer jackets and outdoor shoes. They both checked their hair in the mirror. Emma pinched her cheeks with her fingers. Even though they were already bright cherry pink.

On opening the drawing-room door. They saw Mr Sinclair standing by the piano forte, with the dust sheet over it. He was looking at the pile of music books on the top, tied with a ribbon. He had his back to the door, and started running his fingers over the dust sheet, feeling the outline of the piano keys. They saw he was Lost in thought. Mr Sinclair turned around as he heard the door close. His eyes locked onto Emma; she almost became unsteady for a moment but caught her balance. Her mother thanked him for coming and asked him to sit down.

There was silence for a moment. Then Mr Sinclair opened up and said. 'I have good news for you Ladies. I have come with news of an ideal cottage for rent. In a tiny village called Hawarden, on the Welsh border. From the village, you can see the Cheshire plane. The cottage is near to a wooded area which is very peaceful.'

'Who owns the cottage, Mr Sinclair?'

'He is a gentleman called Mr Glyn. He rents out a few cottages and his tenants have stayed for years, as he is a fair man.'

'We must thank you for your kindness to us, Mr Sinclair.' Lady Pennington said, 'I know our last meeting was a rather difficult one for all of us. Yet you are a Man of great merit to forget it and still come to our aid.'

'You do not have to thank me, Lady Pennington. I miss your Son Robert, a great deal. He and I thought about things in the same way. I dare say, together we would have made our new venture excel. Please allow me to say I have empathy for you both, having to leave your beautiful home and all that you know. Life can be very cruel, especially to women.'

'Yes, especially women.'

'Would you allow me to help you move?'

'I have help, Mr Sinclair.'

'May I tell Mr Glyn that you will be interested in taking the cottage?'

'Forgive me, Mr Sinclair. Money is such a vulgar subject... You understand... Mr Sinclair... we need to live on a smaller budget.'

'I have written the figure down for you.' Edwin hands the piece of paper to Lady Pennington.

Lifting her eyes back to him, 'It is a little less than I thought the rent would be. Yes, we would be delighted to rent the cottage. If you would be so kind, would you do us the honour of speaking to Mr Glyn on our behalf? I can give you good references.'

'Lady Pennington. I know Mr Glyn. He will trust my word. References are not very nice for you to have to countenance.'

'Thank you again, Mr Sinclair, we are most obliged to you.'

'Not at all. I only want what is best for you.' He handed her another sheet of paper. ' Here I have drawn a sketch of the cottage. The outside view and the floor plan. I hope this will assist you to work out where to place your furniture.'

'May I look at it, please?' asked Emma

As Edwin passed the sketch to Emma. His hand gently brushed her fingers. She breathed heavily. His eyes were fixed on her dainty hand. He noticed her breathing had been affected by the accidental touch of their hands.

There was a silence. Which was broken by Sarah as she brought in the tray of tea

When Sarah left the room again. Lady Pennington poured out the tea, then passing Mr Sinclair a cup said. 'I am pleased that you were able to go to the funeral. We received your message from Lord Gilpin. That is why we wrote to you. I have something further on my mind. I wonder if you may help?'

'I will be glad to.'

'It is a bold request Mr Sinclair, yet I must ask.'

'I would view helping you as an honour, Lady Pennington.'

'Would it be in your power, to get in touch with Belinda for me. As you know who she is and where she lives. The dreadful news has to be told to her. Mr Sinclair, she is on my mind.'

'Do not upset yourself, Lady Pennington. I took a trip to London myself, to bear the news face to face.'

'Upon my word, Mr Sinclair. I am all astonished. For nobody had told me.'

'I have never seen such a bright face change to horror as

when I told that poor young woman the sad news. It upsets me to think of it.'

'I wish we had met her.'

Emma asked, 'Was she engaged to Robert?'

'No, I do not think they had got engaged. Robert was planning an engagement in future time. Belinda never talked of a commitment to me, I dare say, she would have if there had been one.'

'Poor young woman. It is very sad... What will you do with yourself now, Mr Sinclair?'

'It is kind of you to ask about me, Lady Pennington. I decided to carry on with the business venture that Robert and I started together. I have found myself a backer. In fact, I wanted to bring up the subject with you. I was finding it rather difficult. So, I am pleased that you have asked the question.'

'Tell me, what is it?'

'I have access to some money that Robert put into the business that has not yet been used. It is fair and just for me to give it back to his beloved mother and sister. It is yours it belongs to you. Can I arrange this transaction for you?'

'Thank you again, Mr Sinclair, you are a true gentleman.'

'Robert would have done the same for me.'

Mr Sinclair stood up and placed his cup, saucer and plate onto the table and said. 'I will take my leave now. Please be assured that I will carry out this assignment for you both. May I request permission to take you to the cottage on the day of the move in my carriage?'

Emma felt her heart beat faster, as her Mother hesitated. She stopped and thought for a moment and then said, 'Yes, we would be most glad of it.'

Mr Sinclair finished his tea, said goodbye and then bowed to Lady Pennington and Emma and left.

Chapter Fifteen

T he two women still dressed in black were holding tight onto each other's arms as the carriage swayed side to side, for it was a very bumpy country road.

Trees and bushes and brambles seemed to flash by. The carriage body was scraped by the longer untamed branches.

We are almost there, Mr Sinclair declared.

There was a damp smell in the carriage from all the rain that had poured down during the last three days and yet again it was raining.

Charles had arrived at the Chester house earlier than he had promised he would. Emma was upset about having to see him face to face. She thought to herself, I never want to lay eyes on him ever again. Emma had felt like boxing his ears, for the cold proud way he had kissed her goodbye. Emma was thinking. Charles is a gentleman. Edwin is not. Yet Edwin behaved more like a gentleman than spoilt cousin Charles.'

Emma thought about the Dale family and was concerned that Mr Dale being frail would lose his job, as she knew Charles wanted to get rid of some of the workers. Emma decided, when I visit Aunt Belvedere, I will pay a call on the Dale family to see what has become of them.

The carriage was climbing higher and Emma could see the view of the Cheshire plane beneath them. They had now arrived at the little place called Hawarden.

Mr Sinclair called out, 'Here is the cottage on the left.'

Emma took the folded piece of paper out from inside her glove and unfolded it and looked at the sketch. 'You have caught its likeness rather well, Mr Sinclair,' She called while waving the paper, so he could see what she meant.

It was not a large cottage, but it was solid, built in stone. It had a pretty garden, fruit trees and a vegetable plot. No lilac trees near the door though, Emma thought.

She could see a few bottlebrush plants that had just finished flowering in the front garden. Which she had learnt about, from one of Robert's books. Now she knew they had come from Australia having been Introduced into Britain by Joseph Banks the plant collector. She had packed that same book and brought it with her, from Robert's Library.

The carriage came to a stop. Sarah and Bess had gone ahead earlier to get things cleaned and make a meal. As the carriage pulled up, they both came out to meet everyone. Raindrops dripped down their necks falling from the low overgrown trees by the gate. Everyone dashed into the cottage. Bess had lit the fire, as the cottage felt cold and damp it having been left empty for a few weeks.

Emma took off her bonnet and gloves and walked from room to room. They too had a smell of damp. It also felt dark after her other home. She went up the narrow staircase and looked out of the window in one bedroom and saw the full view of the Cheshire plane. Going into the next bedroom. Emma observed a swallow's nest by the window and thought how the birds would leave and fly off soon. she reflected how Edwin was downstairs in this very house, how she longed to fly to him, for the want of feeling his arms around her. Yet, soon she would say goodbye, then he would leave here. Yes, dear kind Edwin would leave them, all too soon.

Emma ran down the stairs, just as Edwin Sinclair came through the door with two large cases.

'You look like you have had a shock. Miss, Emma, are you well?'

'Oh I am well, but please forgive me. I am not myself...'

Mr Sinclair put the cases down and said. 'Come in the parlour and sit-down Miss, Emma.'

Emma could hear the others in the room talking. So, she stayed standing in the Hall and said.

'Mr Sinclair, what must you think of me?'

'Think of you? I shall always think most highly of you Emma, Miss, Emma.'

She bowed her head so he could not see her eyes fill up.

'You always show a genuine interest in new things. So, I think with your spirit, you will soon settle in and make it a cosy home.'

'Thank you for your positive view of me Mr Sinclair.'

They were silent for a moment. Edwin tried to catch Emma's eye while he questioned, with some hesitation. 'Miss Emma, may I take the liberty and ask, are you going to marry Mr Greystone after all?'

'I have always remained true to my conviction that I will never marry Mr Greystone. This is why I am here. I could have stayed at my Aunt Belvedere's home with Mr Greystone. But I would rather be poor and live in a humble cottage. On no account will I be forced into a marriage just to gain wealth and status.'

' That shows me that you are a strong woman, I think?'

'I am not strong at all, quite the opposite.'

'You do not feel strong?'

'Mr Sinclair I am afraid.' You know Mr Greystone frightens me. His silence frightens me and his words frighten me.

Emma pressed her fingers to her lips.

Edwin's enquiring eyes followed her fingers.

'Please, Mr Sinclair do not leave us all alone in the world.'

He scrutinised Emma's face.

'I entreat you, dear Edwin. Please let us put the past behind us.'

His eyebrows rose with surprise.

Emma continued. 'Please, do be our guest and visit us soon.'

Edwin said, 'But ... Lady Pennington will object.'

'No, I do not think so, not now.'

He picked up the cases and said, 'Rest easy, I will call on you.'

Emma smiled and took off her scarf.

Edwin took the cases up the stairs.

She hung her coat on the peg and walked into the parlour.

Bess pulled off the dust sheet from the winged chair. Emma sat down and felt the warmth from the fire and Sarah gave her a cup of tea.

Lady Pennington said. 'Ah, there you are, Emma. Do you think you can put up with this cottage?'

'When I first entered, my feelings felt negative, yet now, such a short time later. Mother dear, my answer is an emphatic yes.'

Chapter Sixteen

Emma was standing on a wooden stool trying to hammer a nail into the wall so she could hang up her feathered bird picture, from Mr Dale. As her mother passed her room, she said with alarm. 'Good gracious, do not fall and hurt yourself Emma.'

'Mother, I have found some men's tools in an oak chest. I never knew what fun it is using a hammer.'

'Be careful dear. You should have asked one of the servants.'

'Bess is beating the rugs outside and Sarah is washing the floor. We will have to get our hands dirty and help around the house now. Depend upon it, Mother dear. I understand it is hard for you to countenance it. I can bear it if you wish to go to Aunt Belvedere's for a rest. My dear Mother, I know you have been through such upheaval and this sort of life is a shock to you.'

'I could not leave you, my sweet girl. Especially now, that I have lost my darling boy....'

'May be, we can pretend, we are shepherdesses. who are looking after our sheep and spinning our own wool and also weaving our own clothes? here in the countryside.'

'Pretend games no longer divert me or have the art of pleasing me anymore.' Lady Pennington rubbed her hands together and sighed.

179

Mother dear, 'Would you like to go for a walk together?'

'No dear, I will sort out all the china.'

' The china can wait.'

' No, it cannot.'

'Why do you not want to explore the lanes with me?'

'I need to get these dishes sorted, washed and put away.'

'Mother dear, do you feel all right?'

'I am altogether fine. I will get this room looking pretty.' Lady Pennington started to hum a tune.

'Can you spare me, if I go for a little walk, Mother dear?'

'Yes indeed, I have Bess and Sarah to help me. You go and explore.'

As Emma left the room, there was a mirror on the wall in front of her. She could see her mother wiping tears from her eyes in the reflection.

She needs time alone, Emma thought.

Emma opened the cottage door and went out. She bent her head to avoid large overhanging tree branches by the wooden gate. Closing it behind her, she walked up the narrow lane until she came to a wooded area. Emma walked under the canopy of the trees, then she saw a little pond. She walked up to the edge and looked at her reflection in the still water. It brought to mind her mother's tears that she saw in the mirror. It saddened her heart. Everything had crashed down around them. Emma asked herself, how would she be able to bear all this disappointment? Her dearest brother who meant so much to her had died. Furthermore, she has lost the man she loves. Her mother and her life had changed. Emma no longer lived close to her friends. She had been taken out of her home. Emma knew she would have to cling to hope or she would be dragged down never to pick herself up again. Emma went down and put her hand into the water and felt the coolness against her skin. It reminded her of the breathless feelings she felt at the moment she unintentionally touched Edwin's hand.

Startled by the sound of children's voices, Emma pulled her hand out of the water and just then, a white and grey little dog jumped up at her.

'Down Leo,' she heard a boy shout. 'Sit Leo. Sorry Missy,' the boy said as he picked up the panting dog.

'He is really naughty Missy.'

'Bad doggy.' A girl said. 'I am so sorry lady, his muddy paws have dirtied your coat, whatever shall we do?'

'Oh, it will brush off.' Emma answered. She asked the boy, 'May I stroke your little dog?'

'Yes,' agreed the boy.

'So, this is Leo,' Emma said while tickling the dog under his chin. 'What are your names?'

'Owen,' the oldest boy answered.

The fair-haired boy told Emma that his name was Seth.

Emma looked at the black-haired girl. She blushed as she said, 'Peggy is my name.'

Her smaller sister told Emma her name was Alwen.

'It is so good to meet you all,' Emma said, while she stroked Leo.

'We haven't seen you here before,' said little Alwen.

'That is because I have only just come here. I live in Cherry Wood cottage.'

'What is your name?' Seth asked.

'Emma Pennington.'

'That's a nice name,' Peggy replied.

'We like fishing.'

'What fun,' Emma said. 'Do you mind if I sit down here and

watch you catch your fish?'

'Well, we catch nothing much really.' Answered Owen.

'I dare say, the fish hear you coming. You have to creep up on them,' Emma replied.

She sat down on the grass and Leo jumped onto her lap and settled there. Emma felt more cheerful watching the children fishing, while she stroked Leo. The sun came out, Emma felt the warmth and for a moment she felt tranquil.

It must be delightful having children of one's own, she considered. Emma sat for a while until the children became very excited when one of them caught a tiny fish. But soon, Emma forgot she was wearing mourning clothes, and she started to run around with the children, trying to catch them. They were screaming with delight. They all ran down onto the main lane, just as a Man on a horse was coming along, Emma looked up and saw the horse and then skidded on mud and landed right on her bottom. Her bonnet flew off and her left shoe flicked up into the air and landed on her lap. The children fell about laughing. The male voice said, 'I better pick up this jumble, do you not think, Children?'

Emma looked up alarmed as she recognised the voice of Mr Edwin Sinclair.

Emma put her hands over her eyes and shook her head. 'Oh, dear me, I quite give up, you always seem to catch me when I am not my ordered self. What will you think of me after this,

Mr Sinclair I dare not utter even to myself?'

'Ah, you have said that before. Dear Miss Emma, are you hurt?'

'Only my dignity.'

With that, Edwin picked her up into his arms and put her onto his horse.

The children gathered up Emma's bonnet and shoe. Mr Sinclair placed Emma's shoe back onto her foot while she sat on his horse.

Emma's cheeks flushed hot pink, being aware that the children were all standing, watching the scene. Emma could not enjoy the moment for she felt very ill at ease and said, 'I thank you most sincerely for your help. Mr Sinclair you have been very kind. Please, would you help me down, as I would rather walk back?'

'If you promise me, you are quite well and unhurt.'

'Indeed, I am fine. Perfectly fine, although a bit muddy.'

Edwin helped her down from his horse.

'Thank you, Mr Sinclair.' Emma said.

'You are welcome.'

Edwin Sinclair took hold of the horse's reins. He next told the
two boys to give Emma their arms to steady and help her
walk home.

'Upon my honour, I think Miss Emma Pennington has more
mud on her than all you four children put together, whatever
will her Mother say?' Edwin laughed.

He looked at Emma and winked, but Emma quickly looked
away. The children laughed and agreed that their Mother
would shout at them if they got their clothes that dirty.

As they came to the cottage garden gate. Emma said, 'Would
you like to come in for a drink of lemonade children?'

'Yes.' they declared in unison.

'Please, you must come in and meet dear Mother,' Emma
said to Edwin Sinclair.

Emma told the children to come into the parlour. They
walked into the room in silence. Emma told them to sit on
the rug by the fire. She asked Bess to bring in the lemonade
for the children. Bess looked puzzled.

'These are my new little friends,' Emma explained.

'Bess glanced again at Emma. 'Oh, my goodness, you're
covered in mud.'

'Yes.' Emma laughed. 'Please, bring in tea for Mr Edwin

Sinclair. I shall go upstairs to change.'

Lady Pennington entered the room.

'We have some little visitors, Mother, and Mr Sinclair has come to call on us too.'

Mr Sinclair stood up, bowed. 'I have longed to come and see you and your daughter, Lady Pennington. I wish you to know, you have both been very much on my mind.'

'Mr Sinclair, you are too good to us.'

'Are you well? Is the house suitable for your needs?'

'We are very cosy here, thank you.'

'May I say? You have given the cottage a much-needed pretty woman's touch. Can I ask? Do you need any jobs doing while I am here?'

Lady Pennington said, 'If I could be as bold as to request something Mr Sinclair. Then, chopping down some overhanging tree branches by the gate would be a great help. As I am concerned someone may knock their head against them.'

'I have time to do it right now Lady Pennington.'

'We would be very grateful to you, Edwin you are too kind to us. I see why my son connected himself to you. Thank you.'

'It will be a pleasure to me to be of some service to you both.'

'Please do not rush yourself, first enjoy your tea.'

Then Lady Pennington went over to speak with the children, 'What are your names?'

'I am Owen' said the older boy. Owen pointed to his younger brother. 'This is Seth.'

'So what are your sisters called?'

'The youngest girl said, my name is Alwyn. Are you the pretty lady's Mama?'

'I am Emma's mother, yes, she is pretty is she not?'

Peggy then said, ' Yes very pretty. Thank you for the lemonade; It is the nicest that I have ever had.'

'What lovely manners you all have. Tell me, where do you live?'

'Clover cottage. That's right down the lane, with Mama, Poppa, Nana and Leo our dog. He's in your porch.'

'What is in your jar Seth?'

'A fish.'

'He is a grand fish. My son Robert loved fishing.'

'How old is he?'

'Oh, Robert ... he grew up...'

'Where is he? Is he in this house?'

'No, dear... my son is not here now.'

Mr Sinclair on seeing Lady Pennington's eyes filling up, said to the children.' Finish your drinks for you had better be off now, children. Your Mother will wonder what has happened to you all.'

The children stood to go. Peggy said, 'It is the most beautiful house I have ever seen in my whole life.'

The children left with cheerful chatter.

Emma said, 'Will you excuse me mother, as I need to freshen myself up.'

Lady Pennington whispered to her daughter. 'I think the time has come for you to wear lilac or grey now my dearest.'

'Thank you, Mother, I will.'

Emma went upstairs to get changed.

A short while later. Emma came back into the room.

Her mother was pouring another cup of tea for Mr Sinclair. With that, he looked towards the door and saw Emma. She had on a silk lilac dress. Around her neck, Emma was wearing an Amber pendant. There were amethyst earrings in her ears. Emma looked over to Edwin Sinclair and his mouth fell into a smile.

When her Mother saw Emma, she said, 'I know Robert would not have wanted you to wear black for too long. Not while you are such a young woman. I must say Emma dear. You look delightful.'

Emma looked at the funeral ring on her finger, then said. 'I shall always love Robert. I shall never ever forget him.'

Mr Sinclair said, 'Ah, I agree. Robert Pennington was the best. Such a good fine Gentleman. It was my privileged to know him. May I be so bold to say, dear miss Emma, I long for the day when I may have the privilege to see you again, in the Green printed dress, that your brother brought you from London.'

Emma's eyes smiled as she picked up her cup of tea. Lady Pennington looked at Edwin and frowned.

Seeing her frown, he drank his tea quickly. 'Where are the saw and axe kept?' asked Edwin. Mr Sinclair then excused himself, took off his jacket, and went outside.

Next Bess came in. 'Here are some letters, Miss Emma.'

'Thank you Bess, would you take a jug of beer outside for Mr Sinclair please?'

'Yes, Miss Emma.' Bess said, then she left the room.

Emma looked at the two letters, she recognised the hand of one. 'The writing is Dudley's', Emma said with cheerfulness and opened the letter to read it. Oh, dear-'

'-What does it say?' Her mother enquired.

'Lord Gilpin thinks Dudley is still too young to get seriously attached to Miss Susan Roscoe. So, Dudley is being sent on a tour of Europe for the finishing of his education. His Father says that if their regard for each other continues and gets stronger while Dudley is away. Lord Gilpin will talk with Dudley about furthering the relationship, when he gets back.'

'It is very understandable, Emma. He is the heir, of the title and fortune.'

'Yes, but depend upon it, I shall miss him so much, and poor Susan, how will she feel?'

'Affection needs to be tested, that I do believe, my dear.'

Emma did not answer she now heard the sound of sawing coming from outside.

She picked up the other letter and saw the seal. 'It is from Aunt Belvedere... I do not know why it is addressed to me, rather than you? Mother dear shall I open it, or do you think she meant to send it to you?'

'Pass it here.' Lady Pennington looked at the writing. That is not Martha's hand?'

Her Mother opened it and started to read aloud, it says, 'My dearest, Miss Emma Pennington.'

'Stop!'

'Emma, what is it?'

'Emma got up and walked over to the window. With her back to her Mother, she said. 'It is from Mr Greystone. Is it not?'

Her mother checked the letter. 'Why upon my word? yes, it is.'

'Please do not read anymore. Throw it in the fire.'

'I will not.'

'Please. Mother?'

Lady Pennington found her place and continued to read on. 'I have missed your beautiful face and sweet nature, more than words can say, darling Emma-'

'-Oh Mother, please, please do not read it.' Emma's cheeks started to burn.

'Emma. Are you quite sure you do not actually love this gentleman?'

'No Indeed no.'

'Well, he says, he has arrived back yesterday and is now settled back with your Aunt.'

'Oh no. My Poor Aunt.' Emma said.

'He goes on to write. He has heard of a fine house that he shall go and look at tomorrow.' He then says, 'His only fear is that this other house will not be good enough for his wife.'

'Oh no, please no. not any house...' Emma placed her face in her hands.

'Dear, he adds, 'that no other woman would be more suitable to be his wife than you, glorious Emma.' Glorious,' her mother repeated.

Emma rubbed her forehead with her right hand, shut her eyes and sighed loudly.

Lady Pennington stopped reading it and handed the letter over to Emma.

Emma snatched the letter out of her mother's hand and then carried on reading it. 'I am very desirous of coming to see you to offer you my hand in marriage for the second time. To be sure, that now you have been brought low by your brother's death. I now feel confident that you, my dear Emma, will accept.'

Emma stopped reading, let out a long sigh but said nothing. Her mother went over to the window and watched Mr Edwin Sinclair working hard chopping back the branches for them. Lady Pennington went back over and put her hand on Emma's shoulder and said, 'Mr Greystone will come here, you do realise that... I declare, he will come tomorrow or the day after.'

Emma's colour flushed to a wild pink, she said, 'So that Man takes it for granted. Because I have fallen on hard times. I will now throw myself at his feet and marry him.'

'My dear, you need to think about marriage before you get passed the bloom of youth. I am getting old. This is more than enough for me to cope with, as I am sure it is for you.'

'I wish Father was here.'

'I know, but he is not.'

'How I wish, oh if only Robert was here.'

'We both grieve the loss of them, but we have to decide without them. 'It seems to me that two wealthy men are in love with you. One is a gentleman the other is not. The gentleman is going to renew his offer, and the other is not. One is looking for a family house the other is not. One gave up easily the other has not-

'Dear me mother. Say nothing more.'

'Her mother took the letter, then waved it under Emma's nose. This is the man worthy of your hand. Mr Greystone has only ever spoken of his regard, admiration or love for you if you prefer that word. Why do you not like this gentleman? Your aunt thinks he is a good man. I have only ever heard him flatter us all. Why do you not like him? What has he ever done, Emma?'

'He,... poor Dudley... Oh dear me, It is no good, you do not understand...'

Emma rushed out of the room, shutting the door with a firm slam behind her.

Bess was in the hall holding a tray with a drink of beer that she was about to take outside for Mr Sinclair.

Emma said, 'Bess, I will take it out for Mr Sinclair.'

'Right Miss Emma.'

'Bess, may I ask you a question?'

'Of course.'

'Do you like Mr Sinclair? Answer me please, only from your true feelings, based on what you have seen of him.'

'Yes, Miss Emma. He's polite. Very handsome. A most

likeable gentleman. Did you know Miss, I saw him give those children a coin each.'

'Did he really?... Thank you, Bess. I value your thoughts.'

Emma went outside with the tray.' Mr Sinclair,' Emma called. 'Here is a drink for you. You are most kind to help us in this way, Mr Sinclair.'

Edwin had taken his waistcoat off and neck cloth. He had rolled up his shirt sleeves. The sweat was glimmering on his forehead. He took a cloth and wiped his brow and his brown curls flopped down over his forehead.

Mr Sinclair stopped chopping up the branches for a moment and looked up at Emma. 'Why do you call me, Mr Sinclair? You know what my name is. I am not an outsider or foreigner to you, am I?'

'I...'

'Emma, after all that we have felt. Please do not say that you now view me as a stranger to you?'

He launched the axe in the air and brought it down again and the thick branch split into two.

Emma jumped a little.

Edwin threw the axe aside. Picks up the jug and poured out the beer and swallows it down quickly. While Emma's eyes fixed on his brown curls falling over his glistening forehead, her eyes rested on his uncovered arms, which looked strong. She saw his hands were dirty with earth. Emma stood motionless and said nothing.

'For goodness' sake. Call me Edwin.'

'Yes, Edwin. If you wish it.'

'You sound like you are answering your governess.' Edwin's Brown eyes were flaming at her.

Emma did not know what to say. She looked down, then looking back at Edwin she explodes. 'Do not command me what to say. If I want to call you… Cain or… Herod or whatever. I will. Do you hear me?'

Edwin stood up straight, 'Emma?'

'I am vexed and tired of men telling me what I am to say or do. Men who are not my Father or brother. If it is not men, it is my aunt.'

'Emma...?'

'I may as well lay myself down on the ground here and you might as well, take the axe and chop me in half then both of you men can have half of me.'

Edwin stood insensible, he placed his hands on his hips.

'You, Mr Sinclair and Mr Greystone can both do what you want.' Emma snapped. 'I will be dead.'

Edwin stood in front of Emma and said, 'and you, might as well put an axe through my heart also. From the first time I walked into your brother's house, when I first laid eyes on you, you took my breath away, I knew, I knew I loved you. Just talking with you, I fell instantly and fully in love with you. When I had to leave you, it was like an axe had cut my heart open. Have you any idea how much pain I have felt?' He pounded his chest.

'Do you know how hard it was to see you leave me and not fight against my mother's reasoning?'

Edwin's voice softened. ' You are so...so beautiful and interested in life and the world beyond you. You are such an intelligent woman wrapped in a desirable form. I came here to help you. Yes, for you Emma and your Mother because you love her so. Even though it was her that parted us. I tell you now, my heart never forgot you. I could not sleep for thinking about you. It went around and around my head all the time that Mr Greystone would take you. Yes, take you. O' my dear Emma I love you so much.... Emma ...dearest please come here...' His right hand outstretched to her.

Emma stepped towards Edwin.

He took hold of her hand, and gazed at it for a moment, then he kissed it with tenderness. 'If there was a paradise on the moon, I would pull the moon down for you, right now.'

His left hand took hold of her right hand. She let him willingly. Edwin smiled. 'That moment when you asked me how the new printing machine worked, I knew you were an extraordinary Lady.'

In a half whisper, he continued. 'Can you not understand that you calling me Edwin is all I have left? It was a tiny request that meant a lot to me.'

Emma answered him in a soft, tentative tone of voice.

'I thought you wished to keep a distance between us, forever.'

'Emma, I long to care for you and look after you, but still give you space to flourish. Do you believe that?'

She melted, as a longing for him whispered through her body. 'Oh Edwin, indeed I do believe that. Forgive me, say you will forgive me. I never intended to hurt you. I did not discern you were still in love with me. I really did love you. It was I who requested that Mother should write to you. Dear Edwin, can I explain what has troubled me so?'

He kissed her hand again and whispered. 'Tell me.'

'I received a letter from the awful Mr Greystone today he said, he is on his way to offer me his hand in marriage and is convinced that I will take it, because of my reduced circumstances since Robert's death. He has upset me.'

'What nature of Gentleman does he think he is?' Edwin gasped.

Her inward hope rose.

Edwin edged closer to Emma, and she leant forward. He kissed her on her forehead. Emma felt serene.

Edwin got down on one knee and asked, 'Emma Pennington, love of my heart. I offer my hand to you. Will you marry me?'

'Oh yes, I will Edwin.'

He stood up. She silently pressed her hand to her heart then she pressed her fingers to his lips, he kissed them. He gently put his hand under her chin, Emma shut her eyes and he kissed her lips.

After, they both stood in complete silence for a moment.

With that Lady Pennington came rushing into the garden, 'Mr Sinclair, confound you scoundrel. You ought to be thrashed for this shameful behaviour towards my sweet innocent daughter.'

Emma said in a calm voice, 'Mother dear, Mr Edwin Sinclair and I are engaged.'

'I have just asked Emma to marry me, and she has agreed, dear Lady Pennington.'

'Mother dear, I cannot give him up. Please do not ask me. Edwin is a good man, most gentlemanlike. He loves me and I most certainly love him.'

'But I am confused, Emma, Mr Greystone's letter? Edwin, I thought you no longer loved Emma. Oh, I am lost for words.'

'Mother dear. As you said to me, I must think about getting married. Dear Edwin has asked me and I just could not say no, because it is him, I have loved all along.'

'But Mr Sinclair, she has only a small dowry.'

'What are moneys, when I can have the prettiest most intelligent and engaging young woman in the world?'

'Do you have the means to keep her?'

'Believe me when I say, I am not a poor man. Have you not heard? Large textile factories will be the future. People come from the countryside into the towns to work. Factories need more and more machines. I have the skills to design and make them. Your dear son found a skilled labour force. Good men, who now work for me. I now have a desirable income. I will keep your daughter and you Lady Pennington, in a house and manner that you desire.'

'My dear Edwin...'

'Lady Pennington, we shall marry and you shall come and live with us. If you wish it, of course.'

'Then it just remains for me to say, God bless you both, I cannot help but like you Edwin, my mind has quite changed. I give you my dearest daughter's hand. You have my blessing.'

Chapter Seventeen

The next morning there was singing heard around the cottage, from both Emma and Lady Pennington, they were in fine spirits.

Lady Pennington came into Emma's room and said, 'How do I look in this violet dress? It is time for me to cast away my full mourning attire. I shall wear a few other respectful colours now. Emma dear, you may move out of morning all together.'

'Thank you, I will mother dear. I am sure, Robert would be pleased with the happy outcome of Edwin and his little sister. I only wish he was here to witness it.'

'My dearest Emma, I am sure he would be perfectly satisfied. His little sister with his good friend.'

'I shall wear the Green printed dress that Robert bought me from London, for Edwin said. He was longing to see me in it again.'

Lady Pennington smiled. 'When did Edwin say he would be here?'

Emma glanced at the clock. 'In about one hour's time.'

'Sarah, Sarah,' called Lady Pennington.

'Here I am, Lady Pennington.'

'Would you help Emma get dressed and arrange her hair to look special? Mr Edwin Sinclair is coming to see her.'

'I will make her look like a princess Lady Pennington.' Sarah answered as she went along to Emma's bedroom.

Sarah helped Emma into her favourite dress and pinned her hair into an intricate four chain bun style which made Emma look even more elegant. Emma looked at herself in the mirror. 'What a fine job you have done Sarah. I dare say, I will gain a smile from Edwin.'

'I do like Mr Edwin Sinclair unlike that other new gentleman, who came to your last house. I remember spilling some tea onto his sleeve. He was with your brother Robert in the library at the time. Then he was all forgiveness in front of your brother. But, when I passed him later, in the hallway. He whispered in my ear and told me, that if one of his slaves had been so careless, he would have had her whipped. Really miss Emma, he frightened me. It was an accident.'

'Oh dear me, poor you dear Sarah.' Emma put her hand to her open mouth. 'Oh, no. Mr Greystone is due here any day. I had quite forgotten. Sarah, how I do wish you had told me about that incident at the time.'

'No, Miss Emma. I would not have dreamt of burdening you. I thought you may have had an understanding with him.'

'I see. Promise me, if anything like that happens again, you will come to me.'

'I will. Thank you, Miss Emma.'

Emma went downstairs to have breakfast.

After Emma had finished her morning meal, she went to the parlour and sat down on a chair and got out her knitting, which was her mother's shawl that she had promised her. Emma decided to finish it as her mother could wear it now as a bed wrap.
Emma kept glancing out of the window to see if Edwin was coming. She then glanced at the clock again. Emma contemplated about which people she would have to write to, about her good news. Emma was feeling so excited, she dropped a couple of stitches. So, she got a finer needle to pick them up again. Emma found she could not concentrate on her knitting so she gave up and put it away in her knitting bag.

Her Mother came into the room. 'Emma, I shall allow you a little time alone in the parlour with Edwin when he comes. Only a little time, then I shall come in.'

'Thank you, mother dear.'

Lady Pennington left the room.

Emma was restless. She walked over to the window, then to the mirror and back to the window again. Emma sat down on the wooden chair, then, at that moment she heard a carriage. Emma waiting, looked in the mirror again and pinched her cheeks. Then she turned around as the door opened and gasped as Mr Greystone walked into the room. Bess was behind him, doing sign language with her hands to communicate to Emma that he had marched in straight passed her.

'Oh, Mr... Greystone... What are you doing here?' questioned Emma.

Emma requested Bess to stay with her.

Bess entered the room. Emma was standing by the fire Place. 'Mr Greystone, I did not invite you here.' Standing tall Emma said. 'How dare you walk into my home without knocking and being invited in?'

Mr Greystone frowned.

'I desire you to leave at once and never come here again.' Emma declared.

'Nonsense,' He said as he stepped towards her.

'Go away.' Emma lowered her voice. 'Leave this house now.'

'But my sweet one, did you not get my letter?'

'Yes, that is why I ask you to leave now.'

'I see, you like to tease a man. You like your little jokes. Very well, I confess, you had me. Mr Greystone moved closer to Emma and handed her a gold box with a white ribbon and pressed it into her hand.'

Emma started to push it back and say. 'Please, Mr Greystone. I do not want your gifts. I am saying goodbye to you.' Emma's lip quivered. As she erupted. 'I never want to see you again.'

Mr Greystone stepped back a few steps. 'My dear Emma. You do not understand. I have come to offer my hand in marriage to you, do be serious.'

Emma's face and neck blushed deep pink, she shouted. 'No, please go.'

Mr Greystone shifted towards Emma.

Emma threw the box across the room which landed by the open door.

Mr Greystone, enraged, grabbed hold of her fishu and dragged Emma by the neck towards him.

So Bess grappled with Mr Greystone and managed to pull him away from Emma. But Mr Greystone being stronger, again dragged Emma towards him. Fury flooded through Emma as she beat his chest with her fists.

With that, Lady Pennington came into the room and saw what was happening. She shouted, 'Get out. Get out you devil.'

At that very instant, Sarah came in to the room with Mr

Sinclair. Edwin took one look at the scene and punched Mr Greystone, so he lost his balance and tripped over. Edwin got hold of the bow of his neck cloth, tugged on it, to force him to stand up and Edwin led him out of the room. Edwin then brushed his hands together and said, 'If you do not leave this house now Greystone, I will call for a magistrate.'

Mr Greystone giving Edwin a menacing glare, growled back, 'You will live to regret what you have done, sir.'

Emma was hugging herself and trembling.

Edwin put his arms around Emma, and reassures her. 'You will never see him again. Depend upon it. I will make sure he never comes near you ever again. We shall marry quick, so I can take care of you.'

'Oh dear me. What would have happened if you had not been there?'

'But I was. Do not upset yourself, my dear love. He has gone. Most assuredly, after that scene, he will not be back.'

He helped Emma to the winged chair. Her mother asked Sarah to make tea for them all. She then thanked Bess for protecting her daughter. Then Lady Pennington told Bess to take a rest because she could see, her loyal servant was in shock.

Lady Pennington was quivering herself. She thanked Edwin for saving them from such a man and said to Emma. 'You were right about Mr Greystone after all, and put her arms around her daughter.

'I own that, I was taken in by him.' Lady Pennington kissed Emma's cheek and told her she was her wise daughter with her choice of husband.

Chapter Eighteen

Once again Emma and her Mother were about to move house.

They were moving into Edwin's Sinclair's recently built Regency home. As he felt it would be good for Emma and her mother to be settled in before the wedding day.

Their new abode was in Chester. The windows on one side of the dwelling looked out onto the river Dee. It had no landscaped garden yet. So, it was a blank page for Emma to put her own distinctive imagination on it.

Showing Emma the house. Edwin said, he would order samples of fabric and wallpaper, so they could choose their house decoration together. Emma felt excited as she spoke of her ideas. Before leaving each room, Edwin pressed his lips to her cheek or forehead and kissed it.

Emma explained that her friends Julia and Phoebe, would come to help her get dressed and they would bring fresh flowers for her. Emma said, she now felt there was nothing bad ahead of them. The only thing that disappointed her, was that Dudley was abroad. She told Edwin how Dudley had always been a kind friend to her. Emma even confided, about Dudley being attacked, by orders from Mr Greystone. After talking about it. Emma and Edwin decided to speak no more about Mr Greystone. As they left the last room to be viewed, Edwin took hold of both of her hands and kissed her with tenderness on her lips.

After having viewed all the rooms together, Edwin and Emma joined Lady Pennington in the drawing room. The three of them enjoyed a glass of sherry.

Edwin told Emma to shut her eyes, he put a gift into her hands. It felt cold and smooth. She opened her eyes and saw a gold oval locket. When Emma opened it, she saw a portrait of her on one side and Edwin on the other.

Emma wondered, how did he find an artist to paint her portrait so well, without her sitting for it. Edwin confessed that he was the artist. Emma was overjoyed with the gift and praised his artistic skill.

After dinner, Edwin said he desired to take Emma away to the Lake District. To see the wild mountains and enjoy the tarns. Edwin said, He had been reading William Wordsworth's book called, 'Guide to the Lakes' he now desired to see it together with his darling new wife. He added about his hope to overcome his fear of sailing, so he could take her to Italy. Emma's eyes sparkled. Yet, she reassured him. 'Edwin, I would love to go there yet the truth is I am happiest to be, wherever you are.'

There had been some gifts sent which had been arranged on the large mahogany table for Emma to see, along with letters.

Edwin and Emma spent time together talking about their marriage plans and opening gifts and reading letters of congratulations.

Edwin took hold of another letter and breaks the seal, rapidly his face went pale. His jaw tightened.

'Edwin dear, what is it? Is it bad news?'

'It is just a congratulations letter Emma my darling,' he said.

'Your face does not reflect joyful congratulations.'

'It is of no account. Open the last one Emma my dear.'

She opened the last letter. Edwin put the former in his jacket pocket.

'Oh, it is from Mrs Stubbs. She is a lovely old lady.' Emma passed the letter to Edwin and asked him to pass her the previous one.

Edwin asked, 'Do you think we will have fine weather for our wedding day dearest?'

Emma saw that he was unwilling to pass the disconcerting letter over to her.

Emma without much forethought asked, 'Edwin dear, is it from an old sweetheart, is that why you do not wish me to see that letter?'

'How did you guess?'

He rubbed his mouth with the back of his hand.

' She has not reopened a cruel memory for you, has she?'

'Not at all.' He smiled warmly.

Emma continued saying in a soft voice. 'I need not know of past romances. I understand that most men have had them, never the less my dearest love, you have been unsettled by a letter. Furthermore, it is the last night before our wedding day.'

Edwin stroked Emma's cheek gently, then took her hand and held it tightly.

'Because I love you so much, I have decided to let you read the letter. I do not want you to fret that I have rekindled a love or have a secret admirer. I recognise that you will not sleep if I do not show it to you, yet my love, you will probably not sleep either, when I do show it to you.'

Edwin took the letter from his pocket and offered it to Emma.

Emma opened it and read these words.

Sinclair. You will not have her. Emma is mine. Greystone.

Emma dropped the letter on the floor and Edwin grasped both her hands.

'Darling, this letter is just an idle threat from a coward. Unfortunately, he cannot come to terms with the fact, you do not love him. These empty words are meant to frighten you. Emma, our love is much stronger. Please dearest, put it out of your mind. Do not allow that devil to spoil our wedding day. Can you be strong, Emma my only love?'

'Oh, Edwin your words have soothed me. With you by my side I will be strong.' Emma stepped on the letter as she walked away, she stopped by the door and said. 'Please Edwin, get rid of the letter. I shall not tell my mother about it.'

Edwin picked up the letter and put it in his pocket since the fire was not lit. 'We shall be silent about it, my brave Emma.' He took hold of the silver candelabra and together they joined Lady Pennington in the dining room.

After they had eaten a late dinner. Emma said, she would go to bed early. She looked up to Edwin's eyes, they sparkled with love. 'You are not to see me now until I walk up the aisle. Good night Edwin, love of my life and husband to be.'

Edwin replied. 'Sweet dreams Emma and kissed her with firm pressure on her lips.'

Chapter Nineteen

B ess knocked, then entered Emma's room, and put down the breakfast tray onto the table. Next Bess drew back the bedroom curtains. 'It's a lovely crisp morning, cool, but the sun is out and the sky is blue. This will be the happiest day of your life my sweet Miss Emma. '

Emma sat up.

'It is.' Emma replied with a tone of enthusiasm. 'What woman would not be joyful marrying the dearest man she loves?'

'Mr Edwin Sinclair is a fine man and very handsome to be sure. I am sure you will always be happy with such a good husband. Even more, I know he is a most fortunate man to be marrying you, my dear Miss Emma.'

'Bess you are a treasure. I will always be grateful to you, for looking after me so well. I do hope you are looking forward to witnessing our wedding?'

'Very much indeed. I've only been to a couple. But Miss Emma, I feel I should warn you I cry at weddings.'

'I may even cry with joy myself.'

'Miss Emma, Lady Pennington has told me, to bring your breakfast to your room.' Bess put the breakfast tray onto Emma's lap.

Emma was enjoying her drink of chocolate while Bess arranged her bathing utensils for her. 'This is a comfortable house may I say Miss Emma, Sarah and I will be very happy here.'

'I am delighted. Has Mr Sinclair's servants made you feel at home?'

'I think they are a bit put out about Sarah and me breaking into their little circle. But I'm sure that when they get to know us, they will be fine. There's a young girl called Liz who seems very timid, I shall befriend her, so I can help.'

'I dare say Bess, you will be just like a mother with a daughter.'

'May you be bless soon Miss Emma with children of your own.'

'I do hope so, It is what I have always wish to be, a fine wife and Mother.'

'You will be a praiseworthy Mother I am sure.'

'Stop or you will make me cry with happiness.' Emma felt a lump in her throat although she managed to say. 'After my breakfast, I will bathe and you can brush my hair, then Phoebe and Julia will arrive to help me get ready.'

'Yes, Miss Emma.'

'Is Mr Sinclair about?'

'Yes, he is giving instructions to the head groom about the carriage, and horses. I dare say, he wants it to look it's best for you. I am sure you will enjoy your journey to the Lake district in such a beautiful carriage.'

Only a little time after Emma had bathed. Emma heard excited laughter outside her door.

Bess opened the door and Sarah said. 'It is, Miss Julia and Miss Phoebe.'

'Come in. come in my dear friends.'

Julia gave Emma a hug. 'Who would have believed this special day would have come so soon after all your sorrow.'

Phoebe also hugged Emma. 'I knew happiness would come. Dudley has sent a congratulations letter for you with our post, as he did not know your new address.' Phoebe handed over her brother's letter to Emma.

'That is my one sadness, your dearest brother cannot attend my wedding.'

'Dudley wrote in his letter to us, that he wishes he could be here more than all else.'

'I dare say then, Dudley's letter will have to do for me.'

'Now come over here Em, and sit down in front of the mirror, while we dress your hair.' Phoebe requested.

'My pearl hair band is on the dressing table.'

'Ah, it is very fine indeed Em.' Julia said, picking it up for Phoebe.

Phoebe started to dress Emma's hair until she was happy with it, she handed Emma the hand mirror to check how it looked at the back.

'How beautiful. Thank you. I also love the curls at the front. Just the way I imagined it.'

Bess then checked it over and congratulated Phoebe on such a fine job. For she never knew of a Lady who could dress hair as well as Phoebe had.

Bess next placed Emma's pale-yellow silk dress, along with the matching embroidered pelisse, onto the bed. Followed by pantalettes, short stays, shift, and silk stockings.

The girls grew excited as they started to help Bess dress Emma. First, they helped her into her underpinnings. Next, they helped Emma put on the dress, without ruffling up her hair. Phoebe noticed that the waistline was a little lower than usual. Emma explained it was the new fashion. Julia said, she loved the way the padded puff sleeves stood upright, without flopping over. Julia then bent down to help Emma put on her flat leather shoes. 'Which one would you like on your right foot?' Julia held both the shoes up for Emma to see.
'It does not matter, when I tried them on in the shop, they were both very comfortable on either foot'.

'Yes,' Julia replied, 'They are such soft kid leather, they will quickly wear into shape.'

Next, Bess helped Emma into her pale-yellow pelisse long jacket, which had an oval train which brushed the floor. When Emma was dressed. Julia asked Emma to sit at her dressing table, so she could put some light powder onto her skin. After, she put a tiny bit of pink blush onto her cheeks. Emma thought I am blushing so much that I am sure I do not need it today. But said nothing.

'I have a little black soot paste for your brows and lashes.' 'Oh, I am not sure' replied Emma. 'Dear, it will be very light and you can wipe it off if you dislike it.'

So, Emma gave her friend permission. Julia made a very natural job of it. 'Just a little cherry pink on your lips, just lightly,' explained her friend.

Emma looked into the mirror. She could see that it made her look most agreeable and fashionable. Emma put her pearl earrings on. Now she was almost ready.

Emma said to Bess. 'You must go now and get changed.'

Bess, squeezed Emma's hand. 'Bless you,' she said and went to get ready.

Phoebe commented, ' I like the embroidered feather motifs on your shawl.'

'It was embroidered in the Country of India.'

'Where is India?'

' See in the corner, over there? I have kept Roberts globe. Let me show you. They went over to the globe and Emma pointed to the Country of India.

'Do you not long to travel to all these exotic lands on the other side of the world?' Asked Emma.

'No dear, I would be too afraid to leave the place where I live.' Julia said with conviction.'

Phoebe answered, 'Most truly Yes, if I could take my friends with me. I would like to go with my brother and of course your lovely Edwin and you, Emma dear.'

'Alas, my Edwin dislikes the sea and sailing.'

'Oh.'

'Although hope is not lost. For Edwin told me, he would love to take me to Italy one day if he can manage to push himself to it. He will, I am sure, for I know he does so desire to do it for me.'

'Ah, good fellow.'

'I shall not make it a burden to him. As I am happy just being with him for the rest of my life. How could I ever ask for more? Really, how could I?'

'Phoebe in a thoughtful pose said. ' You are so blessed, to be marrying a man that you love. I wonder what will be the outcome for us Julia?'

The door opened and Lady Pennington came into the room. 'let me see you my dear.'

Emma walked over to her mother.

'My good and sweet daughter Emma. You look Elegant. Your dress and your hair, are perfect. I am so happy for you, my darling. Your carriage is waiting, and Lord Gilpin.'

Emma smiled, 'You look so pretty in pastel blue Mother dear, and I think your turban is most becoming on you.'

'Do you think the ostrich feather goes well?'

' Yes, It makes you look special Indeed, for you are the mother of the bride. Thank you truly, for all you have done for me. Edwin and I have left a gift for you. Which you can open when you get home.'

'Thank you, my dear child. It is time to go,' Lady Pennington said, as she opened the door.

Julia gave Emma her flowers and Phoebe helped her down the wide long staircase. When she got to the bottom, Lord Gilpin kissed Emma's hand and told her she looked splendid. He took her hand and led her into the shining black carriage. After which her mother got in with them.

Emma said, 'Thank you for giving me away, Lord Gilpin.'

'It is a privilege for me to take the place of your dear Father.'

Emma replied, 'You are most dear to me. All of you are. I only wish Dudley was here.'

' Yes, my dear, He is miserable, to be away during your wedding. Be assured of his regards and best wishes. There, there, you will enjoy reading his letter.

'I will.'

'Your Mr Sinclair seems an affable fellow, with gentleman like ways.'

'Indeed he is.'

'This is a very fine Barouche carriage is it new?' Enquired Lord Gilpin.

'Edwin bought it three months ago. The new type of suspension is very forgiving on this bumpy road.'

'Good gracious Emma.'

'I have been reading up about carriages... I dare say,' Emma giggled, 'I sound more like a groom rather than a bride.'

'You are a pretty girl. Just a gentle kind word in your ear. It may be best to hide your intelligence from people my dear, some dislike it.'

Lady Pennington said, 'My sweet Emma gets joy from learning things, do you not, my dear?'

'Indeed I do Mother.'

'Well, well.' Lord Gilpin tapped her hand and said, 'You make a most pretty bride.'

Just then a red and gold leaf flew right into the carriage and landed on Emma's lap. She picked it up and said. 'I will press this it will be my wedding day leaf. Every time I look at it in the future, it will remind me of this lovely carriage drive on my way to my wedding.'

'Charming, delightful.' commented Lord Gilpin.

'A love symbol.' Agreed Lady Pennington. She took it from Emma's hand and placed it in her reticule for Emma.

The carriage started slowing down.

Lord Gilpin said. 'Here we are Ladies. Emma dear, I need to ask. Are you completely sure my dear you want to go ahead and make this vow? This will be your last chance to change your mind. I feel I must ask the question. It is my duty as your step in Father.'

'I understand Lord Gilpin. I have no doubt in my mind at all. Depend upon it, I very much want to marry Edwin Sinclair.'

'Good, very good.'

The carriage came to a stop. Her mother had a tear in her eye. But Emma could not hold back from smiling.

They saw lots of carriages and horses and the sound of crows in the trees.

Lord Gilpin helped Lady Pennington down from the Barouche.

Then Julia and Phoebe alighted from the carriage behind and went to assist Emma. They held up her train as the ground was coated in fallen leaves.

Lady Pennington gave Emma her flowers, while the girls took their places. Lord Gilpin pulled on his sleeves checking they were not creased; he then took Emma's arm.

Lady Gilpin was waiting outside the door for them. She then joined Lady Pennington. The door was opened, the sound of the organ spilled out. Lord Gilpin said, 'Onward, my dear.' They both walked slowly down the aisle. Emma could see people smiling at her as she passed. Emma felt overwhelming joy immerse her very being. At last, she caught her first glimpse of Edwin. The music crescendo with the beat of her heart. As Emma got nearer to her husband to be. She felt fully alive. Lord Gilpin squeezed her hand then let it go. Looking into Edwin's eyes, Emma felt her lower lip tremble with the emotion of the moment. Edwin gave a full smile and whispered, 'You look incredible, my dear love. My angel-'

Suddenly -

A voice shouted 'stop – stop this wedding at once.'

Edwin and Emma looked swiftly around.

 They saw two men who hurried towards them. One was in a uniform another was a magistrate waving a piece of paper in his hands. 'This wedding must not go ahead.'

Edwin stepped forward towards the man and demanded to know what this disturbance was all about?

The Magistrate held up the paper for all the congregation to see. Then proclaimed that the woman called Emma Pennington was already married.

Edwin slapped his forehead with his hand. 'No, no, you have got that wrong.'

Emma clung to Edwin, 'Sir, I am not married and I have never ever been married to anyone.'

We believe that your married name is Emma Greystone.

'No, No, No. That is untrue, I am not married. I would never have ever married Mr Nash Greystone. I hate the man. You must believe me.'

'I see that you know the gentleman that I am talking about then.' Said the magistrate.

Edwin called to Lord Gilpin, Lord Gilpin said to the magistrate

'My dear fellow there has been a simple mistake here. If you go back and research the matter. You will find that Miss Emma Pennington has not been married before. You must take my word as a Lord and a gentleman. I have known Miss Pennington since she was young and I know that she has married no one.'

Lady Pennington was on her feet. Lady Gilpin and others who had known Emma all her life said that she is not married.

Julia and Phoebe were hugging each other while they cried.

The man in uniform said in a loud voice. 'Sit down, or I will send you all to court.'

The people sat down. Only, Aunt Belvedere came towards the magistrate with her closed parasol in the air, 'My man, I shall report you to the highest authority in the land if you do not tell me where you got this ridiculous idea, that my little niece is married?'

'From this, my Lady.'

'But that is a marriage certificate?'

Edwin snatched it out of the man's hands. 'This cannot be true; it must be a cruel joke.'

Emma was shedding tears. Her Mother questioned. 'Please, sir, where did you get this, this marriage certificate?'

Mr Nash Greystone gave it to me, to prove that he married this lady, 3 weeks ago at Gretna Green in Scotland.

Edwin gave the certificate back to the magistrate. 'No, this is a lie. Mr Greystone has done this to get back at me as his revenge. Doubtless, because he wanted to marry Emma but Emma loves me, not him.'

With a grave look the magistrate said, 'Mr Greystone has assured me that you, Mr Edwin Sinclair, are a victim of this lady. Mr Greystone convinced me that you would not have known this lady was already married. It is, Mr Greystones wife, who is in the wrong. So, I have to arrest Mrs Emma Greystone, as she was knowingly about to commit bigamy.' He turned back to Edwin. 'I am so very sorry Mr Sinclair.'

'Sorry! You are so very sorry. Is that all you can say?' Edwin turned to Emma. 'Emma, my love, I asked you to be brave once before. You must be courageous. Do not give up hope. Remember, you are my dearest love and I am yours. I will do everything I can in my power, to get you out of this, this, dirty dealing of Greystones.'

'Oh my dearest Edwin,' Emma Sobbed. 'Mr Greystone has always come between us.'

'Not forever.'

The officer started to pull Emma away from Edwin. Edwin kissed the palm of her hand.

'That's enough.' commanded the officer.

Emma was in a daze.

The officer holding onto Emma marched her to the back of the building.

Edwin shouted at the top of his voice. 'I love you Emma.'

Lady Pennington was holding onto Lady Gilpin crying, 'Help her, help her, somebody, please help my child.'

Edwin's aunties, uncles and cousins and younger brother all gathered around him and they tried to comfort him, but he would not be comforted. 'Where is Greystone? Where is that coward? I will have him thrown into jail, and will make sure they throw away the key.' Edwin's eyes hardened. 'If only I could get my hands on you, Greystone, right now. Edwin shook his fist and was shaking it shouting. Greystone you are a Devil, face me Greystone. Bring him to me...'

The Magistrate went over to Edwin. 'I will have silence, Mr Sinclair.' He scolded.

'Edwin,' Lord Gilpin tapped him on the shoulder. 'I will help you sort this out, my dear fellow. Be strong. We shall go together and see where they are taking poor dear Emma and together we shall get to the bottom of this.'

'I will come too,' Lord Napier added.

Edwin's younger brother Reuben also wanted to go.

Just then the minister closed his Bible. Clapped his hands together for attention and told the congregation and friends to go back to their homes.

Emma turned around and cast a long glance at her beloved Edwin, for she wanted him to know that she meant to be brave.

The officer and Magistrate marched her out of the building, followed by Lord Gilpin along with Reuben, who were supporting Edwin.

Outside, the officer put Emma into a coach and followed her in, sitting down next to her.

Lord Napier asked the Magistrate where they were taking Emma. He told him they were taking her to the local jail. Emma would be held there until they called her to court to answer the charge of, knowingly intending to commit bigamy.

Lord Napier asked the magistrate, if they could go to be with Emma. The magistrate refused. He could only allow Emma's Mother to visit. Everyone else would have to wait. As he needed to question Mrs Emma Greystone alone first.

'Mr Greystone has sworn to us that he is sure Mr Sinclair would not have known of Mrs Emma Greystone's marriage. So, I am letting you know,' added the Magistrate, 'we will not allow Mr Sinclair to visit the lady in question, Mrs Emma Greystone.'

Edwin sat on the low stone wall outside the Church. He covered his face with his hands and started to sob bitterly.

The Magistrate climbed into the waiting carriage and the carriage slipped away.

Chapter Twenty

L ady Pennington had come back from visiting Emma in the holding cell.

Bess tried to hide her tear-stained eyes.

'My poor sweet child, how dreadful she looks. Yet, she is a brave girl. How we must hope for good news. Emma is convinced Mr Sinclair will come and sort the whole mess out. Bess, I hope justice will be on our side.'

Bess gave Lady Pennington a kiss on her cheek. 'Forgive my presumption, Lady Pennington. I just wanted to show how much I care about you both.'

'I took it in the spirit it was meant. You have been with us for a long time, my dear Bess.'

'Yes, and I'll stand in court as a witness for my Miss Emma, I will.'

'Bless you.'

Bess helped Lady Pennington take off her coat and bonnet. Then she said, 'Lady Pennington, there is someone here to see you.'

'Who is it?'

'Lady Belvedere.'

'Oh dear, I could do without her today.'

'She is in quite a state, she was in tears.'

'Very well, I will see her.'

Lady Pennington left Bess and went into the drawing room where Lady Belvedere was standing looking at the painting of Emma.

'Martha dear.' Lady Pennington kissed Lady Belvedere on the cheek and pointed to a chair.

'Martha, please sit down.'

'Charlotte, I am shaking with shock. I am sick of heart.'

'I dare say, Martha.'

'How is little Emma?'

'I have been to see her and I can hardly speak of it... my poor Emma-'

'-My sad little niece. It is pitiful. Charlotte, did she look very ill?'

'Dreadful, but dear, she is being very brave...'

'It is not to be endured.'

'Lord Gilpin has helped us the best he can. He has found a fellow who can advise us about what will happen. My darling Emma must be seen in the best possible light.'

Lady Belvedere wiped her eyes with her hankie chief. 'My dear Charlotte... How will you ever forgive me?'

'What are you talking about? Forgive what?'

'Hoodwinked, I was.'

'I entreat you, Martha, tell me, what do you know?'

'It has distressed me so...'

Lady Pennington stood up wagged her finger at Lady Belvedere. 'Martha, stop feeling sorry for yourself for once. You know something about Mr Greystone and my Emma? Tell me, tell me now or I will go mad.'

Lady Belvedere pattered her mouth with her handkerchief. 'Nash Greystone is a fraud.'

'Whatever do you mean?'

'Nash Greystone. Left a letter on the desk in his room, which I have only just found. Can you believe this Charlotte? He was not at all a friend of my husband. He met him on a ship and got friendly with him. He had the audacity to thank me for the comfortable lifestyle that I kept him in. Yet, he has not paid me for his ball.'

'No.'

He writes, he is furious and distressed about Emma's rejection of him. He threatens us all, saying; He has plans to show his displeasure to Emma and all those who are connected to her.

Lady Pennington swooned and fell onto her knees.

Lady Belvedere called out. Sarah ran in and helped Lady Pennington onto her chair.

Sarah used Lady Belvedere's vinaigrette to help Lady Pennington come to.

'Charlotte, I was taken in by that creature. I am a silly old fool. I will do anything to help you, whatever you need I will do.'

Sarah said, 'Shall I bring you some sweet tea Lady Pennington?'

'Yes Sarah, bring us both tea.'

Sarah left the room and Lady Pennington sat back in her chair. 'What a shock, Martha. What can I do?'

'There there, I will have you stay with me in my comfortable home where I will take care of you, Charlotte we must stick together.'

'I am wondering what to do?' Lady Pennington took another sniff of the vinaigrette. 'Edwin Sinclair is staying with Lord and Lady Napier. I must be gone from here before Edwin comes back to his own home again.'

'I shall organise your things to be packed my dear Charlotte and sent to my address.'

'Thank you, Martha.'

'I will tell Bess and Sarah to do what they can. I will get rooms ready for them tomorrow. But Charlotte dear. I shall take you with me tonight. My whole point in life now is getting my niece back.'

Sarah brings in the tray of tea and says, 'Bess and I want to know if there is anything, we can do for you Lady Pennington?'
  Lady Belvedere and Lady Pennington both explained to Sarah the new arrangements. Telling her to put the plan into action with Bess.

They then heard the house door bell ring. It was Lord and Lady Gilpin.

Lady Belvedere explained what she had intended to do for Lady Pennington. So, Lady Gilpin helped Lady Pennington pack her trunks and bandboxes along with Bess and Sarah, for her journey to her next home.

Chapter Twenty-One

A few weeks had passed since they forcibly took Emma from her wedding ceremony.

They had locked her up in a cell. Emma could not wash as often as she usually did. The food was lacking in volume and variety. She found the stone floors and walls deeply chilling. Her eyes felt strained because of the lack of windows. The place stank of urine, perspiration and boiled meat. Loud screams and cries heard night and day were unending and miserable to tolerate. The very air tasted of doom. Emma had shared this small space with numerous women. She shuddered at the sight of the brazen ill-bred, vulgar, and immoral women as they came and went. Emma cried over pitiable tales she heard from poor women with starving children. She could not believe these women were being thrown into jail for feeding their dying children, on food that they had stolen, only in desperation.

Emma also worried about how the Dale family were coping. Would Cousin Charles have Mr Dale laid off and dismissed from the tied cottage? Would he too, end up stealing food to feed his little children?

Emma could not sleep, she tossed and turned at night. Some women even tried to unpick the silk embroidery thread from her wedding dress. Many poor women had never seen such superior clothing in all their lives. So, Emma turned her dress and pelisse inside out and tied her shawl around her tightly. As the weeks went by her wedding garments and shawl became more greyed with the grime of the place. Which meant her fine clothing raised less attention. Emma spoke little to hide the fact she was a Lady.

The only time Emma got any sleep at all, was when she fell asleep while thinking about Edwin. Emma kept up her strong faith that he would come and save her from this soulless place. But, as the days passed and the only person she ever saw for a couple of minutes, was her dear Mother. Who always came disguised in servant's clothes, wearing a hooded cloak to hide her face. Emma realised that Edwin was not going to save her. Each day that passed, she started to wonder whether Edwin believed her or her enemy, Mr Greystone.

One morning, Emma caught sight of her shadow. It was as someone opened her cell door on a sunny day. Her shadow was hunched forward, rocking back and forth. Emma, shocked at seeing such a negative figure of herself, knew from that very moment she had to change. Emma commanded herself to be stronger and not to allow her thoughts to wither away to desolation.

Emma realised that instead of pushing away from her mind, all thoughts of the trial. She must picture it and practise how she would present herself.

They had warned her she would only have a moment to make a good impression to the jury. They had told Emma that she could have no one defending her, as they caught her in the act of making an unlawful marriage vow. It would be down to the jury to find her innocent. Emma knew she had a hard job ahead to convince the jury of men that she was a guiltless, honourable single lady.

She had never been in a courtroom before. Emma just kept believing her mother and Lord Gilpin would be there for her.

One thing Emma kept asking herself was. How did Mr Greystone get her signature on the fake wedding certificate? Secondly, why did he say that she had married him in Gretna Green? Yet to Emma the most important question was, who did Edwin believe?

For the first time in Emma's life, she was alone. She had to be brave and get her strength from Emma Pennington herself.

Chapter twenty-two

There had been great distress among the loved ones of Emma. Weeks of worry had circled her mother. Bess and Sarah appeared to be most unhappy too.
Both Lady Gilpin and Napier were rather concerned about Lady Pennington's health. As she was getting further anxious and weaker.

Emma's trial was now two days late. Her Mother, Lord and Lady Gilpin, Lord and Lady Napier had been waiting around the courtroom building on and off for a couple of days. They were getting very restless for the time was pressing on. Lord Gilpin asked the clerk if he knew when Emma's trial would take place. Lord Gilpin was told trials could be delayed by a few days. Lord Gilpin looked vexed. He and his wife were too concerned to leave the building as Emma's trial might be called at any time. Lord Gilpin was very much hoping; they would call him for a witness statement. As he was sure it would carry some weight as he was a Lord and Gentleman. Lord Gilpin was concerned for Emma like a Father, for he kept asking if they could see Emma, but the answer was always negative.

Lady Belvedere had gone back home to sleep. Being an older lady, she was weakening. She had just arrived back in the building, when they heard the echo of footsteps coming towards them and saw people leave the building. A clerk came over and said that Emma's trial would be heard during the next group of hearings. He pointed out that they had a lot of trials to get through, so they would only get about 10 minutes or 15 if it was really needed. Lord Napier wanted to know who would judge Emma's case. But the Clerk refused to state who he was. Lady Belvedere asked to know if Mr Greystone was present in the building. Again, the Clerk would not say. Lord Gilpin promised he would do what he could, but he stated that they were going into the courtroom blind with no idea of what folly laid ahead of them.

Just a little later the clerk came and told them that the trial that they had been waiting for is about to start. Lord and Lady Gilpin supported Lady Pennington. An usher opened the tall solid doors. They entered the vast, well illuminated, crowded courtroom, which had an intimidating atmosphere.

Lady Napier held onto Lady Belvedere's arm, who was fanning herself frantically. An usher showed them to the bench where they were to sit.

Edwin Sinclair was sitting only a little way along from them. He was ashen with black circles under his eyes. His hair was overgrown, and he sat with his head bowed resting his fist against his mouth. His younger brother Ruben was sitting next to Edwin, he was scrutinising everyone who came into the room. Yet, when Ruben saw Lord Napier sit near, he nodded to him and his wife.

Lady Belvedere was moaning about the heat and complaining how she was sure that she would faint. Lady Belvedere begged Lady Napier to hold on to her to stop her swooning on to the floor, But, in the next breath she exclaimed that she would throw her parasol at that swindling devil

Greystone and knock his head off.

Then the tall oak door again was opened, and what looked like the jury came in and sat down in a group to the left of the judge's bench. They all looked very well dressed, and all looked like wealthy gentlemen.

Next, Mr Nash Greystone was brought in with a tall, thin man.

There was a shout of, 'All up standing for the judge.'

Everyone stood up. The wigged and robed gentlemen of law and the judge strutted into the room and took their rightful places.

'Silence in court,' came the shout.

The Gentlemen stopped whispering. The Judge said. 'Send in the first.'

With that, through an arched shaped door, Emma was brought in and taken to the bar.

 She stood as if frozen to the spot. The tilted mirror above her head reflected light onto her flushed face. The daylight came from a large arched window at the back of the room. Emma's face was motionless and her slender body now thin.

'I am all astonishment, look at her, how I could weep.' Lady Belvedere expressed as she put a lace hankie chief to her eyes.

Emma's mother had tears streaming fast down her cheeks. She looked pale and sat insensibly. Lady Gilpin put her arm around her.

A gentleman in a white wig stood up and read the charges.

'Mrs Emma Greystone, who went under the name of Miss Emma Pennington. Is hereby indicted on the charge of attempted bigamy. The accused was about to marry a Mr Edwin Sinclair. Knowingly being lawfully married to Mr Nash Greystone.'

Emma shook her head to disagree with what was being alleged.

'What do you plead?'

'Not guilty, Sir.'

'I call Mr Nash Greystone.'

Emma's eyes fixed on to her adversary and her eyes followed him all the way up to the stand.

Mr Greystone was sworn in.

'Mr Nash Greystone. You say that this woman Mrs Emma Greystone was lawfully married to you on the 7th day of October 1820 in Scotland. You made the journey from Cheshire to Gretna Green and did there solemnise your oath in a marriage ceremony over the anvil with two witnesses to this fact?'

All eyes including Emma's, where on Mr Greystone as he spoke the words. 'Yes. You are correct.'

'Where did the alleged ceremony take place?'

'As you said, Sir. The village of Gretna Green, Scotland.'

'In a church or somewhere else?'

'I got talking to a gentleman to ask if the local minister was about. He could not find him. Then the gentleman told me that people often got married over the anvil at the blacksmiths. The blacksmith had married many couples from England and Wales. He had made it quite a business. It was getting late, so I thought to myself. Upon my word, it is not what I had set my heart upon. However, on talking to Emma, she agreed to the handfasting wedding ceremony. I had brought a witness friend with me. So that is exactly what we did, sir.'

'You went to the blacksmiths?'

'We did Sir.'

'What is the name of the person who took the Handfast ceremony?'

'A Mr Robert Elliot, I believe Sir.'

'What evidence do you have of this Handfast ceremony having taken place?'

'Sir, I can provide evidence.' Mr Greystone held up the marriage certificate in his hand.

A clerk took it from Mr Greystone and handed it to the judge.

The judge screwed up his eyes as he read it, then said, 'Well, this looks authentic to me.'

Emma looked up at the ceiling as if she was begging for help.

'The Gentleman prosecutor asked the clerk to give Emma a pen, ink and paper.' He said, 'Now, would you write your name down on the paper?'

There was a hush in the room, while all watched Emma write her name.

The Clerk took the paper from her. He passed it to the prosecutor. Who also received the wedding certificate back from the judge. He then looked at the two signatures side by side. Then he had both the paper and certificate passed to the judge and the judge on seeing them, exhaled and nodded.

Emma was wide-eyed and waited for the next words.

They came. 'Yes, members of the jury. They are a perfect match.' Were the words.

There was a gasp from Emma's family.

Emma's legs buckled, but she held on and straightened up again. With that, Emma caught sight of Edwin. She saw he was shaking his head. He put his palm against his mouth and closed his eyes.

At that moment, Emma knew all was lost. She understood that Edwin no longer believed her.

The prosecutor continued. 'You say Mr Greystone, that you took a friend as your witness?'

'Indeed, sir. I took my friend Mr Duff Campbell as a witness.'

'Did you have two witnesses?'

'Yes Sir. The other was a Mr Stewart Thomson, The Man I conversed with from the village, whom I have already spoken of.'

'You saw him sign his name on the certificate?'

'Yes, Sir.'

'On the 7th day of October 1820. You married Miss Emma Pennington. At Gretna Green, Scotland. Thereafter signed the marriage certificate, along with two witnesses. Is this correct, Mr Nash Greystone?'

'Once again, I say, Yes, I did. That is correct, Sir.'

'Mr Nash Greystone. You have assured the magistrate, the

officer and I. That you are sure in your own mind that Mr Edwin Sinclair, had no knowledge of your marriage to Miss Emma Pennington at Gretna Green, in Scotland, on the 7th day of October this year of our lord?'

'I am certainly sure that he did not know of our marriage.'

'You, yourself did not tell Mr Edwin Sinclair of it?'

'No, I did not, Sir.'

'Why did you not?'

'I was not an acquaintance or friend of Mr Edwin Sinclair. I am a gentleman, he is a trade person.'

'So, did you have any reason to tell him?'

'None at all.'

'You have nothing to do with Mr Sinclair in your day-to-day life?'

'Nothing, I am not from the same social standing as him.'

'To your knowledge, did your new wife Mrs Emma Greystone tell Mr Edwin Sinclair about the handfast marriage over the anvil in Gretna Green?'

'I told her not to tell anyone at all, for we had not yet told her mother and relatives. We agreed that I would tell them in person. I was about to send them an invitation to a meal where I would have announced it to all. But I did not get a chance before my wife was caught as she was about to marry Mr Edwin Sinclair.'

'Pray, for what reason did you not tell them of your marriage?'

'Emma's Mother, Lady Pennington and her Aunt, Lady Belvedere and so-called friends tried to stop me from marrying Emma. They thought I was not good enough for her, for they wanted someone with a grand title. I am a Gentleman, but not good enough for Miss Emma Pennington, in their superior eyes.'

'So even though Mrs Emma Greystone, is now revealed to be an untruthful and unloyal wife? You, Mr Greystone still fully believe in your own mind that your wife did not tell Mr Edwin Sinclair of her marriage to you?'

'No. Emma had told no one, less so Mr Sinclair. She would have worried that if he knew of our marriage, Mr Sinclair never would have wished to marry her. For If she had told him, I am sure, just like any man, he would not have wedded a married woman. It was only three days since we got married.'

'Why do you think she tried to commit bigamy with Mr Edwin Sinclair?'

'I do not know, what man can know a woman's mind? I am

quite at a loss to know the answer, Sir.'

'Did your friend Mr Duff Campbell tell Mr Edwin Sinclair about the marriage at Gretna Green?'

'No, indeed not. I have asked Mr Campbell, and he has maintained he never told Mr Sinclair.'

'Thank you, Mr Nash Greystone, you can step down.'

The prosecutor now called for the witness, Mr Duff Campbell.

Emma watches to see who this so-called witness is. A tall, thin man came to the stand. He had wrinkled skin, and he was holding his hands in a tight fist by his sides.

They then swore him in.

The prosecutor frowned and asked.

'So your name is Mr Duff Campbell?'

'Ay.'

'You are Scottish?'

'Correct.'

'So, Mr Duff Campbell, you went up to Gretna Green with Miss Emma Pennington and Mr Nash Greystone. Is that right?'

247

'Ay.'

'You went as a friend to be a witness for Mr Nash Greystone and Emma Pennington during the handfast wedding ceremony over the anvil at the blacksmith, in Gretna Green in Scotland.'

'Correct.'

The prosecutor held up the marriage certificate and asked, as he pointed to the signature. 'Have a look. Is this your signature?'

'Ay, it is.'

'Who is the other signature by?'

'A gentleman we met, at Gretna Green.'

'Do you recognise Miss Emma Pennington's signature?'

' Ay do '

'You saw Emma Pennington sign it?'

'Correct.'

'Mr Duff Campbell, did you tell anyone at all about this marriage ceremony that you had witnessed in Scotland until Emma Greystone walked into the church to marry Mr Edwin Sinclair?'

'Naw, it was a secret.'

'Did Mrs Emma Greystone tell anyone about her marriage that you heard or came to know of?'

'Naw.'

'Not even Mr Edwin Sinclair.'

'Naw. Mr Sinclair did not know the Lady was wed to Mr Greystone.'

'So you claim, Mrs Emma Greystone fully knew she was about to commit bigamy. You also say that the Man Mr Edwin Sinclair did not know?'

'The man is innocent Ay, but the Lady knew.'

'You may step down Mr Duff Campbell.'

The wigged gentleman sitting next to the judge started to whisper to the judge. The judge started to whisper to the other gentleman sitting on the other side of him.

The judge declared, 'These fellow Gentlemen and I, would like to hear Mr Edwin Sinclair's view on this matter from his own mouth.'

'Yes, indeed judge.'

The clerk called 'Mr Edwin Sinclair.'

Raising his hand, Edwin Sinclair answered, 'I am he.'

'Mr Edwin Sinclair. Would you go to the witness box and get sworn in, Sir?'

Edwin went to the witness box, and he was sworn in.

Emma's eyes focused on Edwin, but he, on catching her eye. lowered his.

The prosecutor now looked at Edwin and asked. 'You are Mr Edwin Sinclair.'

'Yes, Sir.' Edwin replied.

'My question to you is. Did you know or had you heard any rumours about Mr Nash Greystone being married to Miss Emma Pennington?'

'No Sir.'

'You say as far as you knew. The lady called Emma Pennington was a single woman, being unmarried, and so was free to marry you.'

'To my knowledge, Sir. Emma Pennington was not married to anyone.'

'Is there anything you wish to add before you sit down?'

'Well, I have something...'

'Go ahead.'

'I have a letter, I dare say, it is rather crumpled. I received this threatening letter from Mr Greystone, on the evening before my wedding day.'

'In that case, Mr Sinclair, I need to take a look at it.'

The Clerk took the tatty letter from Mr Edwin Sinclair and passed it to the prosecutor.

Emma recalled the letter. She also remembered that Edwin did not want her to read it. She was puzzled as she thought Edwin had destroyed it.

The prosecutor scanned the letter carefully, then he sighed and said. 'Why this letter is the proof we have needed. This puts a very bad light on things. What do you say, Mr Sinclair?'

'Ah, you can see how Mr Greystone was trying to stop me from marrying Emma because he wanted to marry her himself. That is why he sent the threatening letter to me, he thought it would frighten me off.'

'Oh no, Mr Sinclair. I do not see it that way. I am sure the jury will not see it that way either. Mr Sinclair, this is how I see it. The words in this letter say: Sinclair, you will not have her. Emma is mine. Signed Greystone. I think Mr Greystone was warning you when he said, ' You will not have her, or to put it another way. You will not marry Emma, because Emma is mine, meaning Emma is already married to me... Mr Greystone.'

'No, Sir. No.'

'Yes, Mr Sinclair.'

'I do not believe it?'

'I can see by your demeanour that you are sincerely shocked by this revelation.'

'I truly am, Sir. surely, he does not mean that.'

'I can see you did not understand what this warning meant Mr Sinclair. I know Mr Greystone believes the same, too. As he has always maintained that you are not guilty of this charge.'

Emma was shaking her head, tears were filling her eyes. She could see Mr Greystone grinning, with his grey steely eyes twinkling with delight. Emma shut her eyes then opened them and a single tear ran down her cheek. She swallowed hard to hold back the floodgates of the rest.

'I now ask you Mr Edwin Sinclair to take your seat again.' He thanked Mr Sinclair. 'We now must hear what the Lady can tell us.' The Prosecutor looked over and faced Emma at the bar.

Emma was sworn in.

'Your name is, Mrs Emma Greystone?'

Emma looked up and said in a firm voice. 'No, Sir. It is Miss Emma Pennington.'

'You maintain that you were not already married to Mr Nash Greystone, when you were about to marry Mr Edwin Sinclair?'

'I was never married to Mr Nash Greystone. No, never.'

'Are you sure in your own mind? Now I wish you to think hard about this question. Did you marry Mr Nash Greystone, on the 7th day of October 1820? At a blacksmith building, in Gretna Green, in Scotland?'

'No Sir, I am perfectly sure, I did not marry Mr Greystone, at any place.'

'Have you ever heard of a Mr Robert Elliot?'

'Never before you spoke his name to Mr Greystone, earlier Sir.'

'So you claim, that Mr Robert Elliot never married you and Mr Nash Greystone. At the blacksmith's in the village of Gretna Green?'

'Sir, I was never married in Gretna Green.'

The prosecutor picks up the marriage certificate and passed it over to Emma to look at.

'Is that your handwriting? Your signature?'

'It is not.'

'Pray, tell me, how come it matches your signature, not just a little. But your own eyes can see it is a perfect match?'

'I do not know. Please believe me, Sir. It is a great shock to me.'

'So you say, it does look like your hand?'

'It looks like my signature, but it is false. For I did not sign this. Upon my word, I have never signed a marriage certificate in my life.'

'Well then, this is for the jury to decide.'

'Please, listen to me, I am telling the truth. I believe I have been set up by Mr Greystone. Please believe me, I am an honest person.'

'You say you have been set up?'

'Mr Greystone loved me, but I never loved him. I loved Mr Edwin Sinclair. Mr Greystone was furious and angry with me. He is punishing me because of my true feelings towards Edwin. You must see it?'

'Yet, I ask you? Why is it, that Mr Edwin Sinclair is not being punished by Mr Nash Greystone? Does that not seem strange to you? Would he not want to punish both of you? No, he does not. Why is that? I will tell you; it is because Mr Nash Greystone knew that Mr Edwin Sinclair did not know the fact that you are a married woman.'

'Mr Edwin Sinclair never believed I was a married woman. Because I am unmarried and never have, I ever been married to anyone. Emma looked directly at Edwin, hoping to sort some acknowledgement from him.'

'I want to ask about the letter Mr Edwin Sinclair showed us, before. Did you read the warning letter the evening before your wedding?'

Emma looked back.

'I read that same letter, which was not a warning letter. It was a threatening letter to Edwin from Mr Greystone.'

'Was it not a warning letter to tell Mr Edwin Sinclair that he could not have you. The reason being, as you were already married to Mr Nash Greystone.'

'Dear me. No. It was a threatening letter. That is how both Edwin and I saw it. Mr Greystone signed the letter Just Greystone. He never used words like honourable, sincere or faithful before his name. That shows it was a threat.'

'Was it not that Mr Nash Greystone was just writing a brief note to a man he did not know?'

' No, that is not true...' Emma looked over at Edwin and shouted, 'Edwin, please help me.'

'Silence.' snapped the judge.

Emma's lips trembled. 'I am sorry, please forgive my outburst your honour. I just want you to believe the words that come from my mouth are true.'

'Well. You are guilty until you can prove your innocence by what you say. So, I ask you one more time. Did you ever marry Mr Nash Greystone, before you were about to marry Mr Edwin Sinclair?'

'No, Sir.'

'Yet, I say, that this marriage certificate in my hand proves differently. Now, on the afternoon of the 6th day of October 1820. I have a report from a gentleman who knew you. An eyewitness who says he saw a carriage pass him on the lane, going in the north direction. Where he saw you looking out of the carriage, with his own eyes. This was also the day when your neighbours said that your bedroom window curtains were not closed during the night. So, the question is... Did you leave the cottage, take a carriage to meet Mr Nash Greystone and Mr Duff Campbell so you could go with them on the journey up to Gretna Green in Scotland for the handfast wedding ceremony?'

'I was in a carriage on that day. I was visiting my oldest friend. As we needed to check all the arrangements for the wedding. My friend invited me to stay the night and go home the next day. So, the gentleman witness had seen me then.'

'Really, now, do you expect us to believe that?'

'Yes sir. It is the true fact of what happened.'

'Why were the bedroom curtains left open all night?'

'I never asked my servant to shut them while I was away that night at my friend's home. It was unimportant.'

'Or was it because you were running away to Gretna green in a rush? So, you did not dare tell your servant you would be away in Scotland that night?'

'No, I was not going to Scotland. Please Sir, my servant, my friend, or my mother will be happy to stand as a witness to that fact.'

'Servants and women friends will say whatever is needed. I know, some wealthy ladies offer a handsome cash reward for needed testimony at a trial. Mothers will do it for so-called parental love. False loyalty, I call it.'

'Careful, Mr Stamford,' Boomed the judge with a cross look on his face.

'Sorry My Lord.'

Emma's chin trembled as she asked. 'May no one speak up for me please Sir? Am I to stand alone without a witness?'

'Do not speak unless I ask you to answer a question Mrs Emma Greystone. You were apprehended inside a Church... shall I continue? So, you claim that you were travelling to your friend's house where you stayed the night. Also, you say, your curtains were open all night because you did not bother to tell your servant to shut them while you were away at your so-called friend's house?'

'Yes, Sir.'

'Did Mr Edwin Sinclair know that you were staying with your friend for the night?'

'No, I had not told him.'

'Did Mr Greystone know that you were staying with your friend for the night?'

'I had no reason to tell him at all, No.'

'I say, that you left in a coach to meet up with Mr Greystone and Mr Campbell. Joining the two Gentlemen, you all made a journey up to Gretna Green in Scotland. There, you married Mr Greystone. Then the three of you made the journey back to Cheshire. However, on seeing you had left your curtains open while away, you thought up another story to cover your tracks.'

'No, I never did that. Please believe me when I say. I have never married Mr Nash Greystone. Mr Greystone wanted to marry me, he even proposed, but I did not love him, so I refused him. I only ever wanted to marry Mr Edwin Sinclair. As I loved him so, and he loved me. I am telling everyone here in this court the truth.'

The Judge folded his arms over his chest. The prosecutor looked over to the judge. Who then said, 'Come on, Mr Stamford, we have a lot to get through today.'

Gentlemen of the jury. Will you now consider whether the sexual offence of Bigamy was about to be committed by Mrs Emma Greystone? We have heard the words of what happened from the Gentleman, Mr Nash Greystone. We have also listened to the witness, Mr Duff Campbell. Mr Edwin Sinclair was also called to the witness box to give his testimony. We have seen with our own eyes the matching signatures and finally; We saw the crumpled letter written by Mr Nash Greystone to Mr Edwin Sinclair. Which Mr Sinclair misunderstood as a warning. Last, of all, we all heard Mrs Emma Greystone's account of what a woman's mind can mistake as truth.

'My Lords and Gentleman of the jury. You will be failing in your duty. If you take this felony lightly for the reason that this woman is uncommonly refined. This young Lady was seconds away from committing bigamy with an innocent man. So, I invite you all now to consider your verdict. You now need to decide if Mrs Emma Greystone was about to knowingly and unlawfully commit the crime of Bigamy?'

You may now decide.

The Prosecutor sat down. Then the Gentlemen of the Jury all started to huddle together and whisper between them. There was nodding or head shaking and even waving of fingers.

Emma caught sight of a wealthy-looking lady, very fine. Wearing many jewels. She was sitting near to where the judge was sitting. She was talking to the gentleman sitting on her left side.

Emma looked at her and pondered to herself. Who are you? Why would such a fine lady like you be here? It upset Emma for the lady sitting there dripping in her gems and jewels. How could a woman be so thoughtless? Emma had seen with her own eyes that most of the women on trial were very poor and in need. That was often the reason they had stolen food to feed themselves and their starving children. Even the ones who had stolen items were hoping to sell them for monies to buy things for their many children. She looked at the glittering gems and thought, how could a fellow female rub her wealth in the faces of these miserable women, with wretched lives.

Just then, Emma was jolted from her thoughts, when the judge said. 'We have not got all day Gentlemen. For I need sustenance to keep me going.'

Emma felt cross as she thought. This is my life in the balance, and you are distracting the decision makers with talk about a meal. Emma shook her head and looked over to Edwin Sinclair, who was rubbing his eyes with his hand. She then looked over to Mr Nash Greystone, who was talking to Mr Duff Campbell. Emma's mother was wiping her eyes with her handkerchief. Lord Gilpin was talking to his wife, and Lord Napier was talking to, his daughter. Feeling completely alone, Emma looked over to her aunt Belvedere. Her aunt put her hand to her lips then blew Emma a kiss. Emma could not stop herself from smiling back. She suddenly felt unfettered love for her aunt because of that small act of kindness, at that moment, when she needed it most.

Just then, the jurymen started to sit down again in their seats. The clerk walked over and spoke to the gentleman on the first front seat. Next, the clerk waved his hand to the judge.

A voice shouted. 'Silence, Silence.'

Emma felt her hands trembling. She stood up straight. Her blue eyes fixed onto the Judge.

The judge spoke. 'Gentlemen of the jury have you reached a verdict?'

'Yes, Judge.'

'Gentlemen of the jury is the prisoner guilty or innocent?'

Emma's chest tightened, as if a heavyweight, unmovable, pressed upon her.

'Guilty.' Went the cry.

An extraordinary jagged pain ripped at Emma's body.

She exhaled the word 'NO!' which echoed around the room.

The judge turned his gaze to Emma and said, 'Mrs Emma Greystone, you have been found guilty. It now only remains for me to pass the appropriate sentence of the law. You have been caught in the act of committing bigamy. This court must be seen to set an example. So, that is why I am determined to make a warning example of you. You who are a Lady. Since you have no excuse as you do not come from the low rank of society.'

Emma's lips were dry and trembling for she knew her past happy life was at an end. Her childhood life had gone... forever.

The judge continued. 'It now only remains for me to pass the dreadful sentence of the law which is that you be taken hence from here to New Gate prison. Where you will be taken by ship and transported to Australia. To serve a four-year sentence. I have granted you a certificate of remission. I have shortened the length from the usual seven years to four years. For the reason that you never completed the vow or accomplished the consummation of the unlawful marriage. So, you are to be removed from the court and taken directly to your fate. End of case. Next.'

Chapter Twenty-Three

The bolts clattered as the officer opened the prison door. He roared 'What are you doing?'

'Praying sir.' Emma said, opening her eyes.

'A bit late for that.'

'I am not praying for forgiveness. I am innocent of my supposed crime. I am praying for comfort.'

'Oh king George, not another so-called innocent woman.'

'Please believe me, Sir.'

The officer mimicked, In a high tone of voice. 'I'm an innocent angel, I'm an innocent angel, I am just an innocent angel my honour… Of course, I have never heard that before? You, angel. Get up, move, the doctor wants to check you over.'

Emma stood up. The officer got hold of her shoulder and shoved Emma out of the cell and marched her down the corridor. The officer knocked on a door, opened it, and shoved Emma into the room by her forearm. 'Prisoner Greystone, Doctor.' The officer boomed.

The doctor looked up from his writing, on seeing Emma, he said. 'I need to give you a health inspection. We need to check you will not take any sickness onto the ship. He moved towards Emma and said, 'Stand still while I examine you.' The doctor held in his hand a tongue depressor. 'Hold out your tongue. Any sore throats?'

'No doctor.' Emma answered once the implement was removed.

'Let me look at your eyes.'

Emma had to look into the doctor's eyes.

'Any trouble seeing?'

'No, my vision is fine.'

'Let me feel your head.'

'No pain or lumps.'

'No, doctor.'

'Are you with child?'

'No dear me, no Sir.'

'Normal stools?'

'Yes.' Emma blushed.

'Let me see your hands.'

Emma held her hands out to him.

'These are not the normal hands I see.'

'Oh dear me, what is wrong?'

'Well, that is the thing. Your hands show no sign of hard work. I guess you have been brought up as a Lady. So, I ask. What made you fall from grace?'

'Please sir, Doctor, they have accused me of a crime I did not commit. They have found me guilty of bigamy but I-'
 'Come on, angel.' The officer retorted across the room. 'The doctor does not want to hear about you and your angelic cries of innocence.'

Emma said, 'Forgive me, doctor. I only wish you could test me in some way, so you would know I am innocent.'

The doctor went over to the prison officer and lowered his voice. 'Are you sure this young lady is at fault?'

'The court found her so doctor.'

'You must know, it is unusual for a criminal to look at you openly straight in the eye? Do you not agree, Officer? I see she is not the usual sort of female we meet in here.'

'Oh king George, I don't know. I'm just doing my job.'

The doctor rubbed his chin. 'Feed her up a little more. She is underweight.'

'We are not a charity doctor.'

'No, but we are living in the 19th Century now. We do not want a convict to die while aboard a ship, do we officer?'

Holding his chin high the officer said. 'Have you finished with the prisoner doctor?'

'I have.'

The prison officer got hold of Emma's forearm and opened the door, then pushed her through the opening.

The doctor raising his voice said, 'Remember officer, what I have just said.'

When the door was shut the officer marched Emma back to the small dark cell. He flared his nostrils and grabbed a hand full of her hair which he tugged, 'Sooner you have gone angel, the better, I say.'

Emma avoided his eyes.

The prison officer gripped his large bunch of keys and locked Emma's cell door behind him. Walking away down the corridor. Emma could hear the fading sound of the rattling keys along with his footsteps. She let out a sigh.

As Emma sat down, the smell of sodium hypochlorite hit her

throat and made her cough. She could see that someone had swilled the cell while she was out.

How she wished she could hold some lavender to her nose and smell that lovely garden flower scent that she loved so much. Emma thought back to that particular day when she had walked around the Chester garden to collect lavender to make some new sweet bags for her clothes cupboards. That was the very day when she had first met the pitiless Mr Greystone.

Just then, another guard came and opened the door and said. 'You, time for work.'

He pointed to Emma and then the door with his thumb. He grabbed her wrist and held her tightly.

Emma frowned for the guard was hurting her, but she would not complain. He brought her to a large room filled with women. They were picking tar out of old rope. The Guard, let go of her wrist and told her to remove the tar as he threw a bundle of knotted rope at her. Emma rubbed her wrist.

A woman with red knotted hair started to laugh at the top of her voice. 'Look at those silky hands, of miss high in the instep over there.'

An older woman with grey hair said to Emma, 'Take no notice of her dear.'

The red-haired lady continued. 'Pardon me, miss pretty lady, your silky delicate hands will never stand up to this job. There will be blood. Just you wait and see.'

Another lady with fair hair rubbed Jenny Red's shoulder. 'Come on now, darling. We know it is hard for you. But darling, as females we must all stick together.'

'Let the new girl be, Jenny Red.' Said a woman with black stringy hair.

Emma's stomach turned. She kept her head down and said nothing. A little time later. The woman called Jenny Red was proven right; the rope had cut Emma's fingers.

The fair-haired woman whispered to Emma, 'I see your new here but do not upset yourself, darling. Poor Jenny Red is increasing with child; she is very distraught about it. Jenny is a harmless darling, really.'

Then the grey-haired lady said to Emma, 'Did you know that the ladies from the charity will bring you a book to read today?'

Emma replied, 'I did not know?'

'They will leave it outside your cell door.'

 Emma replied, 'Indeed, I love books.' Emma blew on her fingers.

'Trouble is, most of the poor souls in here can't read.'

'How sad not to be able to read-

'Stop talking, you two.' The guards' voice hailed across the room. 'Get on with your work.'

Emma got her head down and carried on picking at the rope.

After 4 hours of hard work. It was time for the women to be taken back to their cells. Emma was blowing onto her fingers again as they had come up in blisters and were throbbing. As she was taken back to her cell, Emma spied a book that had been left for her. The guard gave her the book along with a bowl of soup and a crust of bread. In a sharp tone, he told Emma to stay quiet and educate herself. Locking the door behind him the guard then left. But as he walked away, he rubbed the bunch of keys against each metal bar as he passed. The noise echoed all around the prison. Emma heard the sad sound of poor little babies crying. She longed to cuddle those poor little souls. Emma stood and stretched her legs and back. As she had been bent over the rope for 4 hours. All went quiet again, until the next sounds she heard were sounds of snoring.

Emma sat down on the hard-wooden bench full of sharp splinters to eat the tough bread and bland soup. She examined the book. It was an encyclopaedia, covering letters, A to D. Emma read the book until the failing light when the sun went down. She hoped reading would help her, for she was missing her loved ones so much, it felt painful and agonising. After a little while, Emma fell asleep.

The next morning. Emma awakened to the prison officer shaking her.

'Angel. Move, now.'

'Where are you taking me?' Emma asked, rubbing her eyes.

'The doctor wants to see you again. Unlike me. He must like you angel.'

The officer grabbed hold of her shoulder and pushed her out of the door.

Emma frowned. 'You are hurting my shoulder.'

He grabbed a hand full of Emma's hair, pulled it. 'You are a nobody. You have no opinions. You put up with pain, do you hear me? Angel, I know you are guilty.'

Emma said with strength in her voice. 'No. No. No, I am not guilty.'

The officer grabbed Emma's forearm and dragged her along the corridor to the same place as yesterday. He put his clammy forehead against Emma's forehead. 'You will pay for your outburst, dirty little flea.'

The officer knocked first then opened the door. The doctor told the officer to leave the room as he wanted to speak to the prisoner alone.

'But doctor, I am required to stay with the convict. I-'

'This lady will offer no harm to me. I can assure you.' The doctor replied.

Emma glared at the prison officer. It was one of the few things which brought her delight.

The officer questioned, 'Are you quite sure doctor? This one is rebellious.'

'I will only be a few minutes. Officer wait outside while I ask her to undress.'

'It will not bother me, Doctor.'

'Do as I say, officer.'

'If you are sure Doctor, call if you need me.'

When the door was closed. The doctor spoke. 'No need to get undressed. I just wanted to ask you a question. Where do you come from?'

'Chester in Cheshire Doctor.'

'Do you have a family doctor that you call on?'

'Yes doctor. Doctor Sherbourne.'

'Have you seen him lately?'

'Indeed, he was a wonderful help when my brother Robert died.'

'You still maintain that you are innocent of the named crime?'

'Please doctor, accept as truth, when I say, I am completely innocent.'

'Tell me, why were you brought to court?'

'A gentleman loved me but I did not love him. He became obsessed with me. Yet, I loved someone else, and he loved me too. So, when I was about to marry the man I loved. The other gentleman came into the church with a magistrate and accused me there and then of being married to him. When I went to court. That gentleman had forged a wedding certificate with what looked like my signature on it. He fabricated a story about me marrying him in Gretna Green. So, it seemed to the jury I was about to commit bigamy with the man that I loved.'

'I see… You have passed your medical check for your sea passage. I just want to say. Make sure you get some fresh air when you can, eat everything that is put before you.'

Emma frowned. 'Fresh air at sea?'

'I dare say, you will spend a lot of time in the ship's bulk, locked up.'

'Oh, oh dear me, I see. depend upon it, I understand now.'

'It only remains for me to warn you. See to it, you are not left alone with the sailors or lower officers. Just remember they are not always to be trusted. That is all I wish to say.'

'Thank you kind Sir, Doctor.'

'You can go now.'

The doctor opened the door. 'Officer you can come in.'

'Emma asked, 'When will I be put onto the ship?'

'This afternoon.'

The officer marched in and grabbed hold of Emma's arm. 'I am sorry, Doctor, this one is a bit lippy.'

'Give her more bread when she goes to her cell. She is underweight as I told you yesterday.'

The doctor went back to his seat behind his desk.

'The officer narrowed his eyes. But doctor why should she be privileged with extra food?'

'More bread, I said, officer.'

'Yes, doctor.'

The officer pushed Emma out of the room and banged the door shut.

Outside the doctor's room, the officer put his hairy hand around Emma's neck. But just then, another door opened. Quickly, he removed his hand away and grabbed Emma's forearm and marched her back to the cell in silence. Emma stepped into the cell. The officer banged the cell door shut behind her and locked it. He strode back down the corridor whistling until Emma could no longer hear him.

Sitting down, Emma evaluated. I must never forget what the doctor has warned me about. Emma caressing her throat, thought, I must keep my senses. I wonder why the doctor was so kind to me? His words could mean my safety or my life. I must be strong. Keep my hope bright. I must survive. I will return.

Emma picked up her book, opened it at a random page, and read with interest about different things which began with the letter B.

A little later on, a different guard came and gave her some bread and milk. 'You will be taken to the ship called, The Queen of Sheba, so get this eaten.' He next gave Emma a sack bag with wool and four small thin bone knitting needles. 'You are to knit socks while on board the ship.'

Emma took the bag and food from him.

While she ate. Emma could hear cell doors being unlocked

and the sounds of chains being rattled. The sound of footsteps was getting near to her until, upon eating her last mouthful. A guard opened her cell door. He had a lock and chain in his hand. 'Right, I need to place this on your ankles. Then all you women will be taken to your convict ship.'

Chapter Twenty-Four

As Emma landed her feet onto the wooden decking of the huge ship, she was trembling.

She took deep breaths of air and quickly looked around. Sailors were everywhere. The noise of containers landing onto the wooden deck was thunderous. Men were hurrying up and down rope ladders and steps, and a loud shouting of orders. Emma could smell a mixture of rusty metal, seaside, and damp wood. All the women stood in line. The officer in charge barked at them a list of rules. Emma could hardly hear him. As the wind was blowing against the volume of his voice. Emma hugged her sack of wool, for she felt so alone and more frightened than ever before in her life. Emma kept thinking of how far away Australia was from her home country and all the people she knew and loved. Emma was burning up.

The officer showed them a cat o' nine tail whip. Emma did not have to hear every word clearly to understand what he was implying.

The officer talked on and Emma gazed up at the sky. There were seagulls screeching in the air around the tall masks. As she looked up at the top of one mask, she could see men looking out to sea. Her stomach was churning. A Navy officer now spoke. He warned the women the men were armed, to keep order and to protect the ship. Emma glanced at the women in the line and thought how none of them looked as if they could overpower any man, as all the women looked so thin and worn-out. She saw the grey-haired woman with the red-haired female, who looked very distressed. Emma thought, I do hope that unpleasant person will not trouble me. Next stood up a minister who started to read aloud some passages of scriptures from the Bible. Emma listened intensely because she needed words of comfort. Next, an officer read a list of names; they were told to say, Yes Sir, when they heard their own names. Emma did not want to answer when she heard the name Emma Greystone. But after the sight of the whip, she thought better of it and said, 'Yes Sir.' After they finished the register, the officer told the women they would be locked in the cells, in the ship's bulk. Later, they would be let out for exercise and work.

The officer told the women to stand still while they had their leg irons removed. As they needed to go down steps, into the bulk of the ship. An officer came to undo Emma's lock. He stood very close to Emma, and he stroked his nose and raised his eyebrows at her, and Emma cringed inside. He bent down and undid her lock. She stepped free. He stood and winked at Emma and moved on to the next woman. The warning words of the doctor came into Emma's mind. She wrapped her arms around her body tight for she was determined to protect herself.

A loud whistle blew. Rapidly, the men started to move into order.

Emma and the women were guided down to the bulk of the ship. Emma shivered when she saw so many cells holding countless men. The men started to whistle when they saw the women. An officer shouted warnings at the men and gradually the whistling died down. Emma and the other women were put into a huge cell cage all together. Emma was glad to have the women's company in this dreadful situation. The officer commanded the women to sit down and not cause any trouble.

Emma felt the movement of the ship. Her heart began to bang; it felt as if it was in her throat. Just then, Emma saw the grey-haired woman again from the prison. The woman was holding the hand of the red-haired female who disliked Emma. The woman asked Emma, what was her name? Once she had told them, the grey-haired woman told Emma her name was Mary and her friend is called Jenny, but everyone called her Jenny Red because of her red hair. Emma could now see Jenny Red was well along with child.

Emma said, 'I see you will become a mother soon. I will be happy to help you with your child if you need a rest.'

Jenny Red's face softened. 'I'm wrong and sorry for mocking you, miss. I see you have been brought up a fine Lady, I've always dreamed of being a lady. Jealousy, it's such a wicked sin of mine.'

'Please do not say another word about it,' Emma said.

Mary's eyes widened. 'We are on the way now. I can feel it.'

The wooden beams and panelling of the ship began to make loud creaking noises. The great ship rocked as it slowly came to life.

Some women started to cry and others huddled together.

Mary said, 'Emma, let us make friends. This is not a journey for a woman with no friends.'

'Emma replied,' Yes Mary, I will be very glad indeed, to be your friend and in turn have you as mine.'

'Me too.' Echoed Jenny Red.

Emma whispered, 'Please allow me to tell you something of a delicate nature. Only do not feel shocked. I confer to you this caution for I was given this warning from a kind doctor as a protection for my personal safety.'

'Do tell us. 'Mary said.

'Take care. Make sure you do not find yourselves alone with any officers or sailors. As they may take advantage of you. As I have been warned, they are often morally corrupt.'

Jenny Red began to moan.

Mary put her arm around her and said. 'Do not worry dear. We will look after you.'

'I feel sick.'

'You will be fine when you get used to the rolling motion of the ship.'

Jenny Red continued to moan.

Emma asked. 'Do you want to rest your head on my lap so you can sleep?'

'We are all suffering, now stop fussing.' A round-faced woman bellowed at Jenny Red.

Then, she threw her hands up in the air. 'The wretch has wet herself over me.'

'Heavens above,' Exclaimed Mary to Emma. 'Jenny's waters have broken.'

Jenny Red started to groan and gasp.

The round-faced woman saw what was happening. 'I am sorry, dear. I had no idea.' she put her hand to her mouth. ' You must have help?'

Jenny Red started to howl. 'The baby is coming.'

Mary said to the round-faced woman. 'We need help, can you see anyone in charge?'

'The officers have gone.'

Emma spoke up. ' I may be of help. As I received and read an encyclopaedia, and under letter B, it had a chapter on The Birth of a baby. Emma pleaded. 'Listen please. We need to make more space. It would be helpful to make a circle around Jenny Red, leaving some room so two of you, can stand behind to support her, so Jenny Red can lean back against you and remain in an upright position. I need another pair of you to support her legs. Then another two of you to hold her hands.'

The women acted on Emma's instructions.

The round-faced woman shouted over to the men to turn around the other way. 'This woman needs privacy,' she bellowed.

Jenny Red moaned and threw her head back and wailed. The women held onto her tight.

Next, Mary kindly and carefully removed Jenny's Red's pantalettes.

Emma kneeled down and looked. She could see the baby's head almost out. 'It is coming quickly, Jenny Red dear. Can you push hard during the next labour pain? I will hold on to the baby, so get ready it will be soon.'

With that, Jenny Red let out an almighty grunt, and the head came out.

Women stroked Jenny Red's face. Emma said to Mary. 'When the baby arrives, we will need to tie the cord and cut it with a knife or scissors. We will need help from the surgeon.'

The round-faced woman shouted over to the men. 'Would

you make a lot of noise so that an officer comes down here, as we need to cut the cord.'

All the men started to bang and shout.

An officer came running in and when he saw what was happening. He hurried off again to call the surgeon.

Emma implored, 'Push, Push, give a mighty Push. Yes, ...again...oh, yes! bless you, I have her. You have a beautiful baby girl.' The baby let out a cry and all the women clapped their hands. Even the men whistled with joy.

Emma handed the baby to her mother. Jenny Red took the baby in her arms and kissed her then laughed and cried.

All the noise died down.

A man unlocked the cell. 'I am the ship surgeon. I will deal with it now...' He looked at Emma and Mary. 'You have handled it well.' he smiled.

He tied and cut the cord.

Two officers came with a stretcher. The surgeon said, 'I need to clean this woman and child.'

Jenny Red, looked at Emma. 'I shall call her Mary Emma. I want to remember the two kind friends who looked after me during my time.'

Emma felt the tingle of happiness. She now knew the women had excepted her.

Emma asked the officer if she could wash her hands?

The officer brought her a bucket of water and a rag.

While washing her hands and face. Emma wondered how her own dear mother was coping? She knew it would be a terrible strain for her.

Emma wondered what Mr Greystone was thinking. Was he getting some strange twisted delight out of disgracing her and her family?

She so longed to hear Edwin Sinclair say to her that this whole thing is just a bad dream.

Suddenly, Emma was jolted back to reality.

A stern-looking woman came over with an officer to tell the women which jobs they must do.

She took Emma to one side and told her not to think highly of herself just because she had helped a woman to deliver another future criminal. She narrowed her eyes. 'Far too many babies had already been born on the transportation ships.' She spat out, 'Women from the criminal classes are tough like goats, and need no help to deliver their offspring.'

'Emma retorted. Even goats need company, water and food.

Have you not read about the Angora goats in Turkey? They have the finest mohair on their bodies, which sells as costly yarn.'

'You'll get into trouble with your tongue, foolish girl.'

'I learnt about the angora goats from a book.'

'Be quiet. I tell you. The Gentleman in charge of you women is fearsome.'

Emma's heart sank. She said nothing more.

'He will sort you out.' She hissed, as she tugged hard on Emma's ear lobe before walking away from her.

The woman stood in front of the gathered women convicts and announced it was time for them to be put to work.

During the first half of the afternoon, the women would be taught how to make rope. Then the second half they had to scrub the decks along with the male criminals. Afterwards, they would be given a drink of lime juice and sugar for their health.

This was Emma's first day into a very long journey.

As the days passed by. The convict women had to card wool. Clean boots. Spin wool. Wash laundry. Knit socks. Hang out washing on lines. Sew on buttons and mend clothes. Clean out their cells. Darn socks. Remove tar from the rope. Listen to readings from the Bible. Embroider names into clothes. Peel root vegetables. Polish brass. They had to do these tasks throughout the weeks and spend time in the caged cells. Emma tried to eat all the food that they gave her. Sometimes, Emma felt sick because of the sea swell and also because she felt so anxious about her future. Even so, Emma always remembered the doctor's words about eating and drinking as much as she could to build up her weight. Also, Emma kept the doctor's words of warning in her mind when she was near the sailors or officers. Emma kept her head down and gave the men very little eye contact. She always did the work so as not to draw undue attention to herself. Emma also liked to help Jenny Red with baby Mary Emma, for it gave her joy.

During a storm, the ship was like a jousting knight, only just winning the battle. The Queen of Sheba was bringing its lives safely over earth's seas. Days passed, nights passed, months passed, seasons passed. The moon glowed, the sun shone, rain lashed, and the wind howled and battered. Emma kept up her prayers and Bible reading to gain some comfort. However, Emma could not stop her mind from returning homeward. She thought about her poor dear Mother fretting about her and how she missed her servants Bess and Sarah. Emma often thought about Julia, Phoebe, and dear Dudley. She wondered if he was back home or still away travelling. Would he still want to marry Susan after being away from her? Emma thought about her Aunt Belvedere. But she did not quite know what to think regarding her aunt. Emma thought about Edwin Sinclair; she felt very confused about him. Emma loved Edwin and had believed he loved her. But

Edwin Sinclair had not rescued her. Why did he not come to her aid? Emma kept asking herself these questions.

On the 120th day of the journey. A male criminal got caught stealing a bag of coins from an officer. Everyone had to stand and watch his whipping as a warning. Emma was horrified and almost fainted. During that terrible moment, Emma realised feeling great pain in her heart. Edwin Sinclair would never come and save her. This realisation was as if she bore the pain of being whipped. Emma knew in her heart; no gentleman would ever want to marry her. Not with this dreadful stain on her character.

After the women were sent back down below to their caged cells. Emma fell to her knees and wept bitterly for hours. None of the women could comfort her. Emma understood that she would never again know love.

Chapter Twenty-Five

Ten more days passed, Emma felt like fighting everyone for her very survival. Never had she felt this way before, tired of holding her tongue. The quality of the food was getting worse and they were getting less to drink. No one had even been allowed to wash for a while.

All the people around made Emma think about the poor African slaves who were crammed even tighter into slave ships. They were lucky just to survive their journey. Yet here at least, every person on this ship were about to land in Australia, very much alive.

Then suddenly the shout went up. Land was in sight. 130 days since the start of this journey and now it was about to end.

Emma visualised the time in the library at home, when she and her mother located the new country named Australia, on Roberts globe. Emma also thought back to when she questioned Julia and Phoebe if they would like to travel and visit distant lands. She recalled, Phoebe said, she would only venture with friends yet Julia replied, she would rather stay put, in the place she knew. It was strange that even Edwin disliked sailing on ships. Emma was the one who had longed to see parts of the world and visit far distant places. Yet, how odd it was, she was now, right at this moment travelling to that very most distant place.

Emma went up on deck to do one of her jobs for the day,

gathering washing from the washing lines. Emma saw land coming into view. The gulls started crying overhead. The air felt warmer. When she finished, she picked up the basket of shirts. The sailors were getting ready for action. Emma moved unsteadily along the deck and an officer told her and the other women they must go down below. It was time to be locked in the cells while the crew were navigating the ship near to the land. Emma went down into the ship's bulk and told the other women what she had seen.

Chapter Twenty-Six

The Queen of Sheba dropped anchor in the harbour of New South Wales, Australia. The Governor of the Colony came onto the ship to inspect it. When he had finished his examination and had spoken to the captain and the surgeon. He gave orders for the captain to send the first load of convicts ashore to the Parramatta Penal Centre. The women were to be housed in the jail's Female Factory building.

Once the Governor had finished and had received the information about the convicts on board, he left the ship.

Officers came down to the bulk, to bring the women up onto the deck. Jenny Red wrapped her baby up tight in a blanket. Mary clutched onto Emma.

Immediately up on deck the officers put the leg irons onto the women's ankles, including Emma's.
'Governor's orders.' The officer told them. 'We will not let you lot jump into the sea, or escape.'

Men lowered Emma, Mary, and Jenny red and some other women down onto a boat which was rowed by a few sailors. The baby was crying loudly. Mary said, 'Mary Emma is expressing our feelings very well.' Emma agreed, 'Yes indeed, I feel like howling myself.'

Emma's hair came loose and was smacking against her face. Nevertheless, she took deep breaths grateful to feel the warm fresh air.

After a short time, the boat reached the shore, and the women got out of the vessel. Emma almost lost her balance when she started to walk on land. Two other women fell over and the Sailors laughed at them. Soon all had arrived at the women's factory building.

Each woman was given their personal number. After they had eaten bread and drank lemonade, they were handed a sheep's fleece with a woollen blanket to sleep on. After which, they were given a cotton shift to wear. The women laid down their wool fleece's in rows with very little room in between them, for the room was packed full of other convict women who had arrived there before they came. There was very little room to stretch out. Emma changed into her shift and settled down. Suddenly, she was startled when she saw an enormous spider run out from under her fleece. Emma shivered but managed not to make a sound as Baby Mary Emma had fallen asleep and Emma dared not awaken her, not even for a deadly spider. Emma lifted the fleece to check there were no more spiders. To Emma's relief none was to be found.

The room went dark quickly and the Matron and Officer ordered the women to go to sleep.

Emma felt the solid stillness of the floor comforting. After all the stress of the day that should have kept her awake, feeling exhausted, she quickly fell asleep

Chapter Twenty-Seven

Emma awakened to a deafening sound of chatting, shouting, and arguing. Babies were crying. As Emma focused her eyes, she could see many legs moving back and forth. She sat up. The women were getting dressed or rolling up their fleeces. Emma suddenly remembers where she is and lets out a deep groan of distress.

Mary and Jenny Red were up and dressed.

Emma felt Mary tapping her hand. 'Get up, dear. How can you sleep with all this noise?'

'I must have been in a very deep sleep ... I feel as if all my energy has left me.'

'You need to find it, Emma. We get our jobs today and they shall tell us where we are to go... I do hope we can stay close together.'

Emma stood up. 'indeed, Mary, I do hope so. They gave each other a hug.

Emma took her dirty dress and changed into it, even though it needed washing desperately. It was already very warm and there was a broad smell of perspiration in the air. How she longed to have a wash.

Then a bell rang.

Officers came in to take the women to the dining room. To be given hominy porridge, bread and weak tea to drink. The women sat on a long wooden bench at a scratched and stained wooden table. Emma and the other women sat to eat their breakfast as quick as possible in the short time they had to do so. Jenny Red, breastfed her baby while she ate her breakfast.

The Matron clapped her hands and shouted to make everyone pay attention to what she would say.

'All you convict women with babies and children, are to follow me and I will take you to the Nursery. The rest of you women without children. Remain here with the officer. He will get your accommodation and job routines sorted.'

So, Mary and Emma said goodbye for now to Jenny Red and her baby. As they were to go in the opposite direction.

As Emma and the other women stood to wait for some instruction. The officer called out, 'Would convict Emma443600 hold her hand up.'

Emma held up her hand.

'I have special instruction for you.' He said.

Mary frowned as she glanced at Emma.

Emma shrugged her shoulders.

'You have been summoned by the head superintendent himself.' The officer remarked.

Emma whispered, 'Oh dear, what have I done?'

Mary shook her head.

The officer came and took hold of Emma's arm and led her away from the group of women.

He led her out of the jailhouse. As they walked across the courtyard, Emma said, 'Excuse me Sir, what is the head superintendent like?'

'A very authoritarian gentleman.'

'Oh, why does he need to see me Sir?'

'He would not tell us... Just watch yourself, he is proud, and he likes exceedingly good manners.'

They walked into another large building and down the hallway. They then stopped at a large wooden varnished door with a brass sign engraved with the words, Head Superintendent.

Emma saw that the officer had kind eyes, he said. 'Remember, good manners.' He then smiled a little.' However, I can tell that you have been brought up as a Lady. I can see by your posture and manner. You will do just fine.' He knocked on the shiny wooden door.

'Here is prisoner Emma 443600, Sir.'

A faint voice said, 'Send her in, then go.'

'Right Sir, just as you say.'

The officer said to Emma. 'Go in.' He walked away.

Emma took a deep breath and opened the door.

All of a sudden. Emma immediately collapsed to the floor, out cold.

The Superintendent shut the door and picked her up and laid her on his couch. He opened the window for air.

He rushed to a table drawer and routed for something to bring her around. On retrieving a little silver box, he put his arm around her to lift her up a little and held the salts under her nose.

Emma started to splutter, and she opened her eyes a little.

'No, no, no get away from me, get away from me... Do not touch me.'

'Just a little surprise that is all.'

'No, no... Oh, how can it be?'

'It is a bit of a shock shall we say.'

'Mr Greystone! No, No, Oh what a shock… I, No I cannot believe it, how… how did you get here?'

'Emma sprang up and shook herself free from his arms. She put her head out of the opened window.'

He got hold of her shoulders and pulled her back and closed the window.

'Let me tell you. I left England immediately after the trial ended on the Imperial Sapphire. A journey that only took 123 days.'

Emma was pacing up and down in front of the closed window.

'I do not care how many days it took you… I just, I cannot, … I cannot believe you are here.'

'Now, now, dear Emma, try to control yourself.'

Mr Greystone tried to get hold of her hand. Emma thrashed her arms around, shouting, 'leave me, leave me alone, get away…'

Mr Greystone walked to the door and took a key from his pocket and locked it.

Turning his attention back to Emma. He says, in a soft voice. 'Now, now dear, dear Emma. Listen to me.'

'I do not wish to listen, get away from me, get away from me... You are abominable, it is not to be born....'

Mr Greystone said in a louder voice. 'I will not allow you to marry that, that weaver's son, Sinclair. Not when I have loved you so. When I had lavished so much love and paid much praise upon you.

'You are cruel.' Emma was wringing her hands. 'You do not know what love is.'

Mr Greystone was holding his hand in a fist and thumping it up and down on the palm of his other hand as he spoke. 'I know what love is. Confound it, woman. Most women do not love the man that they have to marry. To be sure. Often, parents choose the man who their daughters marry. Even if you do not feel as I do? Emma. I advise that you marry me?'

'No, we have nothing in common. I know we would never have a happy marriage. I hate your past dealings with the slave trade.'

'There there. Now do be calm Emma dear. I am sorry. I did have to punish you a little... You could not leave me all alone with a broken heart.'

'I am sorry for your heart. But I should not be punished. I have just told you the truth.'

'We can be happy, my dear. I have met so many women. Yet, never have I wished for marriage until the day I met you.'

'No, no, no, Mr Greystone do you not remember? You asked me to marry you, and I emphatically said No.'

'My sweetest dearest Emma. I could not let you go.' He held his palms out to her. 'I just could not.'

'A man has so many choices in life. All a woman has is the opportunity to refuse a man. So, you would take that away from women too?' Emma hugged herself.

'So you can throw yourself away on a weaver's son, a machine maker... A fellow in trade? From some low origin. It is too much for a Gentleman like me to bare.'

Emma turns her back on him to look out of the window.

'You call yourself a gentleman, you are no gentleman. Mr Sinclair behaves in a Gentlemanly way - I have a thorough regard for his character.'

'Why does Mr Sinclair not come to your rescue then?'

'I am too tired.' Emma walks over and flops down on the couch and holds her head in her hands. 'Oh, I want to die. I do not want to live, not if you... not if you are here.'

Mr Greystone pulls a chair near to the couch and sits down. 'Emma, I have had my little revenge. I am able to remove it from my mind now... Emma, dear. Let me look after you. Let me help you. I will tell you about my plan.'

'I do not want to. I do not wish to listen to your plan.' Emma let out a harsh breath.

'You will, my dearest one. If only you knew, how much I love you, sweet Emma.'

'Love, love, how can this be love? Do not use the word love. You do not know the meaning of the word.'

'My love is so deep.' Lowering his head, he asked. 'Do you know what I do every evening?'

'I care not.... Do not tell me, I do not want to know.'

'Emma dear, I will tell you. I draw myself a sketch of your lovely face every evening. So that when I go to sleep it will force my mind to dream about you.'

'Force is a harsh word. Do you force everyone including yourself?

Mr Greystone stood up.

'Emma, do not push me. Speaking plainly enough, I could so easily force you to do what I want. I have the power. Can you not see?' he bristled. 'I only hold back out of my regard for you.'

'Mr Greystone. You call this, holding back?' huffed Emma. 'You are enough to make me repulse life itself. We both know that I am not a convict. I do not belong in this place.

Your love has put me into this place.'

Nash Greystone sits down.

'My new job is here in Australia, in this new country. I left the profession of looking after slaves because you hated it. I heard that they now employ a lot of slave overseers in the convict colonies. So I applied for a position. Yes, I have got fine new opportunities here. I have prestige and a fine social standing. I own land, horses, and a fine house. Yes, Emma. I dreamed of bringing you here to my house as my new bride and wife.'

'I should not be here... You are not listening to me-'

'-I needed you, Emma. Depend upon it, I needed no one in my life before. Only you, sweet Emma.... I can give you the world. You will have houses, servants, carriages, fine clothes, horses, friends from high places. You will have a husband who loves you.'

'No, no. How many times do I have to say NO. Emma stands up and stamps her foot. If I marry you, my incarceration would last my whole life. Not just 4 years.'

'Emma dear?'

Emma gets off the couch and walks over to the door.

'Let me out of this room. Now.'

Emma bangs on the door with her fists. Mr Greystone grabs hold of her and pulls her away from the door and plunged her back down on the couch.

'Let me out of this room at once.' Emma shouts. 'I wish to go back to my friends and do my work.'

Mr Greystone sits down and continues. 'Emma, you yourself have just told me you do not belong in there. We both know you are not one of those low-life characters.'

'Mr Greystone let me go.'

Emma leaps off the couch and goes towards the door again.

Emma rattles the handle of the door. 'Let me out. Please, let me leave.'

'I cannot. I have already arranged for you to work as a servant in my house.'

Emma shakes her head then says. 'I would rather be with murderers, forgers and thieves than do any work in your house.'

Mr Greystone gets up and stands by the door as well.

'Do not be foolish, Emma.'

Emma turns her back to the door and faces Mr Greystone and says. 'I have two women friends; one was with a child who are labelled thieves because they were poor and starving. Both their husbands had died. Their fishing business then failed. They stole food, yes food. Can you believe that they are punished like this for the desperate need of food? Why should they die of hunger? Both women know the command, thou shall not steal. They wept with guilt. Mr Greystone, You and I have never felt that hungry. If we were starving, would we steal food? Think about it, Mr Greystone. Seven years... for starving, terrified women.

'For sure, we must have punishment when rules are broken.'

'Mr Greystone. What if someone is being punished for not breaking the rules?'

'I do not understand you?'

'What rules did the Africans break when they were punished by being rounded up then made to work as slaves on the plantations?'

'Emma, I do not wish to talk about this.' His voice emptied of emotion. 'That is no subject for a young lady to talk about. My plan is to get you away from all those murderers, forgers and thieves in here.'

Mr Greystone guided Emma back to the couch again. He sat back down on the chair by her.

Emma straightened her untidy hair with her hands. Then putting her hands down on her lap, she said. 'There is something I wish to know? How did you forge my signature on the fake marriage certificate that you showed at my trial?'

He went over to a walnut writing desk full of papers, letters, and books. He sat down, fingering his letter brass seal, he said. 'All right then, if you wish to know I will tell you. Do you remember? You signed the visitor's book when you came to my ball, held at your Aunt's house? It was copied from that signature. You see Emma. I met a man who now calls himself, Mr Duff Campbell after he had finished his time in prison for the forgery of bank notes. I found out that he had grown up in Gretna Green and had even helped the blacksmith. He had seen many marriage certificates and had even signed some on behalf of runaway brides and grooms. I could not believe my ears. So, I offered him a reward if he would make for me a marriage certificate with a copy of your signature. I dare say, what a fine piece of art, it was too.'

Emma quickly walked over to his writing desk and stood opposite him.

'You talked about me being with forgers and thieves. Yet, I stand opposite to a forger in this very room... How could you sink so low? How could you do it?

Mr Greystone thumped the seal down hard onto the desk and looked at Emma.

'You must understand. I was angry with you.'

Emma raised her voice. 'You talk about love... Yet, you are cruel.'

He picked up the seal and banged it down harder on the writing desk.

'You, young lady, speak your mind somewhat freely...'

There was silence for a moment.

Mr Greystone's eyes closed.

Emma sat down again. She took hold of a cushion and gave it a couple of thumps with her hand. Then said. 'If I am acting unlady- like you have caused me, to act accordingly.'

Mr Greystone walked over to the couch, narrowing his eyes and pointing with his finger he said. 'Young woman, you must remember who I am.'

'Tell me, please. Why did you not punish Edwin Sinclair?'

There was silence. Then Mr Greystone sat on the couch next to Emma.

He sighed. 'It was not Sinclair I wanted here in Australia; it was you. His eyes glistened. Very well, Emma... Perhaps I was harsh. I am sorry that I had to do it. He took her hand in his. He looked straight at her as he said. 'But please listen to me, now listen to me... I have a plan. I will marry you. You shall have everything that any woman would want.'

Emma turned her head away and looked towards the door.

'Please, I do not know what more to say to you.'

She pulled her hand away and covered her mouth with her fingers.

'Emma listen, I recognise that I will be talked about and looked down on, for marrying a convict... I can bare that... I will bare anything as long as I have you.'

Emma picked up the cushion again and hugged it and hung her head. 'Except, I cannot bear it.' Emma's eyes darkened with pain.

'For sure, you will..., I shall arrange to give you a certificate of freedom. That will mean that you can move around here freely. In addition, through my contacts in high places, I am working diligently to get you, what they call, an Absolute Pardon.'

'Can you not manage to forge that one too?'

He tapped her knee with his hand.

'Emma pay attention to what I say to you. I have finished with Mr Duff Campbell and forgery and everything that has passed. My tune will be somewhat different from the past. I will act in a more Gentleman-like way, my manners will be impeccable. I promise you dear that I will work on qualities you desire me to have. My dear Emma. I confess that I have punished you too harshly, to an over large degree. It was all done because of this sickness that is my love for you. You must believe me.'

'Now Mr Greystone, please hear me… Please get the Absolute Pardon for me. So, I can return to England. I wish to be with my dear mother. She is frail now. Please do not take me away from her? Remember, she has lost her son. Please, Mr Greystone I beg of you. If you truly love me the way you say you do, please, help me get home, to my dear Mother.'

'My dear Emma. I do so want to say yes, just so I can please you. I do desire to make you happy. To love me even. His lip trembled. But how, how could I be without you?'

Clasping her hands together, Emma drops the volume of her voice and says. 'Please, can your spirit be softened? You remember my kind dear Mother. Please, Nash, grant this request of mine.'

He holds her chin in his hand.

'Emma, you have such a beautiful face. You are very fair and lovely.'

Emma runs her hand to straighten her hair.

'I am surprised. How can you still see beauty in my dirty face and dry hair?'

Nash Greystone leant back against the back of his chair. 'To be sure, I am a powerful, strong, serious independent gentleman in powerful authority. Why do you make me feel love sick and weak? Why can I not recover from this attachment of my heart?'

'I think you would be an even stronger man if you let your heart show true love by letting your love go.'

Mr Greystone sits up straight.

'I am afraid that... I know you will go back into the arms of Sinclair.'

Mr Nash Greystone stands up and walks over to the window to look out.

Emma follows him. 'Nash, I have made up my mind. Mr Sinclair no longer cares for me. There you are, I have said it... Sad but true... Now all I wish for is to have a quiet life. Be content to live as a quiet spinster.'

Mr Greystone turns around and gasped.

'So you say, you will not marry him?'

Emma nodded.

'Love only seems to bring me unhappiness. Please let me go home to be with my mother. I will not marry Mr Edwin Sinclair. It is plain that he no longer loves me. So, Likewise, I can no longer love him. He did not help me. As you yourself asked me. Where is he now?

Mr Nash Greystone holds on to the back of the chair.

'Dearest Emma. I want you to stay here with me... Yet... you say you want to go home to your Mother.'

Emma watches his expression.

'I liked Your Mother, but your Aunt... I confess I used her ill. However, for that, I had to put up with her endless complaining and, her chattering.'

'Lady Belvedere was very kind to you. She deserves your merit. My aunt will miss me too. Please, say you will let me go home. Nash, please.'

'You want to leave? I do declare, I have decided - Yes, you may.'

Emma clapped her hands together and smiled.

Nash sits down. 'Yes, I will leave with you.'

Emma repeats slowly. 'You will leave with me?'

'We shall go back to England together.'

'Oh, I am all astonished.'

Nash jumps off the chair and holds the back of it again.

'Yes, my dearest Emma. I shall get another profession. We shall go and live in London. That is a splendid plan. Not what I would have wished for at first. But yes, yes indeed.'

Emma forced a smile.

'We shall quickly tie up ends here. Then board a ship to England. I have plenty of savings. Later I will find something to do, something that I enjoy, and makes you happy my dear.'

Emma said, with a croak in her voice. 'Mr Nash Greystone... you indeed, you have it all planned.'

'I dare say. Emma, you will get used to me my dear. Once in England, I will give you my hand in marriage. I know you will take it. For surely my dear, you will want to indulge me for bringing you home? Emma my love, you shall buy the finest dress in all of London town. Then we shall be married... at last... Yes, we shall be husband and wife for real.'

Mr Greystone sits back down on the couch and takes Emma's hand in his.

Dearest Emma - Say, yes.'

I say... I say yes. What a clever plan.'

'Yes, quite right. My dearest Emma, what a plan.'

He was just about to kiss her hand when there was a knock on the door.

'Yes.'

A man's voice answered, 'Your tea, Mr Greystone.'

Mr Greystone gets the key from his pocket.

'Bring it in, Philips.'

Mr Greystone then unlocked the door. Philips, the secretary brings in the tea tray. He looks puzzled when he sees Emma sitting on the couch.

Mr Greystone sits down on the chair at his writing desk.

'Bring another cup, Philips. As this young female... convict came here to get her job instructions, but unfortunately, she fainted. Sweet tea will help to pull her around. I do declare Philips, it is up to us, to set an example of humility and kindness to others.'

'I am sure you are right, Sir.'

A moment later. Philips brings in the extra crockery and looks Emma up and down.

'Shall I put some used papers under... the person... Mr Greystone?'

'Philips?'

'Well, all I want to say is, your couch may get soiled. I must say, you never know what is living on her, sir.'

'Not now, Philips. When she has finished her tea, would you arrange for her to have a bath? Ask the Matron to get clean clothing for her.'

'For this convict... person, you mean Sir?'

'Yes, I do. Only for the reason that she will be working in my house as one of my servants.'

'Ah, well, that explains it then, sir.'

Mr Greystone straightens up some books on his desk.

'You can go now, Philips. I shall call you back later.'

The secretary left the room.

Mr Greystone puts milk in Emma's tea and passes it to her.

The cup jingled as her hand was all of a tremble. So she rested the saucer on her lap.

'My dear. To be sure, Philips will get a shock, when it is revealed that I will leave with you?'

'Indeed, Nash. I am only afraid, he may think I am, Emma lowered her voice, an immoral woman?'

Nash's face wrinkled in disgust.

'You are nothing like those women. You are most different.'

'I do hope he understands that.'

'Your virtue and nature my dear, are what makes you stand high above other women I have known... To be sure, you remind me of someone else who was very dear to me.'

Emma drank her tea from the white china cup. She watched Mr Greystone as his face paled in colour. Emma said nothing. He walked over and looked out of the window.

'Yes,... I had a dear sister. I was five years younger than her. I looked up to her. She took care of me very sweetly, as a true sister should. Yet, when I was 5 and 10 years old. Something changed everything... We had a gardener... He, that creature, was a slave from Africa... I will never forget the day, that fiend ran away with my sister. I have never seen her since. My Father tried to hunt him down. But... no one, not even he, could find them. I was heartbroken. Nothing has comforted me on losing my beloved sister. That was why I decided to work in the slave trade. I promised myself that when any slave disobeyed an order. I would make them pay, for the reason of revenge on that African slave who took my sister away from me.'

Mr Greystone drank the tea from his cup then walked back to the table and placed his cup and saucer onto the metal tray.

After his words had sunk in. Emma swallowed hard and said, 'I understand how much you must miss your sister. As I miss Robert, my only brother, too.'

'Hum, I did not like your brother. I believe he was trying to find out things about me.'

There was a clay vase on the table with some flowers. Emma went over and started to rearrange the flowers. As she moved them into different positions. Mr Greystone watched her but said nothing about what she was doing.

'I am sure my brother was just interested. Just interested in getting to know you.' Emma said, breaking the silence. Then to her surprise, Emma realised what she was doing, so left the flowers alone.

Emma sat down with tear-filled eyes as she drank her tea. After which Emma put her cup and saucer next to Mr Greystone's on the tray.

There was a knock at the door.

'Yes.'

'It's matron Mr Greystone.'

'Come.'

The Matron entered the room.

'I have brought the clean clothes you asked for, sir.'

'Take this young lady for a bath.'

'Right, sir. Come on you, follow me.' The matron wagged her finger at Emma.

'This young person will work in my house as a servant. That is why she must be clean. Is that clear?'

'Yes, Mr Greystone. Come on, Girl.'

Emma left Mr Greystones room with Matron.

Matron said. 'I hope you realise how much personal interest our Mr Greystone is taking of you?'

'I do.'

'He rarely has time to pay so much attention to a convict girl.'

'Excuse me, Matron. What will be my work?'

'How do I know? But don't you go taking advantage of it my girl. He may look like a toy spaniel but he can be very strict and ferocious like a dingo dog.'

'Mr Greystone told me I will have a certificate of freedom.'

'That just allows you to walk from here to his house. But what I ask myself is… Why you? You need to think upon it, you are a very fortunate girl to be chosen to work in Mr Greystone's house. Convicts normally need to earn that privilege. I warn you always to be on your best behaviour or you will lose this golden opportunity. You will be brought back to the female factory as a punishment.'

'Yes, Matron, I understand. The factory is already overcrowded.'

'As it happens, they are to build a larger female factory soon. As we need somewhere larger to put all you wicked girls.'

Matron opened a door.

'Go in there, girl. There is a barrel of water.'

'A wooden barrel?'

'What did you expect? Did you think it would be a linen covered copper bath? You are not King George's daughter? A wooden barrel will do you, girl. Now wash yourself and your hair. Make sure the back of your neck is clean. Here, take this bottle of stuff. It will kill anything living on you. Be quick girl. I shall sit here, just outside the door.'

A little while later, the door opened again, and Emma walked out. Her hair still wet but she looked fresh and clean.

'Shall I wash the dirty clothes matron?'

'Give them to me, girl. You cannot take dirty things into the fine house where you are going. Do you not know? Servants are given their clothes from the person employing them.'

'Oh.'

'Let's take you back to Mr Greystone, as he asked.'

The Matron knocked on Mr Greystone's door. There was no answer. She knocked again. But suddenly, there was a lot of noise coming from outside the building.

'Oh my, what is going on?' The Matron expressed.

Again, she knocked for the third time. But still no answer.

'Mr Greystone must have gone somewhere. Sit on that chair over there and wait for him Girl. I will have to go out and see what all that noise is about.'

'Yes, Matron.'

After Matron rushed further down the hallway. Emma walked over to a window and looked out. She could see a number of women all crying and hugging each other. One woman was Jenny Red. Emma opened the window and called over to them. 'Whatever is the matter?'

The women explained to Emma that their babies and children had been taken away from them. The children were now to live without their mothers. They were to be brought up in the prison's nursery. The reason given was, so that their mother's crimes would not spoil their children's nature.

It vexed Emma. She understood little children and babies would feel frightened without their natural mothers. Emma thought about little baby Mary Emma. Who she had helped to bring into the world.

Emma shouted to the women. 'I will speak to the head superintendent about it. I can promise nothing. Depend upon it, I will do my best. I must warn you; Matron is coming. Go, go before she arrives.'

The women waved and Emma shut the window. She saw them dispersing just before Matron came out into the courtyard.

Emma sat on the seat near Mr Greystone's room. Then two officers walked past her. They turned back and asked. 'What are you doing here? You should not be on your own.'

'I have been told by Matron to wait here for Mr Greystone.'

The other officer remarked, 'She must be trustworthy or Matron would not have left her here alone.'

'True' agreed the other. 'You will have to wait a little longer as Mr Greystone is busy.'

'Thank you Sir. I will wait.'

When the officers disappeared into a room further on, Emma had an idea. It was rather a dangerous one though.

Emma looked around, on seeing nobody about. She held her breath and turned the handle on Mr Greystone's door. It opened. 'Emma looked around. Nobody was to be seen, so she crept into Mr Greystone's room and shut the door behind her.'

Emma went over to the window. She could see Matron talking to two officers. She quickly went over to the drawers in his writing desk and carefully looked in them disturbing nothing. If she moved anything, Emma put it back in the exact position. She found nothing of interest to her in there. She went over to the window again. Emma could see Matron was still talking. She looked around and next searched the table drawer. There was nothing of importance. Emma shut the drawer and looked around again. Then she saw a writing slope. It had a long drawer, so Emma opened it gently. There it was, the very thing she was hunting for. Emma ran over to the window and saw Matron walking back towards the building. Emma quickly grabbed the paper and shut the drawer, then glanced at it. There in her hand was the fake marriage certificate. She had it. Emma folded it up and slipped it down her front, between her dress and shift and slipped out shutting the door quietly to avoid any noise. She sat down again on the chair. Emma could see Matron coming down the hallway. So, she closed her eyes to look as if she had been resting.

Emma felt a hand slap her shoulder. 'Wake up, sit up straight, girl.' Matron said as she stood in front of Emma. I will have to find someone to look after you as I need to get on, for I cannot wait around all day with you.' Matron started to walk down the hallway to find an officer, just as Mr Greystone appeared from one room further down the hallway.

'Ah, you are back. You may go now, Matron. You must have a lot to do. Leave the girl to me.'

'Are you quite sure, Sir?'

'Yes, on your way.'

Mr Greystone opened the door for Emma and told her to come in.

'Sit down, Emma, my dear. I have just been told that a ship is arriving. It is 3 days earlier than was expected. So, I will be extremely busy as it arrives. I will get you something to eat, then I will arrange for someone to take you to my house. My servants have all been very carefully checked. Do not be in fear of them. They have proved their dependability. So Emma dear you will be quite safe with them.'

'Matron, was rather puzzled because I have not been here long enough to prove my worth.'

'I can deal with her.'

'What shall I say to your servants?'

'Just say to them. You do not know, so they will have to ask Mr Greystone. To be sure, they never do.'

'Are you sure, it would not be best for me to stay in the women's factory?'

Mr Greystone thumped his hand on the desk and said. 'Emma, I do not wish to go over and over this. I have my plan. I shall need you to be on hand, to talk about our arrangements together. Remember, dear. We shall go to England soon. Together. To be Husband and wife.'

'Yes, Mr Greystone,'

'Emma. Call me Nash when we are alone together.'

'Nash, please, may I talk to you about something that concerns me. Would you allow me to speak freely about it?'

'What is it, my dear Emma?'

He came and sat on the chair near the couch.

Emma sat on the edge of the couch and said. 'Nash, something has come to my ears... with great mortification. I am told that when women come here, they are separated from their children and babies. That cannot be right.'

Emma's hair slipped over her left eye. Nash Greystone moved her hair back again gently with his fingers.

'You have the most beautiful hair, my dear love. But it is still damp shall I get a cloth for you to dry it?'

'No thank you, the heat of the day will dry it quickly... Nash, I was asking you about why do the children have to be separated from their natural mothers?'

'Emma, you as a virtuous lady. Cannot understand that we are saving those children from contamination from the criminal nature of their mothers.'

'I have seen with my own eyes how loving those mothers are with their children. Every child needs to be with their own devoted mother. I could understand it, if a mother has hurt her baby or child. I ask you; how many are murderers or dangerous women? Are there many here?'

'All convicts are dangerous.'

'Depend upon it, Nash, my friends are not dangerous.'

'I dare say. But I am telling you there are a few murderers here.'

'A few?'

'If you really must know, Emma. It is a small number, mainly men.'

'To take away babies and children from them all. When it is only a few who should be punished in that way?'

'Emma. What about the prostitutes? They would raise future harlots.'

'You will find most women would never ever want to prostitute themselves. Too often they are forced into it.'

'They are filth.'

'Perhaps men share the blame.'

'Hum.'

'I helped a woman give birth to her daughter on the ship. I saw with my own eyes the bonding between a baby and her mother. Nash, it was wonderful to see. All I can say to you is, please do not take babies away from their mothers.'

Emma suddenly realised that she had her hand on Mr Greystones arm in her fervour. He was looking down on her hand and taking pleasure from her touch.

'I will give it a thought, my dear,' Nash replied.

Slowly Emma lifted her hand away, then stood up and walked over to the window.

Emma turned around and said, 'Thank you, Nash.'

Mr Greystone smiled, but his smile melted away and his brow started to frown. He stiffened.

'Let me say, my dear.' Irritation shone in his eyes. 'You must not speak so freely about subjects that do not concern you. They are not topics suitable for a pure lady like you. For when we are married, I do not wish my wife to think or speak about such things. Do you understand me? I will be your head. So, what I say and what I wish, you will do. Do you comprehend me, Emma?

Emma blushed. She looked down to the floor and said, 'I do.' With her mind, she was thinking to herself. I would rather be dead than married to you. I just need to get home. Then I will have my family, friends, and this time, I will work hard to gain justice.

Mr Greystone got up from his chair. He gave his waistcoat a sharp tug and said, 'Now that I have made my feelings clear to you, I must get a meal for us. I need to get on and sort things out for the incoming ship.'

Mr Nash Greystone left the room.

Emma sat staring at the ornate mouldings on the ceiling. She shivered, for she felt the smallness of the room. Emma felt like screaming. It was as if the walls were coming in to squash the life from her. Emma went over to the window to look out. She saw the convict men sitting in a half- circle, being taught the skill of cobbling. In the sunshine, the teacher was demonstrating how to heel and sole men's boots. Further along, another teacher was showing men how to be spooners. She watched those men making spoons from bone.

Mr Greystone came in with a tray of tea, soup, bread, and beef.

'I had no trouble getting some for you, my dear. They presumed I was getting it for a fellow officer. What are you looking at?'

'I was watching the men. They are being taught to make spoons or mend boots.'

'Come away from the window. They may observe you in my room. Do come here, Emma.' Mr Greystone tapped the chair with his hand.

'We train the men so they can get employment when they leave here.'

Emma came over to the table.

'Do the women, get training?'

Emma sat down.

'Women do not need work. They will be bringing up children and having lots of babies.'

'Yes, Nash, as you say, women will bring up their babies and children...'

'Now, now, Emma dear, eat.'

'I am not hungry today.'

'I insist that you eat something. To be sure, you are rather thin, my dear. I need you to look bonny on our wedding day. So, eat.'

Emma picked up her spoon.

'Nash, what jobs do you wish me to do as your servant?'

Nash put his spoon down. 'Emma, my dear. He tapped her hand. You are not really going to be a servant in my house. I just want you to be close to me. I wish to keep you safe and away from the low life in this place. I need you around so we can make plans for our domestic arrangements.'

'Oh dear, but the servants will think ill of me if I do not do any work. What about my reputation?'

Mr Greystone sprinkled salt onto his soup.

'I remember telling you, my dear Emma. When we first met. Do you not remember what I said? I told you plainly, I will let no one soil your pure reputation.'

Emma quickly sucked in some soup, to stop herself saying what she was really thinking. For she reasoned. You have ruined my reputation for a lifetime. Now I have the stain of this place upon my name. You hypocrite.

Mr Greystone consumed more soup and then said. 'I could give you some knitting and plain sewing to do, for appearance's sake, if you wish. I am sure my dear, you will be busy making lists in readiness for our wedding and reading books to collect ideas for married life in our new home.'

He took a bite out of his bread. Emma kept on eating her soup.

'After we have finished this meal. I will get an officer to take you to my house. There you will ask for Mrs Lydia White. She is my housekeeper. I have asked her to arrange the room for you. I have given her instructions to introduce you to the servants. Emma, my dear, if you need anything, just ask her.'

'Thank you.'

Nash tucked into the beef. 'flavoursome meat, not bad at all. Have you any sensible questions?'

'How long do you think it will be before we leave for home?'

'I do hope, we will be able to leave on this incoming ship, The King Arthur.'

'How perfectly fine. Will I need the written absolute pardon before I can leave?'

'No, No, dear. Once I explain to the Governor, my intention to marry you in England. I declare, he will take my judgment and wisdom into consideration. I am certainly sure I can get him to write a covering letter giving you permission to leave.'

'Oh, Nash. You do not think the Governor would be puzzled. Why a gentleman in your position would desire to marry a newly arrived convict?'

His voice lashed at her. 'There you go again, Emma. It will not do. Asking questions and pushing towards things that do not concern you.'

Emma got up on her feet, narrowing her eyes, she said. 'I believe it concerns me.'

Nash Greystone banged his knife down onto the table just catching his plate, which rings out loud and made Emma jump.

'I will not stand for this.'

'Let me speak Mr Greystone. The Governor does not know me. From his point of view, you have only known me for one day.'

'Sit down.'

'Good gracious, Nash. I should be able to say what is on my mind.'

'Sit down, now.'

'Stop suffocating me.'

Emma strides towards the door then she remembers the fact that she must play a part, so she can get home again. So, Emma shuts her eyes for a moment then turns and says. 'Forgive me please, Nash, it is just that I long to leave this place, of course with you.' Her eyes lifted to meet his. Emma extended her hand to him. 'I do not want your plan to go wrong.'

Emma sat down again.

'I know the Governor. I can deal with him. Emma, you must control yourself. You are not to get yourself into these free-thinking moods. If I say it will happen, it will happen. We can take your Mother to London with us if you wish. But you must leave all the thinking to me.'

'I am sorry.' Emma whispered, although feeling humiliated. She tried to appease him. Emma ran her fingers through her hair and then played with a tendril.

'There is no good to come of it if you get hysterical. I do not want to be paying for doctors, do I?'

'No, indeed.' Emma said, 'I am quite myself now.' She extended her hand across the table towards Nash.

He tapped it, then said. 'Drink your tea. I have to go.' Nash's mood had softened, he asked. 'May I have a smile?'

Emma replaced Mr Greystone's face with Dudley's image in her mind. So, she could give him a natural smile. Emma contemplated, 'Dear Dudley, I long to see you again.'

'Emma dearest.' Nash said, 'That is so much better. Your prettiness is now reflected in your smile.'

'I will soon have reasons to smile more often.' Emma answered.

'Yes, however, I do not want to lose you, my dear. So please, let there be no more hysterical emotions or wild intellectual thoughts and questionings. I want you to leave things to me. A Lady need not spend her time thinking about things that do not concern her. Once you see how much I love you, my dear. You will see the need to obey my authority and do what I wish. The happier I am. The happier you shall be. It is up to you.'

Emma wondered. Why do you not love me for my thinking ability, as much as my appearance? How can you hurt the one you say you especially love?

Nash stood up, tugged forcibly at the bottom of his waistcoat. Then he took hold of Emma's hand.

She watched him kiss her hand then fasten his jacket.

Emma silently considered; you must know I cannot reciprocate your love.

Nash said, 'I shall go and get an officer to take you over to my house.'

Emma thought. Love? It feels like deadly Suffocation.

Mr Greystone left the room.

Emma put her head in her hands. How will I ever manage months on a ship with him?

Lifting her head up, she noticed a world map in a dark oak frame on the wall. She got up and went over to look at it. The map shows the routes of the ships back and forth from England to Australia. As Emma examines it, she asks herself. Should I run away? Her answer was. I cannot because there is the sea at one side and a wilderness to the other. Then she wondered, I could show the Governor the fake marriage certificate? That would not do; As it looks too real, he would never believe it was a fake. Shall I tell the Governor my side of the story? No, for he would for a certainly believe a gentleman who he knows, rather than a female convict. Shall I just marry Mr Greystone and be done with it? How could I, the thought of it disgusts me...? I need justice. He has committed prudery in court and lied to me and everyone. That man has committed forgery. Not forgetting that he has been the instigator of violence against my dear friend, Dudley. He has torn my beloved Edwin from me. Mr Greystone is cruel. I know what I must do. I must keep him believing that I will marry him. I will travel with him on the ship to England, then I will get justice, Emma had decided.

The door opened. Mr Greystone and an officer came into the room. Nash spoke. 'This is Officer Tully. He will take you to my house. Ask for Mrs Lydia White. She will tell you what to do.'

'Yes. Thank you, sir.' Emma replied.

Mr Greystone nodded to Emma and then waved a hand towards the officer. 'That is all officer, off you go.'

Emma glanced at the writing slope with its empty narrow drawer. She wondered if she had been foolish to take such a risk? Yet, Emma felt proud of herself. She had been bold and victorious by taking the forged certificate. Somehow, Emma was determined to prove it was a fake and prove her innocence.

Strengthened by that thought she followed the officer out of the room and the door was shut behind her.

Chapter Twenty-Eight

Officer Tully walked side by side with Emma as he showed her the way to Mr Greystones Residence.

As they were walking along, some creature ran across Emma's path, so she exclaimed, 'Oh, dear me, what a funny looking creature.'

'It is a Kangaroo. The cook's wife feeds it, so it is always about here.'

'I have heard about an animal called a Kangaroo.' Emma said, 'I found it hard to picture it in my mind, now I see why.'

'Do you know that the Kangaroos nurture their babe's in a pocket? Trouble is, Kangaroo's young ones are not safe in this place for it is full of pickpockets.' He laughed.

Emma smiled back, while enjoying a light-hearted moment..

As they carried on walking, the officer said, 'You look remarkable, so tidy and clean compared to the usual females here.'

'Thank you sir, perhaps that is why I have the privilege of working as a servant at Mr Greystone's residence.'

'Maybe, for I don't know how you've done it?' Officer Tully commented.

Emma just smiled.

'Me and the wife have seen people come and go. The key is. Keep your head down, work hard, do as they tell you. The time will pass and you will get your certificate of leave before you know it. How long did you get?'

'4 years.'

'Shorter than most then. There are grand opportunities here. Many freed prisoners have set up fine businesses and have property and land.'

'Sir, may I ask? Do many go back home?'

'Some have. Far more stay here and make a good life for themselves.'

They walked further on. Emma could hear the river and the birds. She drank in the sounds of nature. Even when they passed a house being constructed. The hammering sounds could not drown out the beautiful birdsong.

'That will house Mr Greystones nearest neighbour.' The officer said.

Next, they arrived outside Mr Greystone's Georgian looking house.

'Check you have your certificate of freedom with you always. As they will ask you to show it.'

'I will. Thank you, sir.'

They went up several steps to the door and the officer pulled on the bell. The housekeeper opened the door.

'I have brought, Mr Greystone's new servant girl.' The officer said.

'Yes, I am expecting her. Thank you, officer.' replied the housekeeper.

'For now, Mrs White, I will be off.' He went back down the steps.

'Come in, girl.' The housekeeper said,' Mr Greystone has given you your own room. The news is, when you have seen it, you can have tea in the servant's room down below, where I will introduce you to the rest of the household.'

'Thank you, Mrs White.'

'Mr Greystone has not yet informed me as to what your workload will be.'

'Repairing clothes and household linen, plain needlework mostly.'

'I see, but that does not sound much, anyway, I am sure Mr Greystone will give me a further list when he gets home.'

Emma followed the housekeeper up the wide staircase.

Mrs White opened the bedroom door.

Emma entered and looked around. The walls were painted in pale green. With a white iron fire place. The green-painted window shutters were open and let light into the room. Emma walked across the brilliantly polished wooden floor. There was a large built-in cupboard to one side of the chimney breast. A small chair, by a small wooden table. But the thing that pleased Emma the most was the comfortable looking four poster bed. It took all her strength not to throw herself down onto it right there and then.

'This is a nice room,' Emma said.

'Nice... This fine room is a particularly large and pleasing room.' Replied the housekeeper, as if she thought Emma was not appreciative enough.

'Indeed, Mrs White, I did not mean-

Mr Greystone likes punctuality and faultless manners. The news is, he will not stand for failure in those areas. So do remember that at all times.

'I will. Thank you again, Mrs White.'

Come down stairs with me and have a drink before you start.

Shutting the door behind them, Emma followed Mrs White again down stairs.

Emma was shown into the servant's quarters and sat herself down.

'No, that is not your seat. Move down to that one.' The housekeeper pointed to a simple wooden upright chair.

'Whatever makes you think you should sit that high up, foolish girl?'

Emma quickly realised that the chairs around the large table had a hierarchy to them. She considered. I must take care not to get on the wrong side of the servants.

'Have you been in service before?' asked the housekeeper.

'No, I... I have not Mrs White.'

'I know, I can tell.'

'Oh.'

'We are expected to start a new life. The news is, we must forget our wicked past. For we must make the best of our future.'

Emma contemplated to herself. 'The news is, Mrs White, the last thing I will do is forget about my past.'

After Emma had drunk her tea and eaten some honey cake, which tasted so good, the housekeeper introduced her to some of the other servants as they came in for a drink.

A short while later, Emma was given some shirts and household linen that needed repairing.

The housekeeper gave her a clean plain white dress and told her to change into it.

Emma took the things up the stairs back into her room, she shut the door and jumped onto the bed. Oh, how soft, Emma thought while she laid there. She now noticed the muscle pain in her tense neck and shoulders, so Emma lay still for a moment.

Emma removed the fake folded certificate, from its hiding place and put it down on the bed. She got changed into the clean dress and put the folded paper back into its secret place.

Next she sat down at a table by the window to do some sewing, before settling down to work Emma took a quick scan through the window. She could see the path leading to the gate and beyond to the river bank, flanked by bushes.

Emma settled down to repair the shirts. She noticed the embroidered name tape of N. Greystone. Emma hated that name more than any other. She sighed as her heart sank because of the thought of being trapped on a ship with Mr Greystone, for over a 100 days. Yet, Emma knew she must not shrink with fear from him. She must be courageous.

A little while on, Emma was busy turning a collar when she heard the gate outside. She looked out of the window. There was Mr Greystone coming back home.

Emma took a deep breath for courage. She hated the

thought of the acting she would now have to perform in front of the housekeeper and all the other servants.

Mr Greystone rang the bell and the housekeeper, answered the door. Emma crept onto the landing to peer over the bannister. Screwing up her face she listens hard, to hear what Mr Greystone was saying to the housekeeper.

'Has the new girl come?'

'Yes Sir, although I am not sure how good she will be.'

'Why?'

'Let me hang up your coat Mr Greystone.'

'Why not Mrs White?'

'The news is, the girl has not been in service before sir.'

'I can get rid of her.'

' Sir, I am sure, that the other servants will soon have her in shape. Here are your house shoes Mr Greystone.'

'Is she in her room?'

'Yes, sir.'

'I shall meet her after I have eaten.'

The voices faded quickly as the two of them walked from the hallway into the dining room.

Emma acknowledged to herself. Oh dear, he plans to speak to me after his meal. I must be most careful what I say to him. Keep him believing that I will marry him. Emma checked her face and hair in the mirror. She whispered under her breath to her image reflected in the mirror. I must keep saying to myself. Get on board the ship. Then I am home.

There was another hour due before Emma's meal. As the servants were only allowed to eat after Mr Greystone.

Emma laid on the bed for a moment. Her body felt tight. She had pain over her eyes just thinking about tonight's conversation with Nash Greystone, She kept going from total despair to courage, self-doubt to boldness.

After a while, Emma sprung off the bed, as she had heard the footsteps of Mr Greystone coming up the stairs.

She crept over to the chair and sat down by the window.

The door knob turned and Mr Greystone walked in. Emma was vexed that he did not knock. Although she managed to smile at him and say, 'Nash, you are home.'

Nash Greystone walked into the middle of the room.

'I am, as you can see.'

'Yes indeed. Have all the people vacated the ship now?'
Emma asked. Although, she felt unsure how to proceed.

'Speaking plainly I dare say, you Miss Emma Pennington
would be most interested in a ship being emptied of people.'

Emma was uncertain what he meant.

Mr Greystone raised his brows. 'As you seem to be so
interested. I shall inform you. The last boat of men left The
King Arthur only an hour ago. Speaking plain enough, I have
not witnessed them with my own eyes as I have been doing
paperwork and oh yes... I had to write some important
letters.'

Emma blushed. 'Nash dear, we shall soon leave together on
The King Arthur. Emma stood up, pointed at the chair she
was sitting on. Sit down, Nash, you have been working hard. I
can sit on the side of the bed.'

As Emma started to walk towards the bed. Mr Greystone
grabbed her arm tightly.

Emma halted. 'Nash, you are hurting me, dear.'

'I could break your neck so easily with my hand.' He put his
hand to Emma's throat.

Emma grabbed at his arm and tried to pull away his hand.

Mr Greystones forehead puckered as his eyes narrowed. As

he spat out, 'I was writing some letters. I opened my writing slope drawer. Something was missing from the drawer. Do you know what it is? Yes, you do. For it is you, who has stolen it!'

He took his hand away and walked around Emma in a complete circle.

'What is missing?' Emma croaked. While she rubbed her throat with her hand.

'You know what is missing?'

Mr Greystone got hold of her wrist, then threw her against the bed.

Emma got up and marched back over to him. Looked at him straight in the eye and said. 'Yes, I have it.'

'Have you hidden it in the room? Or is it hidden on you?'

Emma Folded her arms and said, 'I will not let you have it.'

'Yes, you will, Emma Pennington. It belongs to me?' His jaw tightened.

'I have as much right to it. I signed it with my own hand, according to you.'

'We both know you did not sign it.'

Emma fixed her eyes on him.

'What do you want it for Mr Greystone?'

'Never mind, what I need it for. You are a real little thief. I will get it back.'

Mr Greystone forcefully pulled the covers off from the bed.

Emma held onto the back of the chair.

'You should have destroyed it, Mr Greystone. Why would you possibly want to keep it?' Emma croaked. 'After all, when we were married, as you wanted. We would have had a real certificate. So why keep the fake one? Tell me? Tell me why?'

Nash Greystone was pulling off the mattress from the bed.

'Where have you hidden it you wretch?'

Emma ran to the door, but he had already locked it and removed the key.

Mr Greystone's eyes were popping and his face was purple. He now was rummaging through the table drawer.

'I will find it.' He snarled at Emma, 'I will.'

Nash was throwing things about as he searched in the cupboard. He then stormed over to Emma, who was by the door and grabs hold of her arm.

341

'You could only have taken it for one reason you little low life, you wanted to use it against me.'

He lets go of her arm and pushes her shoulders against the door. 'I know you would use that certificate against me, when we got back to England.'

'Nash Greystone, you used it against me in Court, Remember.' Emma said, in a strained voice. 'You are the real criminal here.'

He put his hand around Emma's throat again.

Emma kicked his shins with her feet.

So he grabbed and held both her hands above her head against the door.

Mr Greystone's jaw clenched. Seething, he said, 'Your kicks do not hurt me.'

Emma spoke with full force. 'You are not a gentleman. A gentleman would never treat a Lady like this.'

He moved his legs a little further back from Emma and hissed. 'A real lady would not behave like a little thief. To think how much, how much I loved you. I was sick with love for you. I was even prepared to leave my job, my new country even, yes, to take you home.' He grinds his teeth. 'To think, I longed to marry you.'

Emma roared back. 'I would rather die than marry you because of what you have done to me, my mother, my Aunt, Dudley and Edwin.' Emma was trying hard to wriggle free.

Nash forcibly grabbed hold of her face between his two hands, while frowning he said. 'Emma Pennington, I loved you.'

Emma shouted, 'Say you hate me now. Say it. 'Emma coughed. 'Say you hate me, say it.'

He turned his head away for a moment. Then looking back at Emma, he shouted. 'Tell me now. Tell me where have you hidden the certificate?'

Emma banged on the door with her fists. Mr Greystone let go of her face and grabbed both her wrists again and dragged her to the middle of the room.

Then he said in a low tone. 'It is not in this room, so, it must be on you.'

'Do not touch me. 'Emma let out a scream. Mr Greystone put his hand over her mouth. Emma bit his hand.'

'You little-'

'-Mr Greystone, Mr Greystone,' the housekeeper shouted, 'is everything all right with you Mr Greystone?'

Nash Greystone rushed over to the door and opened it. He

saw the groom and housekeeper coming up the stairs, onto the landing.

'Everything is fine.' Nash said in a calmed voice.

Emma ran out onto the landing shouting. 'No, it is not-'

'-The new girl has taken ill. She is having a turn.' Mr Greystone said. 'Mrs White, I was just calming her down.'

'No, it is not true.' Emma shouted, 'you must help me. Get help.'

'See what I mean, Mrs White.' Nash answered.

'Does she need a doctor, Mr Greystone?' Asked the housekeeper.

'Yes,' dear lady. Mr Greystone then said to the Groom, 'You go and get the doctor.'

Mr Greystone turned to the housekeeper and asked. 'You, Mrs White. Would you put the poor girl to bed?'

'Yes, Sir.' She answered.

Emma was shouting, 'No. I am perfectly fine. I am not ill. Please get the governor.'

Mr Greystone appealed, 'First Mrs White, please go downstairs and get the poor sick girl some brandy.'

The housekeeper nodded and said, 'Yes, Mr Greystone, right away.'

Emma took hold of the housekeeper's hand. 'Do not leave me, please stay here.'

'I will be right back dear. I will be all but one moment. The good news is Mr Greystone will sit with you, then I will be back with a nice brandy to calm your poor nerves.'

In vain, Emma tried to stop her.

Mrs White went down the stairs.

The veins on Mr Greystone's forehead were ready to burst. He gripped Emma by her forearm and dragged her back into the bedroom.

He groaned. 'To think I loved you, worshipped you. Was taking you back to England to marry you. Bringing your mother to live with us. How could you hurt me so?' His eyes flamed. 'You are like my harlot sister. Women are all bad, every single one of them. Nothing but pretenders. He held his hand out.' Give me the certificate now. Give it to me. If you do not give it to me now. I will take it myself. I am not afraid to tear your dress to get it. Give it…'

'No, No, I will never hand it over to you. Even if you tear it away from me, know this… I never gave it willingly.'

'Depend upon it, if you do not hand it over right now. I

promise you; you will never see home again. Believe me, I have the power to do it. Nash Greystone held his hand out.

'I no longer care what you do.' Emma said. 'On principle, I must make my stand to never give the certificate to you.'

'Foolish wretch. Depend upon it, you can forget about any journey home. His eyes flamed. 'just so you understand me. On no account will we ever be married... You can rot in the female factory.'

Sweat was now pouring down Mr Greystone's forehead.

'I would never marry you.' Emma shouted, 'Even if it saved my last breath. I would die before I ever, ever, ever marry you.'

Mr Greystone started to grab Emma's dress. Emma quickly pulled hard on his neck cloth and wriggled out of his way.

Unexpectedly. There was a ringing of the doorbell.

Mr Greystone stopped in his tracks. He and Emma heard Mrs White open the door and say. 'Governor. Officers. Please come in.'

The Governor's voice was heard. 'We need to see Mr Greystone right now. Is he at home?'

'Yes Sir, Mr Greystone is upstairs. I will go and get him.'

'No need dear Lady. My two Officers will go upstairs.'

Nash Greystone's face drained of colour. As he heard. 'Right Governor, we shall arrest Greystone.'

Emma heard the heavy footsteps running up the stairs.

Nash said, 'I command you, Emma. Do what I say.' His eyes were bulging. 'Sit.'

Emma sat down.

Officers burst into the room.

Mr Greystone gave a look of composure when he said. 'Whatever is the matter Gentlemen. Have you come to arrest this little convict thief?'

'Sir, we have come to arrest you.'

One officer put iron handcuffs around Mr Greystone's wrists and locked them.

'There must be some mistake, Gentlemen?'

'No, there is no mistake.' Replied the officer.

'You will find that it is the female convict sitting on the chair who you are looking for, Officers.'

'The Governor knows all about you Mr Nash Greystone.'

Emma could not believe what had just happened. She sat wide-eyed with her hand over her mouth.

The officer asked Emma. 'Are you Miss Emma Pennington?'

'Sir, you said Pennington.' Emma's eyes sparkled with joy. 'Yes, yes, I am indeed Miss Emma Pennington.'

'The governor wants to see you downstairs. If you will please Miss?'

'Indeed, I will.' Emma got up from the chair and glanced out of the window and expressed. 'It cannot be? Yes, I cannot believe it, Blessed be God above.'

Emma ran passed the Officers who were standing either side of Mr Greystone.

She ran down the staircase, passed Mrs White, who was coming up the stairs with a glass of brandy in her hand.

She ran past the Governor waiting in the hallway.

Out through the open door she ran.

'Oh, am I dreaming?'

'No, Emma, it is us.'

Emma ran and put an arm around each of the young men.

'Solomon, Edwin, you have come. God bless you. Seeing you both is more pleasure than I could expect in my whole lifetime. Bless you Edwin Sinclair and bless you Solomon Sherbourne.'

The two men each kissed one of Emma's hands.

Edwin spoke first, 'My dearest Emma. forgive me, I beg of you.'

Solomon said, 'Thank the heavens you are alive.'

Edwin then tapped the physician on the shoulder and said. 'It is this fine fellow, and friend Doctor Solomon Sherbourne, who I shall always be grateful to.'

Emma was listening intently, so he carried on his tale.

'Dear Emma, I was so depressed and lost, after your trial.' Edwin gestured to Solomon. 'This fine friend and Gentleman, never wavered in his belief in you. I am so thankful that he convinced me you were innocent. Solomon told me. I must work hard to prove your innocence. It would be the only way to save you and in turn save me. Emma, Solomon was right. I was like a man looking for clues from a treasure map. This is how your doctor and I have become very close friends over it. When we had found the evidence to prove you were not guilty. Lord Gilpin and Lady Belvedere paid for our crossing to come and get you. Your dear mother is waiting for you. Emma, your Mother has hope now, and is the better for it.' Edwin's voice cracked, so he said, 'Solomon, you tell Emma what happened next.'

'After we had searched for clues. I received a letter from the doctor who practised at London Newgate prison. In the letter, he describes the meeting with you. When he gave you a health examination before you went onto the ship. Do you remember him Emma?'

A faint smile was on Emma's lips, 'Yes, he was kind.'

'I dare say, with his experience of dealing with convicts. He recognised the look of innocence. He believed your tale was true. I am truly glad to say. He wrote me a letter. He believed right that your family doctor would be able to judge whether you would be innocent or guilty of such a crime.'

'Oh, Dr Sherbourne you believed me?'

'I never believed one word that came from Greystone's mouth at the trial. Emma, I knew you were innocent.'

'Solomon, is a better man than I.' Edwin said, his eyes filling up while he pushed his fingers through his hair.

'With that both young men kissed Emma again on her hands.'

The Governor stepped outside to join them.

He said, 'I have the details here. He held up a written document from Solomon and Edwin. I have read their convincing evidence why they feel Mr Greystone is guilty, of

Perjury, forgery, violence, and kidnapping. Mr Greystone has manoeuvred things so he would control you. By being brought to this place with no chance of leaving. '

'Oh dear.'

'What is the matter Miss?'

'I am worried about what will happen to him.'

'You need justice, young lady.' The Governor continued. 'I will lose an employee who is very good at his job. But what he has done to you is just plain wrong, my dear.'

'Emma rubbed her eyes.'

'The only thing we need to find is the fake marriage certificate. If he has not destroyed it.'

'Look no further. I have it on my person.'

'You do?'

'Turn around Gentlemen. Let me get it for you.' Emma retrieved it and unfolded it.

'Well indeed, I am astonished.' Edwin said.

Edwin drew out of his jacket pocket another certificate. He explained, 'I have been to Gretna Green in Scotland, to get hold of a real blank marriage certificate. Here it is, we can compare this real one with yours Emma.'

They all gathered around in a half circle to look at the two together.

'It is a very skilled copy. Except as you can see, the paper is much thinner and a slightly different shade.'

'Yes, said Edwin.' The letter M does not have a curly cue at the lower foot of the downward stroke.'

'Yes, Gentleman, between us we have found a few flaws, even without looking that thoroughly.' Agreed the Governor.

'This is the proof we need for the court case. The court will only hear a case again if we have new evidence.'

'Now we have it,' said Edwin.

'Officers,' The Governor shouted. 'Men, Bring Mr Greystone and put him in the carriage. Miss Emma Pennington. I shall give you a letter containing an Absolute Pardon. You and your gentlemen friends can leave on the ship, The King Arthur. For it will leave here in three days. Miss Pennington, would you come and stay in my home with my wife and I? Gentlemen, you may stay here in Mr Greystone's house, until it is time to leave.'

'Thank you,' Emma exclaimed. 'I dare say, I cannot thank you all enough. Please allow me to say goodbye to my friends first. Depend upon it. It will be difficult for me to say goodbye to them. I know I will miss little baby Mary Emma.'

Mr Greystone was brought out from the house with his hands behind his back in iron cuffs. He fell down on his knees on seeing Emma and pleaded. 'Please forgive me. I was just broken-hearted. Please say you will forgive me dear, sweet, kind Emma?'

'Get up, move.' The officer said. 'Do not upset the young Lady.' The two officers forced Nash Greystone onto his feet.

Mr Greystone shouted louder. 'All I ever wanted was for you to love me.'

The Governor walked to the carriage and said to Mr Greystone. 'I am very angry and disappointed with you. As a Gentleman, you should have known better. Get out from my face.'

The carriage soon disappeared from view. Emma asked, 'they will not hang him, will they?'

'Would you not want to see Mr Greystone hang for what he has done to you?' Asked the Governor.

'I never want to see him ever again. To be sure, but not hanged.'

'Well, my word?' said the Governor.

'Emma sighed hard, I don't think he has ever been right since he was ten and five.'

Edwin asked, 'What happened?'

'His sister ran away with the man she wished to marry against her family's wishes.'

'Was the man poor?'

'Yes, he was a poor African slave who worked as a gardener. I dare say, his sister loved him for the person he was. They wanted to be married, so they ran away together. Mr Greystone has not seen his sister since that day. He misses her so much it hurts him.'

The doctor looked at the marks on Emma's neck. 'I am glad to say, that the marks that devil made on your neck will soon fade. How dare he think he could command you to love him? The trouble was that Mr Greystone had always commanded people to do what he wanted. What happened to his sister is not an excuse to hurt you.'

Edwin added. 'Emma, you are too good for a man like him. Your nature is loving, honest and true... Even I am not worthy of you.' Edwin's voice cracked again. 'I know I let you down. I let you down my love?'

'You are here now.' Emma smiled. 'Edwin, how did you overcome your fear of sailing?'

'Edwin feeling choked with emotion, pointed to Doctor Sherbourne. He cleared his throat and said. Solomon gave me something to calm me down. I think I slept during most of the endless journey.'

'Herbs are wonderful plants,' Doctor Sherbourne said. 'His journey home will be greatly improved upon, by having you dear Emma safely with us.'

Edwin took hold of Emma's hand and as he studied her face with his eyes. He said. 'I want you to take comfort, dearest Emma. The one thing that kept me going the most was the thought of seeing you again.'

'Darling Edwin.'

I know that your dear Mother and Aunt are counting the months in anticipation of seeing you soon.'

Emma put her lips to Edwin's cheek and kissed him. 'It is a dream come true.'

'It is a long journey home.' Doctor Sherbourne said,' but at the end you will be home, safe and loved. He took a cotton bag from his pocket, 'I have the herbs ready.'

Edwin took hold of Emma and swept her back in his arms as he kissed her lips. 'Emma, my brave darling. From this moment on, I shall love you dependably. Yes always, my dearest love.'

The End